DOLBY

LIGHTHOUSE SECURITY INVESTIGATIONS WEST COAST
BOOK FIVE

MARYANN JORDAN

Dolby (Lighthouse Security Investigations West Coast) Copyright 2023

All rights reserved. No part of this book may be reproduced or transmitted in any form or by any means, electronic or mechanical, including photocopying, recording, or by any information storage and retrieval system without the written permission of the author, except where permitted by law.

If you are reading this book and did not purchase it, then you are reading an illegal pirated copy. If you would be concerned about working for no pay, then please respect the author's work! Make sure that you are only reading a copy that has been officially released by the author.

This book is a work of fiction. Names, characters, places, and incidents are either products of the author's imagination or are used fictitiously. Any resemblance to actual persons, living or dead, events, or locales is entirely coincidental.

Cover: Graphics by Stacy

ISBN ebook: 978-1-956588-23-1

ISBN print: 978-1-956588-24-8

❦ Created with Vellum

Author's Note

Please remember that this is a work of fiction. I have lived in numerous states as well as overseas, but for the last thirty years have called Virginia my home. I often choose to use fictional city names with some geographical accuracies.

These fictionally named cities allow me to use my creativity and not feel constricted by attempting to accurately portray the areas.

It is my hope that my readers will allow me this creative license and understand my fictional world.

I also do quite a bit of research on my books and try to write on subjects with accuracy. There will always be points where creative license will be used in order to create scenes or plots.

1

A bead of sweat trickled down Marcia's spine, disappearing into the waistband of her jeans. She wiggled slightly, scrunched her nose at the uncomfortable sensation of sweat-dampened panties, then hefted her backpack a little higher on her shoulders. The brilliant California sun reflected off the water, chasing the early spring chill as it warmed the sand.

She inhaled deeply, then slowly let the air slide from her lungs, relishing the scent of the distant pine trees, mixed with a salty tang of the ocean as the waves chased each other on the shore before they raced back into the sea.

The physical intensity of the hike had been exhausting, but the emotional stretching of being alone in a remote area had been equally as tiring. Her isolation wasn't the concern. In truth, she preferred her solitude. Being around others made her nervous as she tried to think of small talk. She wanted to blend into the background, hoping no one noticed her. Preferring to people-watch rather than actually be *with* people.

But then, she was also more comfortable in her house and not wandering by herself on a long stretch of beach. Out here, she was vulnerable. She was getting stronger, although most would be shocked at how many years she'd worked to get to this point.

Recovery has no timeline. Everyone learns to move forward at their own pace. Give yourself a chance to find your own healing.

The words of her therapist came back to her, although, in truth, they were never very far away. She'd spent sixteen years working to move past the choking fear of being vulnerable with others. And the fear of being in a crowd with people she didn't know. And the fear of closed-in spaces. Or the fear of the dark. Or the fear of... *Stop! Just stop!*

Forcing her anxiety back into the mental box she'd determined to place it in, she continued her sojourn toward the small, abandoned lighthouse secluded in the middle of the preservation land. The landmark was now visible in the distance, a beacon sitting on a small hill.

A cloud temporarily blocked the sun, blanketing the beach in shade while sending a slight chill over her skin. She looked around, waiting to see if prickles on the back of her neck were coming, but no sensation of impending danger arrived. Just the sound of seabirds, the waves crashing, and the breathtaking sight of nature all around.

She continued to the lighthouse, her steps lighter as she neared even as her breath was labored from the exertion. It had taken her almost two hours to get there, and the major accomplishment sent a wide smile across her face. A black lantern room topped the white concrete structure. It was short in stature compared to other lighthouses but sat atop a hill next to the coast. There was no keeper's house. Instead, it was just the beacon.

Due to its remote location, it was rarely visited. Most visitors made the trek in warmer weather, and she'd correctly assumed this would be a good time of year to avoid others. Nearing, she sent a worried glance toward the ocean, seeing the clouds gathering. There was less than thirty percent chance of rain today, but the dark clouds obviously didn't read weather reports.

Her top teeth worried her bottom lip as she hesitated, then shook her head in derision. If it was going to rain, she hardly had time to turn back now since it would take another couple of hours to get home. She'd come this far and was determined to see the inside of the lighthouse. Even though her legs protested, she hurried over the last part of the trail and made it inside before the first splat of raindrops fell.

Several birds roosting inside caused a flutter as they flew out when she entered, and she squeaked, ducking out of their way. The structure was open on both ends, empty of anything other than bird droppings in one corner and a rusty, spiral iron staircase leading to the lantern room in another corner. But it provided the perfect shelter while she waited for the rain to pass. It was filled with light, not closed off, and offered the ability to stay dry while she watched the ever-changing panorama of clouds and the ocean just outside.

She was surprised the inside of the lighthouse was only about fifteen feet on each side, approximately the size of her dining room. The walls appeared sturdy, although some cracks showed near the doorways, and the window openings had evidence of crumbling concrete.

She sat down carefully on the concrete floor, wincing at her tight leg muscles. She dropped her backpack from her shoulders, immediately feeling the ease move through her body. Reaching in, she dug around until she pulled out her food and water. A simple picnic, but as she breathed in the cool, fresh air and let the wind whip the escaping tendrils of hair about her face, she relished her snack of peanut butter crackers and water.

Even with the rain pouring outside her little open-air hideaway, her shoulders relaxed, her chest eased, and a slow smile curved her lips. She held up her phone and snapped several pictures, then tapped on a dictation app and began to talk. She wanted to commit her senses to memory... the smells, the sounds, the view, the experience.

"The blue hues of the sky and water are ever changing...cerulean, Aegean, azure, beryl. The earth tones of brandy, negroni, and maize. The green of moss, olive, blue spruce." She had no idea where she might put this description to use but was determined to record the experience to further her imagination.

A sense of accomplishment filled her at her

successful solitary hike. She leaned back against the concrete wall, stretched her legs out in front of her, and let the peace of the early afternoon rainstorm envelop her.

Dolby trekked along the California trail toward the coast, hefting his heavy backpack on his shoulders. He'd spent several days hiking along preservation lands in Northern California, pitching a tent each night and avoiding crowded areas as he searched for solitude.

Not that he didn't enjoy good company, but as the youngest of three boys, he learned to appreciate some alone time at an early age. In fact, he remembered his mother used to require each of them to read quietly at night before they went to bed. *"Everyone needs time with their own thoughts,"* she used to say.

Privacy was also rare during his years as an Army Ranger, but he wouldn't have traded anything for the camaraderie. Now, as a Keeper for the elite company of Lighthouse Security Investigations West Coast, he experienced that same solidarity he shared with his birth brothers and then his brothers-in-arms in the military with the best group he could work with.

The forest was thick as he walked along, but eventually, the underbrush became more prevalent, indicating the trees were thinning out as he neared the coast. Douglas fir and redwoods, along with pine and laurel, covered the mountains to the east, and he looked forward to the sight of the beargrass, bentgrass, and oat grass covering the coastal prairies.

He stopped and took a sip of water. Stretching his back, he heard it crack along the vertebrae. At thirty-three, he didn't often sleep outside anymore and felt the twinges he'd never experienced in his twenties. As much as he loved outdoor recreation, at six feet five inches and two hundred and twenty pounds, his thick, firm, king-sized mattress would be welcome when he finished his trip and returned home. He'd purchased a modest-sized house where he could spend weekends working on it, and he enjoyed inviting his friends, coworkers, and family to visit. But he also relished the times when he could settle on the deck or by the fire with a good book and a whiskey.

After his last mission, his boss informed him that their office manager, Rachel, had insisted that Dolby take some of his vacation days. Carson Dyer wasn't a stickler for certain aspects of rules when it came to their business, but the health and welfare of the Keepers were of utmost importance to his boss.

Thinking of the office manager, he grinned. Rachel was retired from the Navy and a widow, having lost her Naval pilot husband during a training exercise fifteen years earlier. Hating to be at loose ends, she'd jumped at the chance to work with Carson and keep LSIWC running at maximum efficiency. And being a former Navy officer, she knew just how to handle the Keepers. When she'd said Dolby needed to take his vacation days... that was exactly what he'd done.

He decided the early spring was the perfect time to

hike, camp, see some of Northern California that he hadn't seen in a while, and spend time alone. As he left the wooded, mountainous area heading toward the coast, the hills kept the shoreline from his view, but he could see the darkening clouds in the distance.

Grumbling, he realized how mistaken the weather report had been. He wasn't overly surprised because the weather patterns could easily change this time of year. He prepared for all contingencies in his rolled-up pack on his back.

As he moved beyond the hills, the Pacific Ocean came into view, and with each step, a little more was visible in the distance. Finally, he came to a cliff and, standing on the edge of the world, had the panoramic vista of the ocean with the waves crashing down below and the dark clouds rolling closer. He didn't mind the weather. Hell, as a former Ranger, the weather rarely affected a mission, and if it became a difficulty, they simply altered their plan to accomplish the job.

Sucking in a deep breath of briny air, he grinned. Memories of him and his brothers racing along the beaches during their family vacations rushed back. They'd return to the campground with shells, sticks, rocks, crab claws, dead fish, and occasionally a bird skeleton. His mom would ooh and aah over their treasures, then lift a brow, shake her head, and smile toward their dad. He'd often heard other adults ask his mom if she'd wanted a girl, but she'd always laughed and said, "I was willing to take what God gave me. So boys it is! Couldn't ask for better!" No matter how many times he'd heard her reply, it always made him smile.

Of course, when they were teenagers, racing down the road, dirty clothes sometimes hiding under the beds instead of the laundry basket, or the grocery bill tripling, she'd roll her eyes and grumble playfully, "Boys, you'll be the death of me!" But even then, he knew they were loved.

And when each of them joined the military, his parents stood proudly at their graduations, cheering them on. Now that he was out of the service, he called his parents weekly and his brothers, who were still on active duty, whenever they were available.

He continued, invigorated by the cool breeze hitting his body. After another mile, the ocean was visible in its full glory, and he stopped near a small bluff. He never tired of the view. Even now, the Lighthouse Security Investigation West Coast compound was located at a decommissioned lighthouse on a cliff overlooking the Pacific. Every day when he parked outside, he stood for a moment and took in the sights and sounds of the waves, the sea birds, and the panoramic view of the sky.

And just then, the heavy raindrops began to pelt his body. Looking down, he spied the white, box-shaped lighthouse on the secluded beach. A deep chuckle of satisfaction erupted, and he started down the path as safely as he could. Quickly soaked, he scouted ahead to determine the distance to his destination.

Making a rookie mistake, he took his eyes off the rocky path, and his foot slipped on the loose, wet gravel. Before he could catch his balance, he tumbled downward. Even with the weight of his backpack, his former training kicked in, and he attempted to curl inward, compacting his body to lessen the impacts as he rolled over and over down the steep hill. Trying to protect his head, he felt the small rocks and scrub brush stab at his torso and legs, grateful for the jeans and padded jacket he wore. As he slowed, he reached out, his fingers instinctively searching for anything to grasp to halt his fall. When he finally came to a stop, his bruised body lay in a heap at the bottom, bleeding from a gash along the side of his head, his clothes soaked and covered in mud.

"Goddammit!" he roared. He rolled himself to a seated position, quickly taking stock of his body, discerning that the only thing broken was his pride. Swiping at the water and mud on his face, he glanced around, his gaze landing once again on the small, squat, concrete lighthouse. Having researched the area, he knew it was open-sided and would provide him with some cover. Pushing to a stand, he battled the dizziness that threatened to send him right back on his ass. He shifted the backpack to a more comfortable position, and after swiping his hand over his face, smearing some of the blood mixed with mud, he slightly staggered until he regained his footing and hurried toward the lighthouse.

He'd barely stepped inside when a piercing scream brought his body to a halt, his feet skidding on the concrete floor. Blinking the moisture from his eyes, he quickly dropped his gaze to the woman scrambling to her feet with a wide-eyed expression of fear plastered on her face.

Lifting his scraped and dirty hands, he tried to calm her obvious terror. "Sorry, ma'am. I didn't mean to startle you." From her heaving chest and rapid breaths, it appeared his attempts at reassurance weren't successful. She paled as the blood drained from her face, and she reared backward as her hands lifted as though to ward him off. Just as she rushed to the other opening, he staggered, falling onto his knees before pitching forward, darkness descending.

2

Marcia's heart pounded as loud as the rain beating against the concrete overhead. She stared at the huge, mud-covered man who had lunged toward her before falling to the floor. With her back pressed against the wall, she edged toward the opening. With only a few more feet to go before she could escape, her gaze dropped to her backpack on the floor where she'd left it.

Hesitation filled her as her vision blurred. It wouldn't be the first time she'd fainted when scared, but the idea of being at his mercy had her slow her breathing, dragging in deep breaths until the spots eased from her eyes. The man hadn't moved, and her mind battled the yearning to flee with the desire to have her backpack with her. The instinct of escape took precedence, and she inched closer to the opening. As she looked down again, it was as though her backpack called to her. *Phone. Wallet. ID. Snacks.*

Grimacing, she moved with stealth, keeping her eyes pinned on the man on the floor. As she reached for her backpack, she knelt and felt for the strap with her hand, still not willing to take her gaze from him. *One twitch from him, and I'm gone!*

Inching toward the opening again, she was almost there when he moved slightly and groaned. Chest heaving, she stared at him lying prone on the floor. His head was turned to the side, and while muddy, he appeared to have a streak of red on his forehead. *Blood?*

Pushing that thought to the side, she reached the opening, blinking at the rain that blew in. Taking a step forward, she prepared to run. *Bleeding. He's bleeding.*

She turned to look over her shoulder at how still he lay. *Not my problem. I have no idea what he might be capable of.*

She slipped out of the opening, staying underneath the slight overhang as she focused on the beach heading north. *He won't be capable of anything if I leave him here to bleed to death.*

Taking a step forward, she hesitated again before dashing to the opposite side of the lighthouse to where he'd entered. Peeking around the corner, she spied him still lying on the floor but could see the blood dripping off his face. He seemed even larger. Tall. Wide. Thick muscles evident in his soaked pants and shirt. *I don't know him! How can I think of helping when he could crush me like a twig?*

With her back plastered against the outside, her chest heaved more as she labored to breathe. *Can I leave him here, alone and bleeding? That makes me no better than—*

Crying out in frustration, she whipped around the edge, re-entering the lighthouse. Dropping her bag by the doorway, she crept over and could see the gash on his forehead more clearly. She had little at her disposal to assist, but going back to her bag, she grabbed the couple of napkins she'd included. After sticking her hand out to wet them with the rain, she then bent over the man and gently wiped the blood and mud from his gash. Stepping back, she stared at him. *Okay, I've cleaned it. Good enough?* Grimacing, she turned back to her bag. The bleeding had slowed, but the wound still needed a bandage.

She dug around, hindered by her not taking her eyes off him, until she found the plastic baggie that held bandages in case she'd worn a blister on her feet unused to hiking. Taking slow steps back to him, she crept with caution so she could run in the opposite direction if needed and knelt by his head. She carefully dabbed the wound. Hating to touch him, she was forced to hold the skin of his forehead with one hand while she adhered the bandage. Surprised to find that, in spite of the chilly rain, his skin was warm to the touch. Not feverish... just warm. Her fingers tingled, and she jerked them back quickly, swallowing deeply as she quickly stood.

Okay, that's all I can do. Now I can leave.

And leave him here defenseless?

Squeezing her eyes shut, she tried to still the raging battle of indecision in her head.

"Ma'am, please, don't be afraid."

She squeaked as she jumped backward, her gaze dropping to his face, his eyes now opening as he rolled to his back. Chest heaving, she pressed her lips together but remained quiet as she stepped away.

He winced, then lifted a hand to touch his head. He pushed to a sitting position but didn't stand. He looked up, his eyes blue against the dried mud covering his face. Only the swath where she'd cleaned was free of dirt.

"I didn't mean to scare you," he said. "I was hiking and..." He scoffed, shaking his head slightly before wincing. "I fell down the hill when the rain caused the rocks to slide." He spread his hand out. "That's how I got in this condition. Christ, I can't believe I passed out at your feet. I must have hit my head harder than I realized. I really am sorry."

"Um..." she stammered, uncertain what to say as her body primed to dart outside at the first sign of threat.

He touched his forehead again, his fingers tracing the bandage. "You... you took care of my wound?"

His blue eyes pinned her to the spot, and she nodded. Heat flooded her face at the vulnerable position she was in.

"Thank you," he said.

She darted to the wide opening at the side of the lighthouse base. The rain was still pouring but getting wet was the least of her worries. "Well, I'll just go, and you can... um... stay. Um... I hope you feel better."

He remained perfectly still as though he understood that her flight response depended entirely on his actions. "Please don't leave, ma'am. I know you're uncomfortable, and that makes you smart. I'm going to stand now, and I'll leave. I don't want you to be out in this weather."

His deep and smooth voice was strangely comforting. More emotions began to war inside her, and she hated the idea of making anyone leave in the middle of the storm. *Plus, if he's not trustworthy, how do I know he'd really leave the area?* She kept her gaze on him but could hear the rainfall increase as it pounded the ground outside. If she left now, she'd be soaked before she took ten steps, and she had a long hike back to the house. Plus, it was already starting to get dark.

The man slowly stood and moved toward the opposite wall opening, as far away from her as he could go without actually stepping into the rain. "Will you be all right, ma'am?"

Her head nodded in jerks as she stared at him. With him standing, she once again realized how large he was. She was sure that he was the tallest, most muscular man she'd ever been around. His mud-covered cargo pants and tight, long-sleeved T-shirt were of an undeterminable color but showcased his build as he filled the space, making the lighthouse seem smaller.

"Okay, then, I'll leave you now, ma'am. But please know you have my gratitude. I owe you."

He turned to step outside, and, without thinking, she rushed, "No. Wait." He stopped and looked over his shoulder toward her, his brow lifted in question.

"Um…it was nothing, and you don't owe me anything."

He leaned outside, the rain immediately soaking his

head. He swiped his hand over his face again, removing much of the mud. Stepping back inside, he dragged his hand through his hair, slicking it back. His lips curved slightly, and she blinked at the expression that was both disarming and downright attractive. She blinked as she stared, unable to drag her gaze away. His smile widened, and just like when she touched his skin, a warmth traveled through her.

"Showing up, looking like some kind of mud-covered mountain troll, and scaring you is reason enough for me to apologize. You taking the time to care for my wound is more than enough reason for me to owe you."

A tiny snort escaped at his description, followed by more heat infusing her cheeks. "Oh." Unable to think of something else to say, she simply nodded, glad he hadn't made fun of her reaction. Staring at him, she pressed her lips together, realizing she no longer felt frightened. Cautious, yes. But frightened? No.

He leaned down to pick up his fallen backpack. "If you're sure you're all right, I'll—"

"You can stay." As the words left her mouth, doubt crept in. "Um... it's okay. Maybe if you sit over there, and I'm over here, we can wait until the storm passes." Wiping her sweaty palms on her pants, she swallowed deeply.

His gaze followed her hand wiping, then moved back to her face, his expression holding concern. "Ma'am, you don't—"

"Marcia." Sucking in a deep breath, she let it out as

she straightened her spine and lifted her chin. "My name is Marcia."

If she thought his earlier grin was attractive, the drop-dead gorgeous smile he beamed her way nearly caused her lungs to seize. As dots scattered across her vision, she gulped in another breath, determined not to faint. She hated the weakness, but deep breathing was the only response she'd found to work because she sure as hell couldn't control her body's reaction to nervousness.

He slowly turned and faced her, keeping his body as far away from her while staying out of the rain. Inclining his head toward her, he kept grinning. "Dolby. Jonathan Dolby is my name. It's nice to meet you, Marcia."

Searching deep inside, she once again ascertained no threat. While that might not count for much, she was willing to offer a slight smile in return. Not sure what to say, she breathed a sigh of relief when words seemed to come easily to him.

"Why don't we sit while we wait?" he suggested. "You pick the spot you're most comfortable with, and I'll sit on the opposite side."

Considering the inside of the building was nothing more than a large concrete square with wide openings on two opposing sides, she couldn't imagine that one place would be any more advantageous other than to stay close to one of the entrances. Licking her dry lips, she inclined her head to the side closest to where she was standing. "I'll sit here. Um… with the bird poop over in that corner, you might want to move over there." She pointed at the other cleanest corner in the space.

"Sounds good. That's what I'll do," he said, settling onto the floor next to the other entrance. He stretched his long, muscular legs out in front of him and leaned back against the wall. "And thanks for looking out for me. Not only with the bandage but the bird poop as well."

The grin on his muddy face made his teeth shine out whiter, giving him a comical appearance, but she pressed her lips together to keep from smiling, still uncertain if what she was doing was the smart decision.

With his body slightly reclined, she felt safer, knowing that he didn't appear to be poised to leap toward her. She backed up next to the entrance and stood awkwardly for a moment before she lowered to the floor. But instead of reclining, her body remained coiled, ready to jump up at a second's notice if needed. She kept her gaze on her tightly clasped hands in her lap and him in her peripheral vision, unwilling to stare but not wanting him to make a move without her noticing.

"Smart."

She blinked, her head lifting to meet his gaze. "I'm sorry?"

"You've generously allowed me to stay out of the rain, but you're playing it very smart in the presence of someone you don't know."

She shrugged and wished she had been a little more discreet. "Habit, I suppose."

"That's a good habit to have." He shifted again, settling deeper. "I'm in the security business and am well aware of how we all need to stay safe in unfamiliar situations with unfamiliar people."

"Security business?" She'd always hated small talk, feeling self-conscious, but at his comment, her curiosity piqued, and she couldn't hide her surprise.

He nodded toward the backpack on the floor next to him. "I've got identification if you'd like to see it."

It was on the tip of her tongue to deny the offer, torn between wanting to see his identification and fear of what he might pull out of his backpack. She pressed her lips together, rubbing them back and forth before nodding. "Okay."

He kept his eyes on her. "It's in the small, zippered pocket here in the front. You can watch me pull it out, and my hand won't go into the deeper part of my backpack."

It was uncanny how he could read her mind, seeming to know her fears. He waited until she nodded again. He unzipped the small pocket in the front with one hand, keeping his other hand resting on his side, clearly in sight. Using only his thumb and forefinger, he pulled out nothing more than a thin wallet, and her breath left her lungs in a rush.

He tossed it toward her, aiming it so the leather rectangle expertly landed beside her thigh. She didn't move until he shoved his bag out of reach and placed his hands on his thighs in plain sight again.

Her fingers wrapped around the wallet, and she hoped he couldn't detect her shaking hands as she opened it to see a California driver's license on one side. The non-muddy face staring back stole her breath. Blue eyes. Light-brown hair. Fun smile. Handsome. *Actually, handsome doesn't even start to describe him!* Jonathan Everest Dolby. How can a driver's license photograph look so good? She started to trace his image with her finger but caught herself in time. An employee identification card for Lighthouse Security Investigation West Coast was on the other side.

With a small dip of her chin, she tossed the wallet back to him, but her aim was not nearly as accurate. It would've hit him squarely in the face if his hand hadn't snapped up and caught it in midair.

"Oh, I'm sorry," she rushed out, blushing again. "I'm not... um... not a very good... um.... tosser."

His grin widened. "No worries. I'm glad you let me show it to you. So now you know for sure who I am."

"Yes," she agreed, dipping her chin slightly. "Jonathan Everest Dolby." She'd spoken his name to prove she'd paid careful attention to his identification but found the words slipping easily from her lips, liking their sound.

He chuckled, and his amusement reverberated against the concrete walls of the empty building. It was deep but not as smooth as his speaking voice while still managing to wrap itself around her.

"Jonathan... for my dad's dad. Everest... for my mom's maiden name. But honestly, my friends just call me Dolby."

She tilted her head to the side. "What was your military call sign?"

Now it was his turn to blink as his head jerked back slightly. "What makes you ask that?"

"You... you have veteran listed on your driver's license."

His eyes widened, and he grinned again. "Good catch. And you're right. Army Ranger."

She wasn't surprised he'd been in the special forces.

"How do you know about call signs?"

She grimaced. *And this is why I suck at small talk.* "It's just that... well, on TV, they have names they go by."

He stared, and she battled the urge to squirm under his perusal. Finally, his grin returned. "Mount."

Her chin dipped as her head jerked, and she blinked. "Mount?"

"Not very original, but my drill sergeant called me Mount Everest when he saw my middle name. Then because of my size, Mount just stuck."

She opened and closed her mouth a couple of times before she finally muttered, "Oh."

He laughed, shaking his head. "That's it? Just oh?"

"Well, I guess I can see why you'd prefer Dolby now."

A barking laugh left his lips, echoing throughout the space, and her smile quickly joined his. As their mirth slowed, she relaxed slightly, her earlier fear sliding into the background... but not disappearing entirely. She'd learned to listen to her gut, and while it wasn't sending out signals of danger, she realized this was the first time since fear had overtaken her life that she'd been alone with a stranger in a remote area. Her brow crinkled with worry. *Am I really safe or stupid by being too trusting?*

"Hey, Marcia. You okay?"

Her gaze shot back to Jonathan, but he hadn't moved and was still reclining against the far wall. A shaky breath left her lips, and she offered a smile that felt off-kilter. "Sure. Um... just my mind wandered, I guess." Wanting to keep the conversation off her, she quickly asked, "What does a security employee do?"

From the smile on his face, it seemed as though she'd chosen a subject he was comfortable with.

"My employer takes clients that need short-term protection, and we accept investigative missions, often with the government."

"That sounds suspiciously like a canned promo speech, but I suppose it covers all sorts of cases." She cocked her head to the side as she observed his face. "Do you like what you do?"

He drew his knees up and rested his forearms on top, his pose relaxed. "Love it. I get to go to work each day with people I respect and like and do a job that I find interesting."

She wasn't surprised. His expression had given her that bit of information before his words confirmed it. His smile. His ease. His obvious pride. He held her gaze. The air seemed to thicken, making it hard to breathe, and she dropped her chin, once more staring at her hands, uncertain what to say.

"What about you?"

She winced, now wishing she'd never asked him about his life. Her shoulders hefted slightly. "I work independently. Um... from home. I guess I don't really have to worry about coworkers."

The silence now felt wool-sweater itchy, and she looked up to find his intense gaze still on her. She wondered if he was speculating on why her reply was so evasive. Desperately trying to steady her breathing while fighting the urge to wipe her palms on her jeans again, she let out a shaky breath when he simply smiled and nodded.

"That's cool." He leaned forward, grabbed his pack, then stopped suddenly, his gaze landing back on her.

A flash of worry moved through her at what he might be searching for, but curiosity mixed with concern.

He lifted his hands, contrition on his face. "Sorry. I was going to get something for us to eat. I have it inside my pack. Hungry?"

She pressed her lips together again but nodded. She had a few items but hadn't packed for a prolonged hike. "Yeah. Um… sure."

"Okay, I'll just pull them out nice and easy." He reached inside his pack and pulled out a pack of energy bars. A little sigh of relief slipped from her.

Holding them in his hand, he called out, "I've got peanut butter and almond. What's your pleasure?"

Her mind only focused on *pleasure*, and her breathing shallowed. *The pleasure of your company… the pleasure of seeing if your lips are as sweet in a kiss as they are in a smile… the pleasure of your arms keeping me safe as they encircle me… the pleasure of feeling normal as we—*

"Marcia?"

Blinking, she caught his brow lowered in concern and forced out a laugh. "Sorry… um… I guess I'll take the almond one."

His grin returned as he tossed the bar to her. "Good choice. Now, eat up. When this storm passes, I'd like to know that you'll have the energy to make it back to where you came from."

She nodded as she focused her attention on unwrapping the treat. *Back to where I came from... my lonely home... my lonely existence.*

3

Dolby stretched his legs out in front of him again as he reclined against the lighthouse wall, adopting a casual air about him. A chilly wind blew through the opening next to him. He would rather move toward the corner for comfort, but Marcia's obvious nervousness at his presence kept him from changing his position. Especially since the single room they had to stay out of the rain was less than four-hundred square feet, it afforded him little space to remain separate. The last thing he wanted to do was add more to her fear.

He was a big guy and tried to be aware of his size around others. His mother used to pretend-groan when his father and all three boys would end up in the kitchen of their modest-sized home. *"How am I supposed to move when you four take up all the space?"* she'd playfully grumble, winking at them before his dad would grab her and twirl her around the room, then let Dolby and his brothers take a turn spinning her as well. A smile crossed his mind at the memories.

Unwrapping his peanut butter energy bar, he cut his eyes toward her. By now, he was gaining insight into the beautiful woman sitting across from him. She tried desperately to act nonchalant, but her breathing pattern changed, and her pulse fluttered at the base of her neck whenever she became nervous. And so far, that seemed to be most of their time together. Like an injured animal, she needed space to feel comfortable.

The gentleman in him wanted to insist that he leave and give her privacy to wait out the storm. But the protector in him won out, knowing that he couldn't leave her alone. All he could do was try to put her at ease until the rain passed. Then they'd go their separate ways. At that thought, the bite he was swallowing stuck in his throat, causing him to work just to get it down. He dropped his chin, hiding his rueful chuckle. *Smooth, man. Real smooth.*

Glancing back up at her, he realized she'd already learned more about him, yet she was still a mystery he wanted to solve. And the thought of them going their separate ways settled uneasily in his gut. Something about her drew him in, and it was more than just feeling protective. It was as though a deep-seated emotion called to be with her, and he wasn't willing to let their time together go without learning more.

He'd quickly ascertained that asking her personal questions wouldn't get him very far. She was private and locked up tight. He couldn't blame her since that was not only her right but a smart move for a woman out alone. What he couldn't figure out was why a woman who was so obviously nervous on her own was out in the middle of nowhere. She'd hiked but wasn't an expert hiker, and she'd chosen a remote stretch of beach to walk. *I sure as hell didn't expect to see anyone. She probably didn't either.*

They chewed in silence, then she reached inside her pack and pulled out two water bottles. Grinning shyly, she lifted a brow as she held one out. He nodded, and his hand snapped out to catch the bottle she gently tossed to him. "Seems like we both came prepared."

Her smile widened, and the expression was breathtaking. Unlike many women in California, her complexion was pale, almost translucent, as though she never spent time in the sun. In fact, the pink highlights on her cheeks probably came from her walk today and not from makeup. Her light-brown hair had soft streaks of gold, which matched her eyes. He wanted to see them in the sunlight, having a feeling that the golden highlights would create a halo while her eyes would draw him in further. The heavy sweater kept her figure from being admired, but her slender wrists, neck, and fitted jeans showed evidence of her slim body.

As she lifted her chin and turned the water bottle up, he saw thin scar lines on her wrist. His head jerked at the sight, but he quickly composed himself. He tried to catch another glimpse to discern the scars again, but she lowered her hand, and her long sleeves fell over her wrists, hiding them from view.

Another surge of protectiveness swarmed through him. Pressing his lips together, he fought the urge to stalk over to her side of the lighthouse and wrap his arms around her. While he couldn't tell if the scars were self-inflicted, something had marred her perfect skin. But as skittish as she was, he knew she'd bolt out into the rain if he moved. The last thing he wanted was to frighten her. *She's been frightened before, and damn if it will happen again because of me.*

"What had you taking a long hike today?" As soon as the question left his lips, he held his breath, hoping she'd reply and not shut down. A shy smile peeked out, and the air rushed from his lungs at her beauty.

"The weather was supposed to be nice." Her gaze shifted to the pouring rain outside. "I'd read about this lighthouse and knew the area wouldn't have a lot of visitors this time of year."

A slight crease formed between her brows, and he hoped she wasn't second-guessing her confession. Jumping in, he nodded with enthusiasm. "I know what you mean. I went camping and hiking out here during a few days off to places I knew would be mostly deserted. Sometimes you just want to have some time alone."

The crease remained, but she nodded. "Because I work by myself, I suppose I can't claim to need time alone, but I like open spaces. I thought this beach would be perfect for walking on today."

"And here you are, stuck in the rain, with a mountain troll who's intruding on your privacy."

A giggle slipped out as she shook her head. "Well, at least we have these wide-open doorways and windows in the lighthouse. I don't like feeling closed in, but we're dry. Even if I am with a mountain troll."

Chuckling, he thought about the difference in her initial opinion of him versus what most women think.

The Dolby men were all big, and like his brothers, he worked out. He'd ended up with his mom's blue eyes and her easygoing personality, but his size was all from his dad's genes.

Most women took one look at him, and the flirting began. *Hell, sometimes they don't even flirt... They walk straight up to me in a bar and ask to fuck.* Those offers no longer held any appeal. Sure, when he was younger and in the military, he'd loved the single life. Plenty of women hung around the bases. Mutual flirting and agreements to spend only a night together... that was all he needed or wanted.

But he never took the act of a one-night stand as a compliment. The words thrown at him, "You're built. I love your tats. I can't wait to see if you're this big everywhere," meant nothing. It was just a few hours of fun, and the women didn't care about him as a person. To be fair, he felt the same way about them. It was a physical release. Just sex. But for the past several years, especially since becoming a Keeper at LSI, he'd kept the hookups to a minimum. And after seeing his boss and several coworkers find love, a longing had built inside to have the same kind of relationship as his parents.

His parents had been married for forty years and were college sweethearts before that. His dad had played college ball, and according to his mother, he'd been a player in more ways than just on the field. His dad would roll his eyes, blush, and remind his mother that his previous lifestyle had ended as soon as he'd seen her in the library one day. He was a true one-woman

man, and Dolby wanted that, too. So far, no woman had captured that kind of attention.

Until today.

Looking over at Marcia, he realized he'd grown quiet as his mind wandered, and she was staring at him. Clearing his throat, he threw out, "I'll try to keep my troll tendencies to a minimum."

The tension in her shoulders seemed to relax as she shrugged. "I've never actually been around a troll, so I'm not sure what the tendencies are."

It was the first sign that she was becoming more comfortable around him, and he wanted to keep her at ease. "Let's find out." He pulled out his phone and searched the Internet for the word troll. "Well, it says that mountain trolls are a type of troll in Scandinavian folklore. But the Harry Potter and The Lord of the Rings books brought them to the forefront. Hmm..."

"What?" she asked, leaning forward slightly, her curiosity seeming to overshadow her nervousness.

"Well, it seems there are woodland trolls and mountain trolls."

"Oh. So are you sure that you're a mountain troll?"

He looked up and met her gaze, then speared her with incredulity. "Please, Marcia. Look at my size and tell me you don't think I'm a mountain troll!"

She laughed, and the delicate sound filled his ears, sending an arrow straight through his heart. Her beauty was ethereal, and he wondered if the idea of folklore had muddled his brain. But the pain on the left side of his chest was real, and he stared at the expression of delight on her face, uncertain why it had hit him so hard and why he wanted to experience it again. Looking back down at his phone, he cleared his throat.

"It says that trolls are known for stealing food."

"That doesn't sound like you. After all, you shared your energy bar with me."

Thrilled to keep their playful conversation going, he added, "In Scandinavian fairy tales, it also says they abduct people and use them as slaves."

A strangled noise sounded from the other side of the room, and his gaze jumped back to her face. Her already pale complexion lost what little color it had, and a flash of pain moved through her eyes. Her arms wrapped protectively around her middle in a movement that was both hugging and hiding at the same time. *Fuck! What did I say?* Whatever had frightened her, he wanted to erase it instantly. "But of course, that's not me! I just like to eat, and as you said, I don't mind sharing."

Her head jerked up and down in haste, but she'd lost her easy posture. She swallowed thickly, her gaze down on her hands now clasped tightly in her lap once again. Desperation filled him, hating to see her fear. Her chest moved up and down with her breaths, and she appeared to be counting while struggling to slow the rush of air. Her fingers unclasped and gingerly touched her wrist, and the reminder of her scars hit him.

Before she could see him staring at her, he looked back to his phone, desperate to find something to erase whatever had come over her. As he continued to read funny troll anecdotes, making sure to only read the amusing ones and not mention anything frightening, her arms began to relax. While he kept his tone light, fury settled in his gut at the thought that someone or something had hurt her in the past. After a few more minutes of ridiculous tales, her smile returned, and a touch of color dotted her cheeks again. Pleasure eased through him, knowing he had managed to maneuver her to a place of comfort.

A strong wind whipped the rain causing it to slam through the opening near her, and they both jumped to their feet. Instinctively, he bent and grabbed her backpack to keep it from getting wet. Realizing his hasty action might have caused her distress, she had moved closer to him. Now both standing in the middle of the lighthouse structure, her eyes were wide, but she didn't give off fear... just surprise. He sighed in relief that she was more at ease with him.

"I'm not sure when this is going to pass." She looked down at her phone, but before she had a chance to search, he'd tapped on the specialty LSI radar weather app.

"Damn, it looks like the storm has moved in over the coast and stalled."

She looked up at him, her mouth forming an "O," but no words came forth. It was the closest they had been. The top of her head would tuck just under his chin, making her about five feet seven inches tall. Being this close, a whiff of vanilla hit him, and he battled the urge to sniff her more to see if it was her shampoo, body wash, or just her. Her eyes definitely had the gold flecks that he'd noted earlier—eyes that now held his with uncertainty.

Blinking again, she pressed her lips together as her

shoulders slumped. "I guess I need to go ahead and leave."

While hiking in the rain would be nothing to him, he hated the idea of her soaked and alone. *What if she falls? What if she gets hurt? What if she gets lost?* The reasons they should stay together pummeled him, and he rushed, "Listen, Marcia, let's not tempt fate, okay? I promise I'll stay over there, and we can pass the time like we were. I have more food, and we'll be dry and safe here."

Indecision poured off her, and he stepped back to give her space even though every cell in his body cried out to move closer. He had no idea why he reacted this strongly to a woman he'd just met, but something about her called to him. *Protectiveness?* Yes, but it was more. He wanted more time. More time to learn her secrets, her desires, her background, and her story. More time to gain her trust. More time to let her get to know that he was trustworthy. His breath shallow, he waited.

Finally, with one last look outside at the approaching dusk and pelting rain, she nodded, her brow furrowed. Shifting her gaze up to him, she continued to nod. "You're right. It would probably be foolish to try to get home now."

Letting out his long-held breath, he grinned. "I know you have no reason to believe me, but I promise that my dad raised me to never take advantage of a woman, and my mama would slap me silly if I was lying."

She stared at his face for a moment before laughter erupted from deep inside, bursting forth in a sound he loved to hear. She pressed her hand to her chest, and a sigh of relief escaped from him as he watched her delight. She cast her gaze around the room before turning her attention back to him. "We should probably sit where the rain won't hit us. It'll get colder soon. I never planned on staying out all night."

"Do you have someone expecting you?" As soon as the words left his mouth and her wide eyes hit him, he cringed. "Shit, don't answer that." He reached into his pack and pulled out his wallet. Handing his identification to her again, he instructed, "Text someone... call someone... anyone you know. Tell them where you are and who I am. Give them all my information." He thrust out his phone and his wallet. "Here... take a picture of my ID. Give them my phone number, too."

"Um..."

"Really, Marcia. This way, someone in your life knows exactly what's going on and who you're with."

Her lips were pressed together, but she nodded as she took his phone and the ID. She pulled her phone from her pocket. Snapping a picture of his driver's license and employee card, she then placed her call. He could hear her friend yelling, but Marcia was able to calm them down. When she hung up, she sent a text, and after handing his phone back to him, she let out a long-held breath.

She glanced toward him, then shifted away slightly. He moved back to where his backpack lay to give her as much privacy in the small area as possible. Glad that she'd agreed to stay because he knew if she had tried to leave, he would've followed just to make sure she got home okay, and he had a feeling that those actions would have made her more nervous. And the last thing he wanted was for her to be afraid. *Hell, what I want is for her to trust me. Trust me enough to let me in.* Because for the first time with a woman, he wanted to know whatever secrets she held.

4

Marcia felt sure that if Jonathan knew she only had one real friend to call, he'd think she was a total loser. So far, today had been a huge step for her. *I went for a hike. I'm talking to a stranger. I'm going to spend the night outdoors.* She glanced around at the open-sided concrete structure. *Well, sort of outdoors.* But mostly, she wanted him to keep looking at her as though she wasn't different from anyone else.

"Angela? Hey, it's me. Um… remember how I was taking a hike today? Well, I did, and it was good. At least until an unexpected storm rolled in. I'm at the lighthouse on the beach south of me, so I'm dry and safe, but I'm going to need to spend the night."

"What the hell, Marcia?" Angela screeched. "Are you sure you're okay? I can get someone to come to get you!"

"No, no, that won't be necessary. There's no way someone can get here easily, and I don't want to put anyone out. I'll be fine."

"Marcia, honey, I'm glad you're doing so well, but I don't think spending the night alone in an abandoned lighthouse is the best thing for you. If you—"

"I'm not alone," she blurted.

A few seconds of silence ensued. "What?"

"Another hiker is here, and he's going to stay as well."

"He? What the hell?" Angela shrieked again.

"I have his ID and his phone number. I'm texting his number to you, as well as all the other information. He works for a security company. Lighthouse Security Investigations... um... West Coast. And his name is Jonathan Dolby."

There was a slight pause. "I've heard of them," Angela replied. "The security company."

A rush of relief filled her. "Really?"

"Yes. They're reputable. Send me his information. And tell him that if one hair on your head is harmed, I'll cut off his balls and feed them to the vultures!"

She looked over to see Jonathan smiling. "Um... my friend—"

"I heard her. Tell her that I'm calling my people as well, and you'll be safe."

"Angela, did you hear that? Good. Okay, sending you his info now. I'll see you tomorrow." She disconnected the call and then sent a text. Handing his phone and identification back to him, she offered a little smile. Suddenly, it struck her that he might want her information as well. Swallowing past the lump in her throat, she croaked, "Do you need my info, too?"

He held her gaze for a long moment, then shook his

head. "No. I only want you to share what you're comfortable with."

A shaky breath left her lungs. Nodding, she said, "Thank you. Um… I think, for now, we'll just stick to Marcia. And I promise I'm not a serial killer."

Her chest deflated with another breath as his grin widened, morphing his handsome face into the gorgeous zone. Before she could fall down into the hole of *what-if* and *I wish*, he turned to bend over his large backpack. Her gaze dropped to his ass and thighs, perfectly sculpted by his jeans that were slowly drying although still slightly muddy. He was huge, yet she didn't feel afraid. He could break her in two if he wanted, but she felt safe in his presence.

While she was still musing, he pulled out a tightly rolled sleeping bag and held it out to her. Giving it a little shake, he said, "I know you don't want to get into the bag because it would make you feel trapped, but I thought you could wrap it over you so you won't become chilled."

She hesitated, then reached out and held it in her hand, the thick, soft material immediately bringing thoughts of warmth. The rain clouds obliterated the sunset, and darkness set in even earlier than expected. "It'll be dark soon," she murmured, her hands still clutching the sleeping bag, holding it to her chest.

Squatting, he reached inside his pack again and pulled out a battery-operated lantern. He flooded the inside of the lighthouse with soft light when he switched it on.

"Oh!" She smiled, thrilled to be able to have the

darkness chased away. "What else do you have in your Mary Poppins bag?" She winced, hearing her own words. *God, can I be any more pathetic?*

"Well, this light will have to do even if it's not a floor lamp. And I don't have a tall mirror," he said, placing the lantern on the concrete floor.

Her mouth dropped open as she stared, and he looked up, his eyes twinkling.

"What?" He laughed. "Mom always had us watch the Disney movies when they came out of the vault. And that was after she made sure we read the books."

"That's right. I had forgotten, but before streaming, Disney would only re-release some of their older movies in different years!"

They smiled together, their eyes pinned on each other. And standing in the center of the small lighthouse with the night creeping in and the rain pelting against the exterior, she was drawn to him and filled with an easy longing that didn't frighten her.

"Why don't we share the sleeping bag?" she suggested. Seeing his lifted brows, she hastened to amend, "I mean, we can place it on the floor and sit on it. That way, we'll be warmer than just sitting on the cold concrete."

He stepped back a foot and shook his head. "No, that's okay, Marcia. I want you to be comfortable—"

"I can't be if you're over there getting cold." She winced but refused to take back the words. "Really... I... well, I trust you."

"And your friend will cut off my balls if you're not safe," he reminded.

She blinked, her gaze dropping to his crotch, the unmistakable bulge making it obvious that he was big everywhere. A longing spread throughout her body, one she hadn't felt before. Now blushing for more reasons than just Angela's words, she lifted her gaze to find his lips quirking upward and his brows lifting. A little gasp escaped, and her blush deepened. She quickly pressed her lips together before turning to spread the thick sleeping bag next to one of the walls away from the wide doorway and not under a window opening. Sitting down, she groaned at the comfortable cushion under her tired ass, trying to ignore the sexual tension that had risen in the small space.

Dolby watched her, then settled his large frame down on the bag, leaving room between them. "God, that feels good."

"I was just thinking the same thing."

"I've got more ass-padding than you," he joked, "so I know it must be better for you. I should have thought of this earlier."

They dug into their packs and tossed their combined energy bars, water bottles, cheese crackers, and a chocolate bar into the middle. Without any fanfare, they both ate and drank as an easy camaraderie settled over them.

She sighed as she wiped her fingers on her jeans since she'd used her napkin to clean his head wound earlier. She glanced to the side to look at the bandage. As strong as he appeared, it must have taken a hard hit to his head for him to have dropped earlier.

"Do you think you have a concussion? I didn't even think about that earlier."

"Nah. Granted, I don't usually drop when I get hit on the head. I was dizzy after I first fell, but I'm good now. Believe me, it takes more than a dumbass tumble down the hill to hurt me."

She nodded, not having a reason to disagree, but curiosity had her ask, "I guess you've had other injuries?"

He lifted the water bottle to his mouth, and she became mesmerized, watching his throat work as he drank. Even that mundane movement was gorgeous. And sexy.

"Oh yeah," he replied.

For a few seconds, she couldn't remember what she'd asked. But thankfully, he kept talking.

"As a kid, I broke my arm. Classic tale of falling out of a tree. Tried to jump my grandpa's fence but got caught in the barbed wire. Ended up with stitches that time. Had a concussion during a high school football game. Had some injuries in the Army. Got in a few bar fights in the military, but always in defense of our country, my fellow soldiers, or a lady's honor." He wiggled his eyebrows on the last statement.

Laughter bubbled out as she shook her head. "Why do I get the feeling that you were a really cute little boy who learned early that you could talk your way out of anything?"

Now his deep laughter rolled out, filling the small space. "You're probably right."

She wanted to know more about him. *Hell, I want to*

know everything about him. But questions could invite him to ask about her. *Will that be so bad?* A little sigh escaped, and they fell silent for a moment.

"What would you be doing if you weren't stuck here?" he asked.

Swinging her head to the side, she wondered if he was really interested or just filling time. His gaze remained steady, and she decided that he must want to know. Otherwise, he could have played with his phone and ignored her. "I would probably be inside by the fireplace, reading."

"That sounds nice," he replied with a nod.

"I'm sure it sounds tame to you."

"Really? What makes you say that?"

She jerked slightly at his question. His voice didn't sound irritated, but she realized her statement made an assumption that might have appeared rude. "I'm sorry. I didn't mean to offend you—"

"Hey, you didn't offend me," he assured. "I was just curious." He gently shoulder-bumped her, and she liked the contact more than she expected.

"I guess my statement was more of a comment about myself than you. I tend to spend my evenings alone and assume most people don't. I'm not into parties or bars. I didn't mean to imply that you wouldn't enjoy an evening reading by the fire. It just seems like most people have a much more exciting social life than I do."

"Seriously, Marcia, don't apologize. I guess I do go out a lot, but then I enjoy a good book and being alone at times, too."

Curiosity made her bolder. "So... what do you usually do when you go out?"

"Sometimes I'll go out with my coworkers. They're friends and not just people who work at the same place. We might go to a bar or a game. A couple of us volunteer as coaches at a local high school. About once a month, my boss and his wife like to have everyone over to their house for some fun downtime. Sometimes a group of us will go kayaking, hiking, and mountain climbing. I was always active from the time I was little. Mom always said I came out running. Anyway, I like to stay in shape."

Her tongue darted out to moisten her dry lips at the idea of his *shape*, which was Greek-god worthy. One she wouldn't mind exploring... closely... in depth. Suddenly, the heat inside the lighthouse seemed to rise, glad when he continued.

"For this trip, I preferred my own company. I don't always get as much time just for me as I'd like, so I thought I'd spend a couple of nights in a remote area."

A slight blush appeared to tinge his cheeks, and she was mesmerized. He leaned over and dug something else out of his pack, then pulled out a well-worn paperback. "See? I was reading just last night."

His face held such a heart-stopping smile that it captured her full attention. It was a smile that launched a thousand dreams of hot sex, sweet cuddles, and happily ever afters. Afraid her thoughts showed on her face, she dragged her gaze from him to the book in his hand, recognizing the cover.

"You like mysteries?" She inclined her head toward the paperback by a popular author.

"Yeah," he enthused. "M.B. Burns is phenomenal. Holds my attention every time." He glanced from the book to her. "You read him, also?"

She nodded. "Do you have a favorite?"

"Gotta be the Inspector Marley mysteries. *Night of the Blade.* Yeah, that's my favorite."

Grinning, she continued to nod. "That's a good one."

"I love the way the author keeps me guessing. He layers so many elements into the story, weaving them throughout. Holds my attention every time."

She tilted her head to the side. "Working in investigations, I would think that you might find these fictional mysteries to be rather simplistic... or unrealistic."

"Not at all. That's probably why I like this author so much. His research is good. The characters are like real humans. Sure, it's fiction, but with multiple storylines moving throughout, I keep trying to outguess Inspector Marley."

"Maybe one day you'll figure out the mystery early." With that, she leaned back and munched on the cheese crackers they were sharing, feeling unusually at ease with a stranger who seemed less like a stranger by now. And a little smile curved her lips.

5

The hours passed easily, and Dolby couldn't remember the last time he'd felt so comfortable with a woman he'd just met. Maybe it was because there was no expectation other than making conversation, sharing a snack, and keeping warm. At some point, they'd scooted closer to each other, and he'd made sure she appeared at ease with their proximity. As a large man, he was naturally warmer, so he sat where he could block the breeze blowing through the lighthouse structure, glad that the cool temperature wasn't cold.

She squirmed several times, and he spied the blush on her cheeks. Anticipating her need and source of embarrassment, he was glad the rain had stopped. "I'm going to head outside to take a break. I'll go to the left, and if you need to do the same, you can go to the opposite side of the building. I'll leave the lantern in here."

Nodding, she enthused, "Oh yes, please. Thank you."

Making sure to give her privacy when he finished,

he pulled out his phone and called LSIWC headquarters, knowing the call would forward to whoever was on duty for the night.

"Hey, Dolby. How's the vacation?"

He recognized Hop's voice. "Good, man. Taking time for myself. Wanted to let you know that I'm at the Lost Coast Trail beach at the old lighthouse. Got caught in a rainstorm, and I'm still here. A lone woman who was hiking got caught as well. I didn't feel right leaving her by herself, so I'm staying through the night."

"Damn, man. Only you'd go off to be alone and end up with a woman."

"Nah, it's not like that. She's pretty, sweet. Real quiet. Private. Not into talking about herself, but good company."

"So not like the typical Dolby dame?"

A rueful chuckle slipped out at the poor joke. It seemed because he was a big guy with a friendly smile and outgoing personality, the women he tended to attract were loud and brassy. Not that he didn't enjoy an up-front woman, finding it easier to have a hookup with someone understanding the boundaries. But Marcia was interesting in a way that made him want to spend more time with her. "No, it's not like that at all. She's definitely not a typical Dolby dame."

"You need some help?"

"Nah. But it's chilly, and she was unprepared. I thought that maybe if someone was available in the morning, we could get a lift so she didn't have to hike the whole way back."

"I can do that. I've got your coordinates, and I'll bring my small bird and can get you back to your vehicle."

Dolby grinned. "Thanks, Hop. That'd be great. We can fly to my vehicle, and I'll take her home. That way, I can be sure she's taken care of."

Hop laughed. "And get to spend more time with her and see where she lives, right?"

"Absolutely. See you in the morning, man. There's no rush, so oh-eight-hundred will be early enough." Disconnecting, he shoved his phone back into his pocket and headed into the lighthouse, pleased to see Marcia back on the sleeping bag, her soft smile turned up toward him.

He settled next to her again, sitting closer so their legs almost touched. They wrapped the sleeping bag over their legs, cocooning to hold in the warmth. Grateful that the temperature was not freezing, he still wanted to make sure she was comfortable.

Eventually, her head dropped to his shoulder, and her breathing slowed. Unusual emotions swarmed through him, emotions he was not used to. Warmth filled his chest, and he battled the urge to lift his free hand and cup her face just to feel her skin. But he remained still, hoping she could rest. He liked the feeling of her just leaning on him—not flirting, or trying to grope his crotch or grab his arms, or get him to sleep with her. Marcia was real. Fragile, yet he could tell a steel cord ran through her. He glanced down at her wrist, but the long sleeve of her sweatshirt still covered it. Something had hurt her in the past, and he wanted to annihilate the threat, even if it had come from within her.

She shifted slightly. "Thank you," she whispered so softly he wasn't sure she'd spoken.

"For what?" he whispered in return.

Sounding barely awake, she breathed, "For just being you and letting me be me." Her body grew heavy as she gave him her weight, and her breath became slow and even.

His heart seized, and he lifted his hand to cup her face, then halted and rubbed his chest instead. Leaning his head back against the hard wall, he stared up into the dark, decommissioned lantern room, thinking of all the lives it had saved over the years. *And now, two strangers meet where the light used to shine, guiding them toward each other.*

Marcia blinked her eyes open, seeing the barest hint of daylight coming through a nearby opening. The momentary confusion cleared, and she remembered where she was, what had happened, and who she was with. It was still dark outside, but the black had morphed into a shade of dark gray. Six o'clock, according to her phone.

Taking stock of her position, she realized she had slid down and was lying on the sleeping bag. Twisting slightly, she could see that Jonathan was also lying down, but he was on his back with one arm thrown over his head. She grinned at the little-boy visage he presented in his sleep. Then she remembered the words she'd overheard when he was on the phone.

"Real quiet. Private. Not into talking about herself... No, it's not like that at all. She's definitely not a typical Dolby dame... We can fly to my vehicle, and I'll take her home."

She tried not to let the words prickle. After all, she wasn't in the market for a relationship. Or a date. Or even a hookup. And as he indicated to his friend, she was not his type.

The last thing she wanted was to be there when he awoke and endure the awkward now-we're-in-reality conversation. Plus, she hated the idea of his friends arriving. It was one thing to meet during a storm and spend time together. But she wanted to leave before he saw her in the morning light, more lacking than ever. *And I don't want him to know where I live.*

With more stealth than she knew she had, she crawled to the side and managed to gather her bag. She was just to the lighthouse entrance when she stopped and turned back to stare at him. Swallowing deeply, she thought of how he'd made her feel so normal. She'd started her hike to prove she was brave enough to take the risk. Then running into Dolby, she'd given her trust to a stranger for the first time ever, and he'd wormed his way into her heart.

Glancing down at the book lying on his pack, she tiptoed closer. She took out a pen from her bag and carefully opened the front of his paperback to scribble an inscription. She left the book open where she'd found it and slipped outside. Lifting her face to the sliver of sunrise, she stood for just a second to breathe in the fresh air before hurrying on her way. She wanted to be almost home when his friend flew in, so she hiked quickly and determinedly. After about ninety minutes of nonstop hustling, she reached her rental house on the coast. Chest heaving, she panted as she climbed the hill to the gate and entered the code to let herself through the security fence.

Her phone rang just as she walked into the house. Grinning at the caller ID, she answered, "Good morning, Angela. And, yes, I'm home."

"Already? I was going to call for the cavalry if you didn't answer! I supposed your mystery man drove you home?"

She hesitated for a few seconds, and that was all it took for Angela to jump on her.

"What's wrong?" Angela barked, sounding like a mama bear even though they were close to the same age. "Do I need to kick some ass?"

"No! It's just that I left really early, and he was still sleeping." She dumped her bag onto the kitchen counter and walked to the refrigerator, trying to ignore the ache in her legs.

"What's going on, Marcia? I'm worried about you."

"Don't be," she assured, staring at the contents of her refrigerator. She should be hungry, but the thought of sharing protein bars with Dolby crossed her mind. Sighing, she pulled out two eggs and a bottle of orange juice. Adding butter and jam to the counter, she tried to think of what to say to Angela that would make any sense. Giving up, she deflected. "Listen, I'm pretty tired and really need a hot shower and some breakfast. How about you come over later, and I'll tell you everything?"

"Okay, but I'm going to hold you to that. I'll bring something for lunch at about one o'clock, and you can tell me all the details."

Relieved that her tenacious friend was giving her a break, she readily agreed. "Perfect. See you then." Disconnecting, she placed her phone on the counter. She gazed at it for a few seconds, then pressed the photo app and stared at the picture of Jonathan's driver's license that she'd snapped. Tracing his face lightly with her forefinger, she chewed on her bottom lip and sighed. "It was really nice meeting you, Jonathan Dolby," she whispered.

Blinking out of her memories, she quickly fixed a breakfast of scrambled eggs with toast and jam. Once full, she walked into her bedroom, ready for a hot shower. The distant sound of a helicopter approaching caught her attention. With her heart in her throat, she raced to the windows overlooking the beach and watched as a small helicopter flew by. Suddenly, she stepped back to ensure no one could see her and waited until it passed out of sight. Scoffing at the notion that Dolby might be looking for her, she shook her head.

A few minutes later, she stood in the shower, the hot water pounding her tired body and working out the kinks in her muscles. Closing her eyes, she let her mind fill with the memory of him standing in front of her in the lighthouse. Even though he'd gone outside in the rain to clean off some of the mud, traces remained on his face, neck, and clothes. But it had only served to make him more endearing. She snorted. *Endearing.* Shaking her head, she thought of other descriptors. Hot. Stunning. Gorgeous. Alpha. Sumptuous. A leader of men. A commander. A chief. The kind of man who would spark the imagination of writers, historians, poets, and musicians. A muse. A muscular, virile, all-male protector like Dolby would hardly be described as endearing by most women.

Snorting again, she flipped off the water and stepped out of the shower. Time to get back to work.

Hours later, Marcia sat with Angela in her living room, their lunch finished, and now talking over wine. Leaning back, she turned her gaze from the window that filled the room with light to her longtime friend and editor. For a day off, Angela dressed in casual elegance. Her style sharply contrasted Marcia's desire to blend into the background. Angela's blond bob swung just above her shoulders, and her blue eyes took in everything around her. And right now, those blue eyes were pinned on Marcia. Shrugging, she sipped the rest of her wine and placed the glass on the end table, having finished her adventure tale. "And that's pretty much what happened."

"Humph!" Angela scoffed. "Only you would save a gigantic, gorgeous specimen of a man, spend the night in a deserted lighthouse in the middle of a storm with him, and then slip out before he wakes!"

"Life isn't a romance novel, Angela." She sighed, her shoulders now slumping.

"No, and it's not always a suspense thriller, either," Angela shot back.

Unable to hide her wince from her friend, she wasn't surprised when Angela leaned over and placed her hand on Marcia's leg.

"Oh, honey, I'm sorry. But you know what I mean. You've accomplished so much. Come so far. You're successful, smart, and independent. But I'd like to see you happy as well."

"I can be happy without a man, you know."

"Oh, believe me, I know," Angela said with a harsh bite to her tone. Grimacing, she sighed heavily. "Sorry."

"Are things not any better with Roger?"

Angela shook her head. "No, but I don't want to talk about my husband right now. I want to talk about you."

Huffing, Marcia insisted, "I am happy. And I thought you'd be proud of me for stepping out of my comfort zone yesterday." She was referring to the long hike, but in truth, the whole day and night hadn't been just a step but more of a speed race out of her comfort zone.

"I am!" Angela waved her hands dismissively in the air. "Just ignore me. Listen, from what I know about Lighthouse Security and believe me, they keep a low profile. I know someone who had them work up a security system for them. They're all hired because they're the best at what they do and are also outstanding people. No way would any one of them have taken advantage of the situation." She finished her wine, set the glass next to Marcia's empty one, and grinned. "But a little harmless imagination can keep the fires burning. Who knows? He might end up in one of your books."

Marcia looked out the window to hide her own smile. Little did her friend know that Jonathan had definitely sparked a new muse. *I may never see him again, but I won't forget him.*

6

Dolby couldn't believe it. *Me? How the fuck did that happen to me?* A former Ranger, he'd slept outdoors on dirt, rocks, beaches, mountains... hell, anywhere needed. And he'd trained to sleep so lightly that he could jump into action at a few seconds' notice. *Yet Marcia managed to wake and leave without me hearing anything.*

He'd woken, stretched, noted the sunlight was peeking through the openings, and then rolled to the side. As soon as he realized she wasn't there, he saw her bag was gone and raced outside to see if he could catch sight of her. But all that was left were small footprints in the sand heading north.

He stomped back into the lighthouse, anger racing through his veins. Anger at himself for letting her get away. He realized he hadn't told her about his friend coming to get them this morning. He hadn't taken the time to assure her he'd see her home safely. *What the fuck was I thinking?*

He knelt by his backpack to gather his items and noticed his paperback was on top. Picking it up, he spied the script on the inside cover. His breath stilled in his lungs as he stared at her delicate handwriting.

Jonathan, Here's a favorite quote from Shannon Adler: "God built lighthouses to see people through storms. Then he built storms to remind people to find lighthouses." Thank you for sharing the lighthouse with me. Marcia

He didn't move for a long moment, his heart beating an erratic pattern as her words tattooed their print deep in his chest. "Jesus, could you have written anything more perfect?" he wondered aloud.

The sound of a helicopter in the distance jolted him out of his musings. Grabbing his pack, he stalked toward the entrance. He twisted his neck, looking over his shoulder one last time, scanning and memorizing the space where he'd met the enigmatic woman. Turning forward again, he jogged outside to meet Hop as he landed the small bird on the beach. Hop had been an Air Force Special Operations pilot before working for Carson. Another Keeper, Bennett, had been an Army Ranger sniper and was in the back of the four-seater.

Hop immediately barked out a laugh. "What the fuck happened to you? Looks like you went ten rounds mud wrestling… and lost."

"Did the mysterious lady hiker take you down in the mud?" Bennett's laughter blended with Hop's.

"Shut the fuck up," he grumbled. "She cut out on me this morning. Head north. Maybe we can find her."

Bennett shook his head. "She skipped out, and you didn't notice?"

Hop's brows leaped to his forehead as Dolby sighed. "Yeah. How the fuck she managed to wake up and leave without me being aware of her movements, I'll never know. But her footprints head north. She wouldn't have left in the dark, so she's only been gone for two hours at the most."

He kept his eyes pinned to the beach and the surrounding hills but caught no sight of her. They came to an area where homes were perched, overlooking the beach and neighborhoods fanned below.

"Damn," he grumbled. "I can't believe she got away." As soon as the words left his lips, he could feel Hop's gaze boring into the side of his head.

"Sounds like she's more than just a stranger you met and passed some time with," Hop surmised. "Thought she wasn't a Dolby dame?"

Inhaling deeply through his nose, he let it out slowly, trying to think of how to describe his feelings without sounding like a crazy person. *Who just meets someone and feels something deeper?* "She wasn't. But then, that's what had me so fascinated. I just want to make sure she's safe. She wasn't used to hiking and certainly not used to sleeping on concrete."

"You sure that's all?" Bennett asked.

The inscription in the paperback in his bag seemed to burn its image in his mind. "She was... I don't know. Different. Nice. Hell, not just nice. She was a natural beauty. Not a flirt but shy. Fuck... not shy." He searched for the right word. "More like really cautious."

"Afraid?" Bennett asked from the back.

"No. I mean, kind of. Shit, I'm not making any sense."

Hop laughed. "Sounds like she's got you tied up, man."

"She was obviously cautious, being a woman alone, and then saddled with a man my size who was a stranger to her. But even after we started getting to know each other a little bit, I realized I had done most of the talking. She gave very little away."

"Clever woman," Hop said. "Even if she was beginning to trust you, you were still a stranger. Giving you too much information wouldn't be smart."

He nodded. "I know you're right. I got the feeling that her caution wasn't just due to this situation but simply her way. And damn if I didn't want to know more." He looked over to see Hop's grin. Glancing to the back, he found Hop's expression mirrored on Bennett's face.

"By the way, nice bandage." Hop laughed.

He reached up to touch the bandage on his forehead. "You wouldn't fucking believe it, but when I fell down a cliff and got to the lighthouse while covered in mud, then discovered it occupied, I managed to scare the shit out of her before landing unconscious for a few minutes at her feet."

"You were unconscious?" Bennett snorted from the back seat. "That's probably why you didn't even hear her leave this morning. Must have hit your head harder than you thought."

"I was dizzy as fuck. While lying there, she cleaned the gash and put a bandage on it before I came to."

"She must have overcome her caution to come near a mountain like you," Hop said.

Nodding slowly, he agreed. "Yeah. I wouldn't have blamed her for hightailing it outta there. But she stayed. When I came to after just a moment, she was spooked and ready to flee. I offered to leave, and then we both stayed." He remembered the look of fear on her face and hated that he'd been the one to put it there. "We can head home," he finally admitted, his chest deflating, realizing she was well and truly gone.

"You got a name?" Bennett asked.

"Just Marcia. And before you ask, no, I don't have her address, phone number, or last name."

"How about thinking with the head on your shoulders?" Hop asked, shooting a smirk toward Dolby. "We're investigators. So investigate!"

"And you don't think that sounds a bit stalkerish?" he bit out.

"Hell, yeah, it's stalkerish," Bennett replied. "But if you find her, it'll be worth it."

Hop nodded his agreement with Bennett. "Of course, if she finds out, you might have to spend some time convincing her that you're not some crazy man after her." Barking out laughter, he added, "But then, maybe you are."

"Great," he grumbled. "Just what Carson needs is for me to get arrested for stalking a woman." He remained silent for the rest of the flight back to where he'd left his car, turning the possibilities over in his mind. He thought of spending time in the area, hoping he might run into her, but he honestly didn't have that kind of free time right now. Plus, she said she didn't go out much. Scrubbing his hand over his face, he decided he'd ask Jeb for advice. While they were all skilled in IT security, Jeb was their guru as well as being a former SEAL. If anyone could find her, it would be him.

An hour later, he stood in his bathroom staring at the reflection of his disheveled appearance. Eyes wide, he didn't move for a full moment taking in the sight. Then he slowly dropped his chin to his chest, closing his eyes in mortification. He didn't usually spend time perusing himself in the mirror. He also didn't worry about his appearance. He just dressed for the occasion. For a tactical mission... cargo pants or jeans, boots, a tight T-shirt, and, if needed, a coat and cap. Besides that, his only concern was the equipment required for the job. He'd dress comfortably or fancy for a security mission—whatever the occasion and client dictated. For a night out, it was just jeans, a T-shirt, boots, and a smile for the ladies.

Now, as he lifted his head and looked at the dried mud streaks over his face and neck, his dirty clothes, and the way his hair stood on end with bits of mud stuck on the tips, he audibly groaned. "Oh yeah, man. I'm sure Marcia was super impressed with you," he growled at his reflection. After shucking the dirty clothes and tossing them to the floor to be washed, he stepped into the shower, grateful for the hot water.

Scrubbing the trip off him, he emerged several minutes later, refreshed and much cleaner. Peeling the bandage away, he observed the bruising was more from hitting his head than the small cut that had bled. He winced at the memory of her scrambling across the floor trying to back away from him when he first entered the lighthouse. Thinking of her caring for him in spite of her fear made him want to find her even more.

Once dressed, he threw his clothes into the washing machine, checked his emails. He saw one from his oldest brother who was stationed on the East Coast, so he quickly answered, never knowing when Frazier might be sent on a mission and would be out of contact. As a former Ranger, he knew the drill and never missed an opportunity to keep up with his family. Deciding to send one to his other brother, Dalton, as well, he then closed his laptop and headed into the kitchen to fix lunch.

He'd just finished eating when his phone rang. Grinning, he answered, "Hey, Mom."

"Sweetheart," she exclaimed. "How are you? How was your time off?"

"Good, really good."

"Did you read any good books?"

Chuckling, he replied, "Yeah. I hiked for a couple of days and at night had a chance to finish the last book I was reading." As soon as he mentioned the book, he thought of the quote Marcia had inscribed for him… before she left him.

"I know you enjoyed having some time to yourself."

"Well, I was with someone last night. Another hiker got caught in the rain, so we spent the night at an old abandoned lighthouse."

"Oh, lovely. Where was he from?"

"Uh... well, it wasn't a *he*," he replied with a wince, knowing his mom wouldn't let that statement rest. He was used to sharing his life with his family but now wondered if he should have kept his mouth shut.

"A *woman?*"

"Yeah. We had a nice time talking—"

"How old was she?"

"I don't know, Mom. I guess in her mid to late twenties. You always said it was rude to ask a woman her age."

"Was she pretty?"

A vision of Marcia with her dark hair and shy smile filled his mind. "Yeah, she was."

"Your voice tells me that you're interested. Are you going to see her again?"

He gave up trying to escape his mom's inquisition just when he heard his dad in the background shouting, "You might as well confess all, son. She's not going to give up!"

Sighing heavily, he confessed, "Mom, there's not a lot to tell. Her name is Marcia. She's sweet, pretty, and I have to admit that I really liked getting to know her. And yes, I'd love to see her again. I just have to see if that's what she'd like, too."

When he was afraid that his mother was going to continue her loving but inquisitive conversation that might lead prematurely to wedding bells and grandchildren, he was rescued when she suddenly said, "Oh, darn. Aunt Sue is calling. She's probably lost her glasses again and needs me to find them. But don't think this conversation is over, Jonathan!"

Glad to say goodbye, he leaned back in the chair, Marcia filling his mind. Growing restless, he wasn't expected into work until the next day but decided he couldn't wait to start his search.

He drove to the Lighthouse headquarters, greeting Rachel as he went through her outer reception area.

She lifted her brow, then narrowed her eyes as she took him in. "First of all, you have another day on your leave. And second of all, what the hell happened to your head?"

He sighed and dropped his chin to his chest, shaking his head. "Yes, ma'am, I'm aware that I'm here off the clock. But I needed to check on something. And believe it or not, I fell down a hill."

He looked up when she didn't offer a response but spied the way her lips twitched upward. "I know, I know," he grumbled.

A stocky older man with a steel-gray military haircut walked into the room, stopped and stared at Rachel, then Dolby, then back to Rachel. Theodore "Teddy" Bearski was their equipment manager, and Dolby watched as Rachel's face pinkened slightly.

"What the hell happened to you?" Teddy asked, his gaze back on Dolby.

Sighing once again, he said, "I fell."

"Hmph," Teddy grunted before turning to Rachel and offering a little smile. With a dip of his chin, he muttered, "Ms. Rachel."

Dolby watched as Teddy lumbered out of the room, and Rachel's eyes followed him. She jerked her attention back to him and jumped slightly. Clearing her voice, she said, "Take care of your injury, Dolby. And keep your business short today since you're still on vacation." With that, she began clicking on her keyboard, and he knew she'd dismissed him.

With a grin, he moved through the security panels that led down the hall to the conference room. Entering the compound's main room, he spied Carson, Bennett, Rick, and Jeb. His boss had served with the Army as a Special Forces Green Beret, and the latter two were former SEALs. His greeting was warm, each of the Keepers being friends as well as coworkers. He hesitated for only a second, then headed straight to Carson.

With a glance toward a grinning Bennett, he said, "I guess you've already heard about my misadventures."

Carson held his gaze before his lips quirked upward, losing the battle to hide his smile. "As usual, it's hard to keep a secret around here."

"Yeah, well, I didn't exactly make a great first impression, but the woman I met managed to overcome her fear and take care of me." His hand lifted to the clean bandage he'd placed on his forehead, but he thought of the one she'd used.

"You going to look for her?" Carson asked.

"I'd like to, if you don't mind me using some resources, boss. If you do, just say so. The last thing I want to do is misuse company resources."

Carson chuckled at the comment and shook his head. "I'm pretty sure you remember what I was doing to find out about Jeannie. Hell, Chris, Leo, Rick, and Hop have all used resources. I trust my employees to be discreet, not take advantage of anyone, and handle themselves professionally. I don't see any reason you won't continue to do that, so use whatever you need."

He offered Carson a heartfelt smile, proud to know his boss trusted him on a personal level that went beyond the profession. Carson's wife had started in the middle of a mission, and his boss had done his best to give in to his feelings for the pretty nurse.

With a chin lift, he stood and walked over to Jeb.

Jeb twisted around to look up at him and grinned. "What name have you got for me?"

"All I've got is Marcia."

"Spelling?"

It hit him that there was more than one spelling of the name, but her inscription in his book was branded onto his brain. "Marcia... m-a-r-c-i-a."

"You want to try for home titles or driver's licenses first?"

"Oh, hell. She didn't say she was a California resident." Dolby inwardly curses at his lack of finding out more about her. With his skills, he could have easily had her divulge bits of information without her becoming suspicious. *Instead, I just let her lead the questions and talked about myself.*

Jeb cut through his recrimination. "Bennett has already told me the area you were in, so I'll see if I can find any houses owned by a Marcia in a ten-mile radius."

"I don't expect you to do all this on your own, Jeb. You have plenty to work on. Show me what I'm looking for, and I'll work on it."

With a nod, Jeb showed him the database that listed

the recorded deeds in the counties he was interested in. Once they'd typed in the parameters, he waited while the program sifted through the data, drumming his fingers on the table as anticipation moved through him. He finally narrowed it to four, yet looking at their driver's licenses, none matched her.

Jeb looked over and cocked his brow. "No luck?"

He shook his head. "She could be visiting someone, a renter, or just vacationing in the area." Sighing heavily, he grabbed the back of his neck and squeezed.

"Didn't take you for giving up so easily," Bennett said, walking over.

Growling, he shook his head. "I'm not. I'll go through all the California driver's licenses with her name and description, even if that takes forever." He began the next program, using the filters he knew. Marcia. Brown hair. Brown eyes. Between five feet five inches and five feet eight inches. He'd guestimated her to be about five-seven but wanted the wider filter. After adding in what he thought her weight might be and the parameters for her possible age, he sent the information into the program. It immediately began calculating the possibilities.

He leaned back in his chair, his back cracking as he stretched. He cast his gaze about the room, but then his attention was grabbed as photographs began flashing up on the screen. He shifted forward, his focus narrowed to the screen. After just a few minutes, he squeezed his eyes shut and shook his head. There was still pain from the previous day's fall, so he decided to scroll at a slower pace.

Moving through each photograph, he stared carefully, dismissing each one. Hair is too light or dark. The face is too narrow or too round. Cheeks are too plump or too hollow. Lips are too full or too thin. Not about to give up, he kept going for over an hour. Just when he was ready to take a break, his finger halted over the mouse as his gaze raked over another photograph. Heart-shaped face. Pale skin. Dark hair falling over her shoulders. Light-brown eyes that held a hint of caution visible even in the DMV photograph. *Her. It's her!*

Marcia Blackburn. He looked at her address, then checked the records. The deed to the house wasn't in her name, so he wondered if she was renting. Looking at the map, he shook his head. It was in one of the neighborhoods located on the edge of the preservation beach. *She must have hustled to get there before I flew by this morning.* He choked out a grunt. "This morning." He couldn't believe he'd only met her yesterday and had now spent the entire day searching for her. *I must be crazy.*

As soon as that thought crossed his mind, he immediately dismissed it. *No... something was there. An interest. A spark. A feeling.* He was willing to admit it might be one-sided, but he wanted to make sure. If she didn't want to have anything to do with him, he'd respect her wishes. But to not take a chance just wasn't in him.

With a grin, he printed off her information and stood. Waving it in the air, he called out his goodbyes and accepted their good wishes. He hurried home with a purpose, barely stopping when he barreled through his back door. He made a beeline to his bedroom, where he'd laid the paperback on his nightstand.

Opening up the front cover, he stared at the inscription, memorizing the words as they were now branded on his heart. He had no idea what he thought staring at the words would do, but perhaps her secrets would suddenly blossom forth from the pages.

He added the driver's license photograph to the book on his nightstand and got ready for bed. Once under the covers, he stared at the picture, wondering what haunted her eyes.

Tomorrow... I'll see you tomorrow.

7

Marcia was sitting at her desk, her fingers poised over the keyboard, but no words came forth. Instead of the scene running through her mind, all she could focus on was Jonathan. Tall, gorgeous, and drool-worthy. Even covered in mud with blood smeared on his face.

When she'd left him in the lighthouse the previous morning, she'd memorized the sight of him and his face peaceful in slumber. It had crossed her mind for only a second to go over and kiss his cheek softly, just to know what his skin would feel like underneath her lips. But the temptation couldn't outweigh the need to disappear.

And so she'd left, slipping away without thanking him properly or giving him a chance to say goodbye. Sighing, she shook her head. *Well, it's too late to go back and do anything differently.*

Even with that thought, she couldn't imagine what staying would have accomplished. An awkward wave. Watching his back as he walked away. Or him insisting on walking with her when she knew he'd rather be on his way.

Emitting a slight growl, she shook her head. *Get your mind back in the game, girl!* Rereading the previous paragraph, she began typing. The words might be crap, but she knew she could clean up the manuscript later. What was important now was just to stay busy.

She finished the chapter, saved it to several devices, and then stood, stretching her arms above her head. Walking into the kitchen, she peered out the window just as her security alert sounded. It was the tone that indicated someone was at her gate. She walked over to the panel and pressed the button. "Yes?"

"I'm looking for Marcia."

The voice was male, and not for the first time, she wished she had the ability to see who was there. When she'd rented the house six months ago, the landlord had assured her of the security system. She discovered the audio worked perfectly, but the video camera didn't always engage.

"And who are you?"

After a slight hesitation, the reply came through. "Marcia, this is Jonathan Dolby. There's a camera attached to this security panel. Can you not see me?"

Her chin jerked downward. "Jonathan? What are you doing here?"

"I wanted to talk to you again, but please answer the question. Can you not see me?"

"No, it doesn't work all the time." She immediately winced, realizing she had just admitted that the security system was lacking. "You—" Clearing her throat, she began again. "You wanted to see me? Did I forget something at the lighthouse?" Having left something was the only reason she could imagine he'd searched her out. And how he'd manage to do that, she had no idea. Swallowing deeply, she wondered what else he knew.

"Yes, you did forget something at the lighthouse. Would it be possible for me to come through the gate?"

Her finger hesitated over the button to unlatch the security gate at the end of the driveway. She couldn't imagine what she'd left at the lighthouse, but if he'd gone to this much trouble to bring it back to her, it would be rude to leave him standing outside. She snorted. *Rude is the least thing I'm concerned about.* The chance to see him again filled her mind.

"Yes, yes, of course." She jabbed at the button, then turned and raced down the hall, through her bedroom, and into her bathroom. Snagging her hair tie out with one hand and grabbing her brush with the other, she swiped it through the tresses, attempting to tame her hair. She hadn't bothered to blow-dry and style her hair earlier, but she rarely did unless she went out. *Ugh!* A headband lay on the counter, and she quickly pushed it into place, at least giving the appearance of grooming.

She gazed down her body and grimaced at her sweatpants and baggy shirt. She stripped quickly and pulled on a pair of leggings and a tunic top. Satisfied that her clothes were at least clean, she looked at her face in the mirror. She wore no makeup but lightly brushed a hint of blush on her cheeks and added a swipe of lip balm. Rolling her eyes at the ineffectual effort, she ran back to the front door, then stood for a few seconds, attempting to catch her breath. With a final exhale, letting the air rush out, she threw open the door just as he walked onto the covered portico.

All thoughts of playing it casual flew from her mind as her breath halted in her throat. Seeing him in the bright light of the day, clean and smiling as his gaze landed on her face, caused her insides to somersault. With only socks on her feet, she was even shorter than when she'd met him, and her head leaned back as his blue eyes stared intently at her. And while he'd seemed big in the lighthouse, she had a better idea of how large he truly was as he filled the doorway, almost blocking the outside light. Without the dried mud, she could now see his short hair was thick and sandy brown. She instantly decided the next character she wrote would be described precisely with his hair and eyes. Reminding herself to breathe, she took all of him in, still in disbelief he was on her stoop.

"Why doesn't your security camera work?"

Blinking at the harsh tone of his question, she jerked her chin back slightly as she was thrust into the present and out of her musings. "Um... it... this is a rental." She stammered her explanation, realizing it wasn't an explanation. Starting over, she continued, "I rent this house. The security is good, but the camera hasn't worked since that last lightning storm." She shrugged, still holding on to the door. "I just haven't contacted the owners."

"I'll have a look at it," he declared.

She blinked. "You'll have a look at it?"

His expression, as well as his tone, softened. "Yeah,

Marcia. I work for a company that plans out security, remember?"

She remembered every detail about him, every thing he'd said to her the previous night but wasn't about to admit to that. Swallowing audibly, she tried to think of something to say, but all she could focus on was his beautiful eyes.

"How about we start over? Hello, Marcia."

His deep voice had an almost playful tone as he restated his greeting. She was still hanging onto the doorknob, more out of fear that she might fall at his feet if she let go. He was everything she remembered and more than she could've dreamed of. Cleaned up, freshly shaven, and utterly gorgeous. And why he was standing on her porch, she couldn't imagine. Seeing his slight grin, she curved her lips in response. "Hello. Would you like to come in?"

He grinned wider, and she felt his smile right down to her toes, which were curling into the floor.

"Yeah, I would. But it might be easier if you'd step back."

Jumping slightly, she felt her face flame. "Oh yeah. Sorry." She immediately moved out of the way. Uncertain of what he expected, she led him through the open entryway toward the living space, feeling his eyes on her back the entire way. The house she was renting was large, much more than she needed by herself, but it was the location and privacy that had drawn her to it. She'd left the search in Angela's capable hands and hadn't been disappointed.

Now, the walk to the living room felt as though it

was taking forever just knowing *he* was there. It became harder to breathe, and when she glanced behind her, she sighed in relief to see that he was not following too closely.

He halted, his eyes roaming over her face. "I don't wanna make you nervous, Marcia. I can leave if you'd prefer. Or if you want to call someone to be here while I'm here, that would be okay, too."

She was surprised that he picked up on her nervousness so quickly, but as she searched his face and only found sincerity staring back, she swallowed down her nerves. "I don't normally allow people to come inside when I'm alone, but considering we were together the other night, I feel like I can trust you."

"You can. And I hope I'll have the chance to prove that to you again."

She waved her hand toward the sofa. "Can I get you something to drink?"

He shook his head, still smiling with his gaze on her. He sat where she indicated, and she perched on a chair facing him, her hands clasped in her lap. She wanted to stare at him and allow her gaze to roam over every inch, further committing him to memory. Now, with the bright sunlight streaming in from the windows, she could fully see his blue eyes twinkling, his firm jaw, and his body that rivaled a Greek god as his muscles strained his shirt. Thighs stretched the denim of his jeans, and biceps threatened the material of his sleeves. Glancing down at his booted feet, she remembered comparing her own feet to his the night before. *Twice the size of my shoes.*

He looked down at his boots with a crinkle across his brow. "I'm sorry. Should I have taken off my shoes?"

With a flaming face, she shook her head. "No, no. I was just looking... well, just thinking... you have big feet." As soon as those words slipped out, she wished the floor would open to swallow her whole. "Oh God, that's not what I meant."

He burst out laughing, and in spite of the embarrassment coursing through her body, she smiled at the sound. Blowing out a clearing breath, she tried again. "I have little feet." Before embarrassing herself further, she smoothed her palms over her thighs. "You said that I forgot something, Jonathan. I can't imagine that I left anything."

"Yes, you did." He waited until her gaze sought his. "You forgot to say goodbye."

Her body jerked slightly, and she opened her mouth before snapping it shut, uncertain of what to say.

He lifted his hands in a placating manner and said, "I know I'm being presumptuous, and I apologize. When I woke yesterday morning and you were gone, a part of me was shocked because, as a former Ranger, I should've heard your movements. But then, I was just saddened you'd left so quickly, and we didn't have a chance to say goodbye. I would've made sure you got home safely." He looked around before turning his twinkling eyes back to her. With a boyish grin, he added, "I confess, I would've liked to have had your phone number, too."

Heart beating an unsteady pattern, she tilted her head to the side as she stared. "My phone number?"

"Yeah, Marcia, your phone number. I really liked talking to you." He shrugged before adding, "And I would've liked to have more time getting to know you."

While his words caused her heart to sing, she narrowed her eyes as another thought hit her. "Jonathan, just how *did* you find me?"

His confident air dropped away, and he shifted on the sofa, his expression like a child caught with his hand in the cookie jar. His shoulders slumped slightly. "All I knew was your first name and what you looked like," he began.

"You're also an investigator," she stated, crossing her arms over her chest as understanding settled in. "You investigated me."

He winced, nodding. "I used a search for a driver's license in California. I should apologize for invading your privacy, but I wanted to see you again, Marcia. But if you tell me to leave and never come back or contact you again, I promise I'll honor your wishes. I really hope that you won't, though."

Her body tightened, her muscles brittle, threatening to snap. "And just what else about me did you investigate?"

The surprise on his face seemed genuine, and the way he jerked back his body as though punched made her think that perhaps her address was all he'd discovered.

Lifting his hands to the side, he shook his head and spoke softly. "Marcia, I promise I didn't investigate you in any way other than to find out where you lived so I could visit. I don't know anything else about you." He stood, his expression now defeated. "I'll leave. I never wanted to make you uncomfortable, and it's apparent that I have. I hope you'll keep my phone number in case you ever want to contact me, and I really hope you do. But I'll leave it on your terms."

She barely breathed, standing on a precipice, not unlike the cliffs outside her window. Only instead of the beach at the bottom, this precipice felt as though it could be lined with jagged rocks just waiting to tear her to shreds.

She jumped to her feet and stared as time stood still and the world stopped revolving. Their gazes held, neither looking away. It was only the two of them in the center of the universe. Neither moved, both holding their breaths as the seconds ticked by.

A slow, sad expression crept over his face, and he finally offered a dip of his chin. "Goodbye, Marcia. It was truly a pleasure to have met you."

Her chest rose and fell as the air left her lungs, but as he turned to walk out of her house, all the oxygen and light disappeared from the room. The room felt colder, darker.

She never made snap decisions, always thinking everything through carefully. The instinct to protect herself kicked in, but reality slammed into her. *If he walks out of my life, I'll regret it forever.* Deep inside a strength grew, surprising her.

"No, wait!" she cried out, her arms lifting toward him.

He stopped and turned slowly, his expression carefully blank but his gaze penetrating. Saying nothing, he waited.

"Please don't go. I can't explain it. I'm usually... well, in the past... it's just that I'm always very cautious. But there's something about you... something that makes me want to know you more. I'm afraid, but I don't wanna be so afraid that I don't give you a chance to be my friend." Her words rambled, and she shook her head slightly. *How can I write such prose yet can't speak what I'm feeling?*

He turned the rest of the way to face her and slowly walked to where she stood, giving her every opportunity to halt him. But she didn't want him to stop. When he was directly in front of her, she leaned her head way back to hold his gaze and discovered once again that nothing about him frightened her. Warmth and light moved in with his presence, surrounding her again.

"Are you sure, Marcia? I don't know what's happened in your past to make you fearful, and I hope that one day you'll share it all with me. I can't even explain this draw that I have toward you, but it's there, and it's real. I've spent too much time on the battlefield honing skills of listening to my inner voice. And while it might serve me on missions, I'd be a fool to ignore it in my personal life as well."

Her brow furrowed as she pondered his words, his larger-than-life persona filling the room, encircling her. Self-doubt crept in. "I'm not a very exciting person, Jonathan. I'm introverted and timid, and I know a lot of men don't want to spend the time it takes to get to know me. I guess I don't know what you think you see in me."

"What I see is a beautiful woman whose strength shines out despite a haunted specter in her eyes."

She jerked at his succinct words, surprised he seemed to see within her and describe her so perfectly.

"I see someone who challenged herself, moved past her comfort zone, helped a stranger, and made me want to know more about you. That's what I see when I look at you."

Nothing he said had ever been spoken before. She'd had men who thought they knew who she was, often thinking that if they tried to force an introvert to socialize, she would become an exciting person. Or men who discovered more about her and thought they knew who she was based on what she'd been through. She met a few opportunists in the past, only serving to have her pull inside herself even more.

But she'd never been stared at the way Jonathan stared at her. She'd never had someone see the real her. And while there was much he didn't know, she was willing to take a chance for the first time. A chance with life. A chance with him. She pressed her lips together, fighting the urge for them to curl into a smile while keeping their trembling hidden. "Okay."

"Okay?" he asked, brows raised.

"Yeah, okay." She nodded, her head light as she tried to remember to breathe. "I'd like you to stay. I'd like to get to know you, too. Whatever we felt the night at the lighthouse, I can't deny it was special. So maybe, just maybe, it's time to step out of my comfort zone again."

As she said the words, she prayed she wouldn't regret them. But continuing to stare into his blue eyes that reached into her soul, searching and soothing at the same time, she was filled with a certainty that she would not regret letting him into her life. Friends? *I hope so.* More? Unable to stop her lips from curving upward now, she was willing to think that more could be exactly what she needed.

8

Dolby wasn't often surprised, but everything about Marcia so far had caught him off guard—including how much he wanted to get to know her more. Nerves had slithered up his spine as he'd driven up to her house. Doubt wasn't his usual emotion, and sweaty palms weren't what plagued him, but now he was afflicted with both.

As soon as she'd answered the security call and he'd heard her soft voice, he'd had an overwhelming desire to vault over the gate just to see her again. But when the camera on the security panel didn't work, he wanted to jump over the gate for another reason, and that was to make sure she understood that her security system needed to work to its fullest capacity. The house she rented was obviously prime real estate, and the owner should take steps to make sure she was safe.

Then she'd opened the door. He'd locked his body into place, fighting the urge to pull her into his arms.

The confusion and uncertainty in her eyes gutted him. And when her wide eyes stared into his, and she finally admitted she trusted him, it was all he could do not to rush inside. Following her down the hall slowly, he devoured her with his gaze, struck with her beauty in the full light of day. Her hair was down, the silky tresses shining in the sunlight pouring in from the windows. Her leggings showcased her legs while the long shirt hung below her ass and fell off one shoulder, exposing the black camisole strap. Her feet were encased in fuzzy pink slippers. Easy. Comfortable. And understated sexy.

He'd wanted her to sit next to him on the sofa, but she'd perched on the end of an opposite chair, her hands clasped tightly together in her lap. The last thing he wanted to do was make her more cautious. Almost always jovial and at ease, he had to work to adopt a casual air. Then she'd asked about how he'd found her, and he felt fear in his gut that she'd reject him. But as his dad flashed through his mind, honesty was the only thing he would offer.

I was eleven when I overheard my mom ask Dad where he'd gone after work. "Honey, I went to the bar with some coworkers. Sam was retiring, and they decided to take him for drinks."

"Did you forget that we were supposed to have dinner with the neighbors?"

His face had registered shock and then regret. "Oh, sweetheart, I did forget. And it's all on me. I could have told them no since his official retirement party is next week anyway. I'm so sorry."

His mother was irritated and didn't hide it, but by the time they went to bed, they were holding hands again. The following day, I asked Dad why he didn't fib and just say he got held up at work.

"Son, I'd never lie to your mother about anything. To me, she's the most important person in the world besides you boys. And lying about something simple just leads to lying about something big." Dad placed his hand on my shoulder and looked me in the eye. "You'll know one day when you find the woman who owns your heart. Never lie to her. 'Cause that'll cut deep into trust, and you want that woman to trust your words."

He wanted to know what had happened to Marcia that caused such anxiety, but he'd never force her to relive something that she wanted to keep private. Even though the scars on her wrist were hidden by the long sleeves, he knew they were there, and his chest hurt. Lifting his hands to the side, he gentled his voice even more, seeing her ready to bolt while visibly struggling to stay strong. Promising that he'd only searched her enough to find her address, he observed the fear moving through her eyes. With regret pulling at his core, he stood. "I'll leave. I never wanted to make you uncomfortable, and it's apparent that I have. I hope you'll keep my phone number in case you ever want to contact me, and I really hope you do. But I'll leave it on your terms."

Marcia didn't move. In fact, her chest barely lifted when she breathed, even when she jumped to her feet. Neither of them spoke, but the air was thick as emotions seemed to swirl about the room. He couldn't ever remember being this nervous, but she still didn't move as he stared. With a heavy heart thinking he'd messed up his chance with her, he finally said, "Goodbye, Marcia. It was truly a pleasure to have met you."

He turned and walked toward the front door, knowing he'd never see her again and hating that he'd caused her pain while his own heart ached in his chest.

"No, wait!"

Those words slammed into his back like a shot, and he turned slowly, thrilled she might call him back and also terrified she was angry. He could barely believe his ears when she begged him to stay, admitting that she was cautious, something he already knew. And then, when she said she wanted to have the chance to be his friend, it was all he could do to keep from crowing that he hoped they could be a lot more.

Walking toward her, he didn't stop until his large feet were just in front of hers. She held her ground and his gaze at the same time. He wanted so much for her to trust him. To tell him what had happened to hurt her in the past. His inner voice let him know it was something big. But no matter what it was, he wanted to right the wrongs of the past. He almost laughed when she wondered what he saw in her. Christ, if she only knew. Giving it his best shot, he replied, "What I see is a beautiful woman whose strength shines out despite a haunted specter in her eyes. I see someone who challenged herself, moved past her comfort zone, helped a stranger, and made me want to know more about you. That's what I see when I look at you."

She just stared, and his palms began to sweat as his fingers twitched. Sucking in a deep breath, he needed to leave before he fell under her spell even more. And then she uttered one word that caused his heart to stutter. *"Okay."* All the air rushed back into the room, and he gulped to suck in the oxygen. From the look on her face, it appeared she had to remind herself to breathe as well.

She licked her lips, and he noticed her open her mouth a couple of times before she finally pushed through and said, "I'd like you to stay. I'd like to get to know you, too. Whatever we felt the night at the lighthouse, I can't deny it was special. So maybe, just maybe, it's time to step out of my comfort zone again."

Grinning, his heart much lighter, he reached down and covered her small, delicate hands with his own, bringing them between their bodies. Holding on for fear of her disappearing, he said, "It might be crazy to want this after we only just met, but I'm glad you're taking a chance on me, Marcia."

Her lips curved upward before breaking into a wide smile. Inclining his head back toward the sofa, he asked, "Can we sit?"

"Let me get us something to drink first."

"You don't need to serve me. I'll come with you."

She nodded shyly and turned, walking past the kitchen island that divided the kitchen space from the living room. He glanced out the window, and the view of the ocean was spectacular. "Wow, I can see why you wanted to rent this place."

She reached into the refrigerator and pulled out a pitcher of iced tea. Pouring two glasses, she handed one to him. They walked back into the living room, settling on the sofa with their bodies angled toward each other. "I had sold my house and wanted to live closer to my good friend. She and her husband have a house near here. I'm looking to buy but want to find just the right place. Until then, renting was the perfect solution."

"Where did you used to live?"

He noted a slight hesitation before she replied, "San Francisco. Well, south of the city. I had a nice and quiet condo where I could work. But then the land around was sold, and several high-rises were being built. It became noisy and crowded. I'd visited this area where my friend lived and fell in love with it. I'm renting now but hope to find a nice home to purchase." She held his gaze. "What about you?"

"I live and work in the Big Sur area. I bought a place. It's not on the water like this, but it's got a great mountain view, and the ocean is only a couple of miles away."

"That sounds lovely." She glanced around and sighed. "While this is nice for now, I can't wait to have my own place again. Somehow renting makes me feel like I never actually can decorate or call a place my own."

Grinning, he nodded. "How would you decorate?"

"Bookshelves!"

Laughing, he realized it was the first time she'd answered a question without any hesitation. "And you'd fill them with M.B. Burns mysteries."

She blushed and shrugged. "I don't know. Maybe I'd fill them with all romance novels."

"Oh yeah? What kind of romance books?"

As soon as the words left his mouth, her blush deepened, and her mouth twisted slightly. She shrugged again before sucking in a deep breath and letting it out slowly. Straightening her spine, she lifted her chin and held his gaze. "All kinds of romance. People can be so judgmental about books. If someone is reading self-help, biographies, mysteries, paranormal, or nonfiction… no one seems to think anything about it. But as soon as someone mentions romance novels, many people roll their eyes as though you've just admitted you read something unworthy."

Throwing his hands up in defense, he shook his head. "You won't get book snobbery from me, Marcia. My mom is a librarian. She raised my brothers and me to read anything and everything we wanted. As far as I'm concerned, all books have value. Hell, especially romance."

Her brow furrowed as she stared at him. "I can't tell if you're serious or not."

He shifted closer so his knee touched hers, and his arm lay on the back of the sofa, his fingers dangling near her shoulder, itching to touch her bare skin. During the night they'd spent in the lighthouse, they'd sat close to each other for warmth, but he didn't want to make any assumptions now. "Books are a reflection of life. And none are more important than those about relationships. Friendships. Family. Couples. Love."

He knew it wouldn't be the answer a lot of men would give. But he'd seen firsthand the way a true relationship could shape a family and the next generation. He'd seen the other Keepers who'd fallen in love and the rest of them who'd fight to protect that person, bonding their friendships forever. But he wondered what her response to his statement would be.

She pressed her lips together, her gaze never leaving his. It was an interesting dichotomy with Marcia. In his experience, people who were introverts and cautious around others often didn't make eye contact. But with her, she peered deeply into his eyes as though wanting... well, he wasn't sure what she wanted, but he hoped she found whatever she was searching for.

Reaching out, she placed her hand on his arm. The touch was butterfly light, but he felt branded, more so knowing she probably rarely offered physical contact to others.

Smiling, she said, "I like that, Jonathan. I think that's the nicest description of romances I've ever heard."

He grinned, loving the smile on her face and knowing he had put it there. "Well, my mom would have my head if she heard me dissing any genre of book."

They sat in silence for a moment, and it dawned on him how comfortable he felt. There was no awkwardness, no desperately trying to find something to say. There was just the peace of the afternoon as they sipped their drinks.

"You only have brothers?"

Chuckling, he nodded. "Yep. Two brothers and I'm the youngest."

Her eyes widened, as did her smile. "Three boys!"

"Yeah, we were hell-raisers. Oldest is a Navy SEAL now. The next one is a Marine. Recon."

"Wow, I'm impressed. Tell me about them... well, about all of you."

His smile widened at the interest he spied on her face and shifted to face her more fully. "Frazier is the eldest. Calm. Quiet. Big fucker—uh... big guy."

Her mouth dropped open. "You're calling someone else big? Bigger than you?"

Looking at her slender form, he could only imagine what he looked like to her. He scrubbed his hand over his hair, remembering the dried mud sticking to the ends yesterday, and hoped she thought he looked better today. "I guess we're about the same size. Maybe it's just because while growing up, he just seemed bigger to me since he was the oldest."

She leaned back, her attention riveted on him. "That makes sense."

"Anyway, he was tasked with keeping an eye on Dalton and me, but we were all three daredevils. Dalton, two years younger, always felt like he had to do what Frazier did. And I was two years behind him and pretty much stayed right with them. What they did, I tried. Riding a bike before I could balance. Driving before I had my license. Trying to kiss a girl before I knew what the hell I was doing. Going into the military."

"It sounds competitive, but in a good way."

"Hell, we were all competitive, but we had each other's backs. If anyone messed with one of the Dolby boys, they had the others to watch out for." He was still grinning as he watched her smile. He was close to his brothers, and in truth, he missed them. He harbored a secret desire that one or both would get out of the military and want to work for LSI. Shaking his head, he looked over to find her attention riveted on him, and smiled. "Best brothers anyone could ask for."

She blinked, her smile faltering slightly then appeared to settled right back in place so quickly he wasn't sure if he'd imagined the change or not. He wanted to ask about her family but halted, still afraid of stepping on an emotional landmine.

"So you were the youngest. Was that always good?" she asked, her voice soft.

The easy "of course" reply that was ready to fall from his lips hesitated as her gaze seemed to penetrate deep inside him. Instead, honesty prevailed. "Most of the time, yeah. But... well, you can imagine that the competition I mentioned before wasn't always so great." Unsure why he was willing to bare his thoughts, he continued. "Everyone thinks the youngest child gets away with everything. Is always easygoing and sometimes doesn't care. But I found sometimes it was really hard not to be able to do what they were doing. I put a lot of pressure on myself trying to follow in their footsteps."

"It was hard to live up to, I would suppose," she said, squeezing his hand.

"My family is great. My parents always wanted each of us to forge our own destinies. And Frazier and Dalton were always supportive and never placed expectations on my shoulders. I guess I'm just driven to match up to what they've become."

"I think you've succeeded, but mostly, I think you're

wonderful just being you," she admitted, her smile curving, turning her beautiful face into gorgeous.

His heart stuttered, both at the gentle touch of her hand in his and the smile on her face. He wanted to kiss her more than any other woman he'd ever met but didn't want to do anything that might be more than she was ready to handle. But he had no doubt... *I will be kissing her when the time is right. Kissing and a whole helluva lot more when she's ready.*

"Your parents must have enjoyed having such a big family."

He blinked, returning his attention to the conversation and off her luscious mouth. As her comment sank in, he was surprised. Most people responded with comments like, "Your poor mother," "Did they keep trying for a girl?" or "Your parents' grocery bill must have been huge!" But Marcia's smile indicated she thought having a large family of all boys was all good.

"Mom and D̲ad probably wondered what the hell they were doing with all the testosterone in the house, but they survived and so did we."

Another flash of something dark moved through her eyes but was once again gone so quickly. Her smile was still in place but now appeared more practiced. She glanced out the window, her body held a little more stiffly for a moment, then sighed.

Turning, she surprised him when she spoke again. "My friend told me that she'd heard of your company. She said your boss was known for only employing the best."

Pride glowed from within whenever he thought

about his fellow Keepers. "Carson Dyer is our boss. He hires mostly from former military special forces. Honestly, I've never worked with a better group of people in my career. I know it sounds like I'm bragging, but the Keepers are truly the best."

Her head cocked to the side, interest flaring in her eyes. "Keepers?"

"For Lighthouse Keepers. Those whose duty it is to guide others to safety." He smiled softly. "Kind of reminds me of the quote you left me."

Her eyes widened, and she twisted around to face him fully, leaning closer so he could see the gold flecks in her eyes as the bright sunlight beamed through the window. "I have always loved that quote." Her gentle smile threatened to steal his heart. "And I have to admit the idea of a company named for lighthouses is intriguing."

"The original Lighthouse Security Investigations company started in Maine. Their leader had been raised near lighthouses and was fascinated with their history. He ran a successful business and then partnered with my boss to open a West Coast branch."

"You mentioned the security on this house. Do you set up systems?"

"No. We design sophisticated systems that go much deeper than what most systems do. We contract out to expert companies who do the installations based on our specifications."

"Oh." She held his gaze, then smiled softly. "You really like your job."

Her statement was true, but he was already able to

read her. She was interested in him, but unlike a few other women he'd gone out with, she didn't try to find out everything he did. He sometimes wondered if they were more interested in how much money he made than who he really was. "I'm a lucky bastard. Love my job, boss, and coworkers. Can't ask for more."

Once again, Marcia had managed to get him to talk about himself while he still knew so little about her. He hesitated as the desire to question her in a friendly interrogation just to know more overwhelmed him. Yet he had no doubt she'd lock down if he pushed too hard.

All he knew was that she worked from home and rented a house that offered no insight into her personality. She only had one friend she mentioned she could rely on to tell that she was spending the night in the lighthouse with him and didn't have family in the area. Not much information, considering he'd discussed his work and family in detail. He had no problem sharing but didn't consider himself indiscreet. But everything he shared had come from her questioning. *Who's the master interrogator? I think more her than me!*

He glanced around the room, searching for clues to her. She worked from home, yet the kitchen, dining area, and living room gave no proof that anyone did anything in these rooms other than eat and relax. Taking a risk, he asked, "Can I ask what you do?"

Uncertainty replaced the smile on her face, and he winced, hating that the simple question did exactly what he didn't want to have happen. The silence was no longer comfortable, and he shifted on the sofa. Her gaze dropped to her hands in her lap, and he noted how tightly she clasped her fingers. He opened his mouth to assure her that she didn't have to share anything she wasn't ready to when she stood suddenly. Holding his breath, he waited.

"Follow me."

It was only two simple words given as an order and not a request, but he leaped to his feet, anxious to see where she was taking him.

A door opened from the side of the living room, and as soon as they entered, he was engulfed in a room so different from the stark one they'd just left. Built-in wooden bookshelves filled the back wall of the study, and windows overlooking the ocean view lined the opposite wall. A heavy wooden desk sat in the middle of the room facing the windows, with a desktop and two laptop computers, notebooks, colorful sticky notes, and cups of multicolored pens covering the top. A filing credenza sat opposite the door with a small leather loveseat nearby.

The room was lived-in, slightly messy, and was an intimate look at the woman who was now standing in the middle of the room, her gaze holding his. She wasn't smiling. Instead, her nerves poured from her as she twisted her fingers together again. It struck him that she had invited him into her private space, probably more intimate than where she slept. And he was also hit with the thought that other than her friend, probably no other person had stepped into this room. *Christ.* The realization of what she presented to him nearly took him to his knees.

Finally, dragging his gaze from her eyes, he forced

his legs to move. Walking past the desk, he hoped to gain clues as to what she did but wasn't about to open one of her notebooks or lean too close to see what she'd written on a sticky note or computer screen.

The top of the credenza held a collection of bird figurines, and moving closer, he could see they were all doves. Some ceramic and some carved from wood or stone. "You like birds?"

She was silent, and he turned to peer over his shoulder at her. Her lips were pressed, rubbing together. He looked back down at the collection.

"I like doves," she finally said.

Not wanting to make her nervous, he offered a little smile.

"Mourning doves," she continued, walking next to him and picking one up. "I like their symbolism."

His head cocked to the side as he waited, hoping she would elaborate.

"A visit by a mourning dove represents encouragement." Her gaze held his, and she swallowed deeply. "It's supposed to be gaining hope from a loved one. Um... one who's... gone before."

He tried to steady his breath as she opened up a small part of herself, and it was like she was giving a gift to just him. With slightly curved lips, he squeezed her hand and then continued to peruse the room.

When he turned, the bookcase captured his attention next. His breath halted in his throat as he stared at framed awards, bestseller lists, and prominent reviews hailing the author's talent. Rows of print books snagged his attention as he recognized the covers... and the name underneath the titles. M.B. Burns.

The air rushed from his lungs as he swung his head toward her and gasped, "You. You're the author of the Inspector Marley mysteries? You're M.B. Burns!"

9

Marcia's mouth was dry as she led Jonathan into the study. When Angela discovered the house for rent, this room sealed the deal for Marcia until she found her own place. The rest of the house was just for living, but this room was her sanctuary. Her space for creating. The room where she could make it her own, giving it life and, in turn, having it give life to her characters and their stories.

But standing in the middle of the room as his penetrating gaze glided around, taking in the contents, she wondered if she had lost her mind in bringing him in here. *We've just met. What do I really know about him?*

He walked to her dove collection, and she blurted about their meanings. Something about him made it so easy to reveal things to him. *Maybe I can do this.*

Next, he moved toward the bookcase, and she noted the instant that his body jerked, and she winced. Leaning closer, he moved from the frames to the books on display.

Her breathing became so shallow dots appeared before her eyes. Suddenly, he whirled, his eyes bulging as his intense gaze pinned her in place. His voice held a touch of incredulity as he gasped, "You. You're the author of the Inspector Marley mysteries? You're M.B. Burns!"

Unable to speak, she simply nodded her head in a jerky motion, praying she wouldn't faint. His expression gave her nothing other than stunned shock. Lightheaded, more spots filled her vision.

Then his face transformed into a beautiful smile, making his blue eyes twinkle and her heart race. Her expression didn't change, though. It was locked into a terrified, what-have-I-done, I-think-I'm-going-to-be-sick expression. Suddenly, she blurted, "I don't know why I showed you. Please... you can't tell anyone!"

His brow lowered, but before he had a chance to speak, she continued to plead. "Please, I'm begging you, don't tell anyone!"

He stepped closer, stopping only when a tiny space remained between them, yet she didn't feel crowded. Nor did she feel afraid. Still holding her breath, she waited.

"Marcia, you don't have to beg me to keep your secrets. I know we're still new to each other, so I'll give you this... I'm a man of my word. As a former Army Ranger, a current LSI Keeper, and the son of two people who loved me but would've kicked my ass if I told a lie, I give you my promise that I won't ever betray your trust."

He leaned closer and put his hands on her shoulders,

dropping his head so all she could see were his eyes. "But I need you to do something for me," he said.

At that comment, she would've done anything he asked.

His lips curved as he said, "Breathe."

She gasped, sucking air into her lungs, trying not to cough. The black dots filling the perimeter of her vision finally cleared. Letting the air out in a rush, she breathed several more times deeply until, finally, her world stopped spinning.

He straightened but kept his hands on her shoulders as he inclined his head toward the bookcases. "I have to tell you, I'm so fucking surprised and so fucking impressed! To know that you're the author and creator of those wonderful characters and those amazing stories! I'm so humbled you shared this with me."

Finally, with his words and acceptance, her lips curved ever so slightly. "Thank you." She winced slightly at the poor thanks she'd given in light of his effusive praise. That had always been the way with her —*it's so much easier to write than speak.*

"Then I think it's even more awesome," he admitted with a wink.

She jerked, realizing she'd spoken aloud. Shrugging, she decided she might as well go ahead and confess all... or at least more. She stepped away, and his hands fell from her shoulders. She instantly hated the loss of his comforting touch. Continuing toward the bookcase, she waved her hand nervously toward another row of print books below the mysteries. "These are also mine."

His brow furrowed as he followed her, then leaned

down to peer more closely. Jerking again, he widened his eyes, and another smile split his face. "You're also Marcia Black? A romance novelist?"

She nodded again, uncertain what to say, noting it wasn't a trait that Jonathan suffered from.

"Damn, woman. You've got two pen names and write best sellers under both! I can't imagine how you do that. I can't imagine how you keep everything straight." He glanced back over at her desk, and his grin widened. "Of course, I know you have to be dedicated and disciplined, but it looks like colored pens and colored sticky notes help."

At that, an unbidden giggle erupted, and she felt the oppressive weight lift off her shoulders. "It's really all I do, so staying organized is not hard."

He continued to peruse the books as they stood side by side. "I'm stunned to realize you created one of my favorite characters. Jesus, Marcia, you're amazing."

She looked up at him, warming under his praise. Years earlier, she'd discovered that awards and best-seller lists were nice, but the praise from her readers meant the world to her. A smile curved her lips again as her cheeks heated with a blush. "Thank you."

As they moved away from the bookcase, he reached for her hand, and they walked over to the small loveseat and sat down. The touch was casual yet warm, the tingles moving up her arm. They sat close together, their hips and thighs touching, and he slid his arm around her. He was huge next to her, but instead of the usual crowded and overwhelmed feeling that had her ducking away from people, she forced her body to relax. Glancing up, she caught his smile.

"Can I ask how you started writing?" he asked.

She shrugged, her lips pressing together. It was such a simple question, one she'd been asked numerous times when giving written interviews arranged by Angela. "I always enjoyed writing, and when I was younger, I enjoyed... enjoyed... wanted..." The words came to a stumbling halt as she swallowed deeply. Unable to hide her distress, Jonathan shifted so her body faced his.

"Hey, it's okay. You don't have to talk about it if you don't want to."

Holding his gaze, she spied the sincerity in his eyes.

"Honestly, Marcia, you don't have to talk about anything you don't want to. I want to know about you but never want you to feel like you have to offer me your secrets."

Her tongue darted out to moisten her dry lips, and his gaze dropped to her mouth. Swallowing deeply again, she blurted, "I have these canned answers to questions when doing written interviews. But... in truth, I've always loved to read. My... um... mom read to me all the time when I was little. My... dad teased that I always had my nose in a book. I loved mysteries... especially British mysteries." Snorting, she amended, "More like I devoured them." She quieted as her mind drifted back to when memories were all she had, and some were only slightly less painful than others. She cleared her throat. "Anyway, um... life... well, when I went to college, I needed to find a creative outlet. And so..." She shrugged, heat flooding her body. "I majored in English Literature and minored in Creative Writing. It was a way to... put life into... um... fall into myself."

Her body tensed at her admission, praying he wouldn't ask more about her family. *Why did I bring them up?* She worked to steady her breathing.

His arm tightened around her shoulders, and her attention snapped back to his face. His eyes captured hers, and she wondered if it was possible to drown in someone's gaze. She'd certainly written those words before, but never until that moment did she believe they were true. Just staring into his eyes, she knew he wouldn't ask for more. It was as though he'd realized she'd given all she could about her early life. Finally looking down, knowing it was the only way she could focus on what she was saying, she continued.

"It's hard to break into the publishing business, but I met Angela. She loved the story I'd sent to her. She and I worked on my first book deal, and I was able to publish with a major publishing house. They were only interested in the mysteries. I release my romance novels as an indie author."

"I'm embarrassed to confess that I always assumed M.B. Burns was a male. Jesus, that's such a chauvinistic concept."

"That's how it used to be for a lot of female hardcore mystery or suspense authors in the past. Not so much anymore. But I wanted to write with a pen name for privacy, so the initials worked for both concepts."

"M.B. Burns and Marcia Black. Pretty clever. I'd never think of them as being the same person. Has anyone else?"

She shook her head. "Lots of authors write in multiple genres. Different pen names aren't unusual." She sucked in a slightly shaky breath before letting it out. Unused to talking about herself, she felt more confident in his presence.

"I can only imagine that protecting your privacy is of ultimate concern. I know we've planned security systems for others in the public eye."

"Oh, no one knows that I'm the one who writes these books. Staying out of the public eye is... um..." Silence ensued as she struggled to find the right word.

"Important, right?" he provided.

"Yes." There was more she could say, but so far, today's confessions had exhausted her.

"Angela is the only one who knows?" he asked, his penetrating gaze searching while his gorgeous lips curved.

The importance of their conversation wasn't lost on her. Until this moment, Angela was the only person who knew that Marcia Blackburn was the author of two bestselling series. She should be terrified that she'd given away her secret. Perhaps she should be afraid, but staring into his face, all she felt was calm. And, in truth, also another emotion she hadn't given in to in a long time... desire. She leaned forward just enough to see the indigo ring around his light blue irises. His lips were so near. Fear of the unknown and brazen longing warred within. The former emotion was one she understood intimately, but the latter was new for her.

His gaze dropped to her mouth again, but she held still. There was no way she was going to initiate a kiss, but she prayed that it was something he wanted and was willing to go after. His chest rose and fell with each second that seemed to stretch into eternity.

"Marcia."

Her name falling from his lips sounded as though pulled from the depths of his lungs, and she had no idea what to say.

He swallowed, his gaze moving from her eyes to her mouth again. "You've gotta give me the words."

Brows knitted together, she blinked, still not knowing what he expected.

"I want to kiss you," he said, his breath wisping across her cheeks. "But I don't want to fuck anything up. I need to know what you want."

"I want that, too," she whispered, not trusting her lungs to speak and breathe at the same time. "I want you to kiss me."

She watched the resolve flee from his eyes a second before his lips landed on hers. He left no doubt he knew what he was doing with the soft kiss. His lips moved over hers before his hand glided through her hair and cupped the back of her head. He angled her just enough to seal their mouths together. His tongue darted out to trace the seam of her mouth, and she opened underneath his silken assault. Her body vibrated as lust coursed through each nerve. Her hands clutched his shoulders, fingers gripping until her knuckles were white, anchoring to something steady as the current of passion swept her away.

She'd written countless kissing scenes, but nothing had prepared her for the onslaught of desire. She never wanted the kiss to end. She'd had rushed, hurried kisses before. Years earlier, she was anxious to step into the adult world and mistakenly thought sex would ease the pain, only to find that with an uninvested partner, it barely sparked a light, much less a flame. But Jonathan consumed her with fire and made her want more.

This man could make her believe that someone would want to tenderly put back the pieces of her that had been broken so long ago.

10

Dolby had plenty of experience with flirting... both giving and receiving. But with Marcia, flirting just to tease or initiate sex had not crossed his mind. Since meeting her at the lighthouse, he knew she wasn't fake. Shy. Cautious. Giving away little about herself. Now that he knew she was a famous author guarding her privacy, he could understand her reticence.

Yet he felt something else besides the desire for privacy that cast a haunted specter through her eyes.

With each moment they'd spent together, his attraction and interest had grown, but he had no idea if she felt the same. Not until she leaned closer, her gaze dropping to his mouth. On any other woman, he'd read the signals, but with Marcia, he desperately needed to hear what she wanted.

"I want you to kiss me."

He wasn't sure he'd ever been so anxious to hear a woman's response before, and when he heard hers, all other thoughts flew from his mind. His fingers glided through her silky hair to cup the back of her head as their lips melted together.

The kiss began slowly as he felt her timidity, but then she leaned deeper into him, allowing him to take charge. He had no desire to plunder but, instead, wanted to give her everything he could offer in a kiss. In the ensuing moments, he lost all other thoughts other than to continue kissing her as his body reacted in ways he'd never felt before.

Oh, he'd expected his cock to react. Hell, that was basic biology. But it was as though every cell in his body was electrified as tingles raced along his nerves. Desire flashed like lightning behind his closed eyelids. He wanted to drag her across his lap, wrap his arms tightly around her, and continue kissing until neither knew anything other than the feel of the other's mouth moving in sync.

As his cock swelled, pressing uncomfortably behind his zipper, he refused to take things further. Not now. Not today.

Marcia was no fuck. No easy lay. No one and done. He knew that before he'd knocked on her door today, but then he also hadn't assumed he'd be kissing her, either. But now that he had a taste of her kiss, he wanted to savor each sensation.

Unlike some men who preferred not to kiss, he didn't avoid it. Granted, it implied intimacy but usually was nothing more than a precursor to sex. But with Marcia, the kiss had a life force of its own. If he did nothing more than kiss her, taste her, and memorize the feel of her lips and his tongue in the warmth of her mouth, he'd leave a happy man. But then, he also knew it would flame his desire to be with her more, and he could only pray she felt the same.

Nibbling her bottom lip, he pulled back slightly to see her closed eyes, flushed cheeks, and slightly swollen lips. Her eyes blinked open at their separation, filled with a hint of confusion mixed with lust. *Jesus, she's beautiful.* Just as uncertainty shifted through her expression, he applied slight pressure with his hand to pull her mouth back to his.

She moaned, and he swallowed the vibration, anxious to keep hearing that little noise, wondering if she'd make the same sound when she came. He desperately wanted to find out but was willing to take things at a turtle's pace if that was what she needed.

She shifted slightly on the small sofa, moving her body closer until their chests pressed together. With one hand still cupping the back of her head, his other hand slid down her back to her ass, digging his fingers into the flesh. Her arms encircled his neck, and he felt her short fingernails scrape along his scalp, sending tingles down his spine. His cock threatened to burst the zipper of his pants.

Wanting to touch her skin, he slipped his hand underneath her sweatshirt and nearly crowed as his fingers glided over her silky-smooth back. Angling his head again, he took the kiss deeper, his tongue thrusting as it explored her warm mouth, tangling with her tongue and memorizing each taste, touch, and feel of this woman who'd captured his attention.

He wanted her underneath him in his bed, but more

than that, he wanted *her*. But not this way because the last thing he wanted was for her to look at him with regret filling her eyes instead of desire and care.

Moving both arms so his hands were on her shoulders, he gently pushed her backward until their lips parted. Both breathing hard, they stared at each other for a long moment, neither speaking. Her eyes were seeking, and he never wanted her to doubt his desire.

"I didn't come over here today to seduce you."

Her tongue darted out, dragging the moistened tip over her dry bottom lip. Still breathing hard, she nodded. "When you walked in, I was surprised but thrilled to see you. But I never expected to share my private life with you."

"I'm glad you did. I want this to be the start of something."

She stared, blinking, then pressed her swollen lips together. "Something?" she whispered.

"Us."

A tiny crinkle formed between her brows. "Us?"

For a man used to telling a one-night partner what he needed or expected and having them understand exactly what he meant, he struggled to find the right words for Marcia. "I want to see you again. This isn't just for now. I really want to begin *you and me* together. Decide if what I feel and what I hope you feel is lasting. You know? *Us*."

A light-pink blush filled her cheeks, and a gentle smile curved just the edges of her mouth.

"I want us to find out more about each other. Explore more—"

At that, her smile dropped as her breath hitched. The air was warm between them, their breaths mingling as they still fought to ease the pounding of their hearts. "I will never betray your trust, Marcia. I want to know all your secrets, everything about you, and hope that, in time, you'll share."

A flash moved through her eyes, but she snapped her mouth closed and nodded slowly.

He was aware he'd have to earn her trust and stood with her in his arms. Gently setting her feet on the floor, he kept his hands around her waist until she was steady. "I hate like hell to leave, but I want everything between us to go at the right time and the right speed. And if I stay, I'll be tempted to toss those good intentions to the side. While I wouldn't regret being with you, I'd regret not doing it the right way."

Her eyes widened as her lips parted, and his chest nearly burst with pride at the look of hero worship in her eyes. Shaking his head, he said, "I'm not a hero, Marcia. I'm just trying to be a man worthy of you."

Her top teeth landed on her bottom lip as though to keep from smiling, but she lost the battle, and her lips curved upward. "I think that might be the sweetest thing I've ever heard."

"Hell, sweetheart, you write romance novels. I have no doubt you've written much sweeter things than I could ever think of saying. But one thing to know about me… if I say it, I mean it."

Her smile slid away as her expression became serious. With her palms flat on his chest and her gaze staring straight into his, she shook her head. "Jonathan,

I write many things for my fictional characters. Many things come from the heart, but the words that go between two real people who have feelings for each other in real life are the most glorious things ever heard."

"Shit," he muttered. Seeing her raised brow in surprise, he quickly added, "I'm gonna leave now before I give in to my baser instincts and scoop you up on the way to finding your bedroom. But that's not what this is about. Not now." He bent and kissed her lightly again, loving the familiarity of her lips. Straightening, he linked fingers with her and led her out of the office, through the living room to the front door.

Turning, he stared down at her guileless face and leaned over to give her one last peck, knowing the memory would have to last for a week. "I want to see you again as soon as we can."

Her brilliant smile eased the ache in his chest at having to leave her. "I want that, too."

"I live about two hours away, but that's not a big deal. The problem is that I'm leaving to go on a mission tomorrow. It's in the country, nothing major. Just security analysis for a client." He watched the disappointment cross her face and was struck once again by how she easily offered her real emotions without artifice.

"Does it sound strange to say that I think I miss you even though I've never really had you?"

He shook his head. "Hell, Marcia, I already miss you, and I haven't even walked out the door yet."

She laughed, and he decided she didn't do that often

enough and wanted to be the one to bring more laughter into her life.

He pulled out his phone and looked at her. He entered her number as she gave it to him and sent a call to her, hearing her phone ring from the kitchen counter. "Now we have each other's numbers. My week will be boring during the evenings. Can I call?"

Smiling again, she nodded. "I'd like that."

Bending, he kissed her again. Then, with a promise to see her next weekend, she pulled away, sighing heavily. He jogged down to his vehicle while ordering her inside before he left. Driving down her road to the highway, he knew the past couple of hours had just changed his life for the better. Grinning, he turned up the music, already counting down the days till he could see her again.

11

"Girl, you've got to give me more details! Kissing Mr. Gorgeous. Right now, I'm living vicariously through you!"

Marcia stifled her grin at Angela's comments. She was sitting on Angela's kitchen stool while her friend loaded up a platter with crackers, cheese, chips, dip, and cookies. Brows raised, she knew that for Angela and Roger's usual guests, she would create a charcuterie board that would rival any restaurant. But tonight, Angela wanted to let her hair down and simply drown her anger in junk food, which was fine by Marcia. Although she had no idea how they would eat everything she'd set out.

As much as she wanted to tell Angela more about Jonathan, she hated to share too much excitement in the face of Angela's marriage difficulties. But she should have known her closest friend would recognize her hesitation and the reason for it.

"Oh no, Marcia. Just because my husband has turned

out to be a real asshole doesn't mean you have to hide your happiness." Angela leaned over the counter and grabbed Marcia's hands, her fingers lightly grazing over the scars on her wrists. "In fact, honey, you deserve to be happy more than anyone I know."

Tears filled her eyes, threatening to overflow, but she fought them back and placed a wobbly smile on her face instead. "I don't know what I'd do without you."

"I'd like to think that you'd be a penniless author desperately trying to peddle your novels, but you and I both know that's not true! I only helped you get your foot in the door."

"That's not what I'm talking about, and you know it. I'm talking about your friendship."

Angela squeezed Marcia's hands and grinned. "I know. And because of that friendship, you're going to give me the details I'm craving!"

They carried the platter and glasses filled with wine into Angela's family room. Her massive house had a formal living room used only when they entertained, but the family room also overlooked the ocean and was much more comfortable. As many times as Marcia had been in this room, she was always struck by how much of Angela was in the decor. It seemed Roger's penchant for pretentious furniture didn't extend to this room or the kitchen.

They settled on the sofa with their food and drink on the coffee table in front of them and a view of the sunset just to their side.

"I was stunned when he found me, Angela. I know

he's an investigator, and it probably wasn't very hard for him, but I admit I panicked a little bit."

"I'm sure you did. Are you afraid of what all he might have discovered?"

"Absolutely! Even though I decided to share with him about my professional life, that was my choice." She shrugged, then sipped more wine. Leaning forward, she grabbed cheese and crackers, munching as she recalled her feelings about the afternoon Jonathan appeared.

"It's one thing for you to decide what you want to share with someone, but something quite different to feel like he's invaded your privacy," Angela said. "But considering you're not panicked, I assume he knows nothing else about you."

She nodded but remained quiet, something her friend rarely did.

"Do you see yourself ever sharing?"

"Maybe. I mean, yes, of course, I will. With the right person and after enough time that I know I can trust them. After all, I did with you."

Angela's smile widened as she nodded. "Marcia, you have no idea how glad I am that you met him. In just a couple of days, you've taken brave steps that you haven't in a long time… the hike, staying with him. And kissing him!"

Blushing, she shook her head. "I swear, this is embarrassing. I'm almost thirty years old, and we're talking about a kiss as though we're a couple of teenagers. But it was nice."

Angela's brows lifted to her forehead. "Nice? Girl,

how can you be a bestselling romance author and describe a kiss as nice?"

"Okay, much more than nice. Toe-curling. Soul-searing. Moan-inducing." Laughing, she covered her mouth with her hand, shaking her head again. "God, I don't understand it. How can I write scenes that readers love, and I can't even describe my own kiss?"

"Maybe because it was everything you felt deep inside, and you didn't have to try to analyze it. You weren't worried about a clinical analysis."

Unable to keep her lips from curving wider, she nodded. "Believe me, I wasn't worried about anything with his lips on mine!"

Angela hooted, slapping her thigh with her hand. "Now that's a description of a kiss!"

They finished their wine, and Angela poured more. "When do you see him again?"

"This weekend. We've talked every night on the phone, and I admit I can't wait to see him again."

"Well, don't forget to tell him you're not at your home, and that you're staying here."

The previous day, a water main had burst down the street from Marcia's house, so the neighborhood would be without water until it was repaired. Angela had invited her to stay at her house for a few days.

"I haven't said anything to him yet because I thought maybe I could return to my house tomorrow."

"Well, that's a perfect segue into what I wanted to talk to you about this evening."

Angela's voice no longer held her usual mirth, and

Marcia was curious as to what was going on. "Is this about Roger?"

"Oh yes. This is all about Roger." Angela set her wineglass down, then settled back into the soft cushions of the sofa and held Marcia's gaze. A calculating smile settled on her friend's expression. "Well, I guess I should say it's about Roger, his mistress, his illegal activities, and my revenge."

Marcia's chin jerked back as her mouth dropped open at Angela's statement. She'd listened over the past couple of months as Angela complained about Roger's impromptu trips, his underhanded business dealings, and her growing anger with her husband. But Marcia had no idea things had gotten so bad. "Um... okay... wow... you've got my attention!"

"Well, in a nutshell," Angela began, lifting her hands to use her fingers to check off her list of Roger's transgressions. "After months of wondering about his spending *our* money, I hired a forensic accountant and now have evidence of Roger squirreling away money in a secret offshore account, presumably to keep it from me if we divorce. Considering I had money when he married me... much more than him, I might add, his stealing from me is unconscionable. And in the process, we've uncovered some of Roger's less-than-legal ways of obtaining money that I'm sure law enforcement would be very interested in. Believe me, a divorce should be the least of Roger's worries at this point. But a divorce will be a definite since we also uncovered evidence of Roger's multiple affairs, most recently with his assistant." Angela made the final tick with her fingers and dropped her hands.

Marcia's mouth hung open for a moment. She'd never warmed up to Roger but was stunned to find how underhanded he was being. "Are you sure?" As soon as the words left Marcia's lips, she knew Angela would have had all her ducks in a row. "I mean, that sounds like a crazy plot for a book that you'd tell me was too far out to be believable."

Angela nodded. "Hell, it'd be laughable if it wasn't all so pathetic."

Angela's expression was calculating and hard, but Marcia could see through the anger, knowing her friend was hurting. Leaning forward, she placed her hand on Angela's arm. "Oh, honey, I'm so sorry."

Angela inhaled deeply through her nose before letting the air rush out. "Well, I should have listened to my mother years ago when she said Roger was a snake in the grass. Who knew how right she would be?"

They remained silent for a moment before Angela shook her head slightly and turned her gaze back to Marcia. "And this is where you come in."

"Me?" she squeaked, having no idea how she could assist.

"I'm heading to Los Angeles tomorrow morning to start divorce proceedings with my attorney and will be there for at least two days. Roger is in Hawaii, supposedly for a symposium which I now know is code for *I'm on a trip banging my assistant in a five-star hotel on my expense account.* I hope you'll stay here in the house until I get back, even if they've fixed the water main in your neighborhood. I have a registered envelope from the private detective that will need to be signed for when it's delivered. I might be back when it arrives, but in case I'm not, you can sign for it if you're here."

She quickly acquiesced, nodding. "I can easily do that, Angela." Snorting slightly, she confessed, "I thought you might ask me to hide in a bush somewhere with a camera to catch his indiscretions!"

Angela barked out a laugh. "Oh no. I paid a premium sum to have the best private investigator dig out his secrets. The funny thing is that Roger has no idea that I've changed my Will and Trust beneficiary. That little turd won't get away with anything by the time I'm through with him."

"I'm really sorry, and I'll do whatever you need me to. God knows you've always been there for me."

"Can you work from here?" Angela asked.

"Of course." With her laptop, she could easily write anywhere, and staying in Angela's mansion was no hardship.

Finishing their *I've got a new guy,* and *I've caught my husband* wine and snack, they hugged good night before retiring. Once in the guest bedroom, Marcia snuggled under the covers and held her phone, hoping Jonathan would call. Half an hour later, she was not disappointed.

"No, I'm not fucking kidding. My grandparents met at some hippie concert that was like a Woodstock knock-off." Dolby laughed. "Believe me... I tried to tell myself they were just two average, boring music lovers there. In reality, I overheard my granddad say that when he saw the gorgeous girl rolling in the mud with her top off, he knew she was the one for him."

"Oh my God, Jonathan!" Marcia gasped before joining in the laughter. "Are you serious?"

"Hell yeah. I still try to erase that image. If you think it's hard to imagine your parents as sexual beings, try imagining your grandparents!"

Her laughter was becoming one of his favorite sounds. He only wished they were in the same room… hell, in the same state. But he was in Nevada with Adam and Leo, two of the original Keepers, working on the security design for a multimillionaire head of an engineering firm who helped design military aircraft. The client's massive estate was one of the reasons three Keepers were working on the assignment at the same time.

They spent their days analyzing and designing and their evenings in one of the guesthouses. He had to admit that the large four-bedroom guesthouse, complete with a private swimming pool, a game room with a billiards table, and a widescreen movie room, was a helluva lot better than a hotel room. And it came with a cleaning staff and a cook who would prepare supper for them daily.

Plus, he had plenty of privacy to chat with Marcia in the evenings, an activity quickly becoming his favorite part of the day. "What did you do today?" he asked.

"I managed to get another few chapters written. I'm still at Angela's house. She left this morning to spend a couple of days in LA. She's going through a bit of a rough time personally, and I want to help her in any way I can."

"Sounds like you're a good friend," he commented.

"Oh, it's the least I can do," she enthused. "She's taken on my baggage and quirks, so it's only right that I support her as well."

It was on the tip of Dolby's tongue to ask about the baggage and quirks she'd mentioned, but he hesitated. *Trust has to be earned.* It was hard to go slow when she was all he thought about. They'd talked on the phone for hours over the past week, and he couldn't wait to see her again.

"Since you're there by yourself, how's her security system? Does the camera work?"

She snorted. "Yes. In fact, it's in perfect working order. She set it when she left, and since I haven't gone anywhere, it's still set."

"You haven't gone out on a deck or anything?"

"Goodness gracious, Jonathan. You can trust me to take care of myself, you know. But no… it's been raining here for the past two days."

"Sorry," he mumbled, not really sorry at all.

"It's okay," she said. "It's kind of nice to have someone checking on me."

"You can count on that." He looked over and saw that Leo and Adam were almost ready to go out. They were making a nighttime perimeter check of the estate. "I hate to go, but we've got some business to attend to tonight. I'll talk to you tomorrow night, and then we'll be back the day after that. Since that'll be

Friday, I'll plan on driving to see you then, if that's okay?"

"Sure," she agreed easily, her voice soft. The one-word whispered reply wrapped around his heart, then she continued. "I was hoping you'd want to."

His chest ached with a longing never felt before. He knew most people would scoff at the suddenness of his feelings, but he'd seen his boss fall just as fast. *Hell, so did my grandpa!*

After saying goodbye, he disconnected and jogged out to the SUV in the drive. Adam drove, so he climbed into the passenger seat with Leo in the back.

He never asked her about what she was writing or even what book or series she was working on. They'd only known each other for a week, and even though feelings and interests were already involved, he was careful not to pry into her professional world.

The three Keepers had barely begun their drive around the perimeter when Adam sang, "Another one bites the dust."

"Fuck off, man." He laughed.

"Seriously, Dolby? Based on what I've seen this week, Natalie has started the pool on how long it will take before you're officially off the market," Leo said.

"Don't you have anything else better to do than talk to your woman about me?"

"I do, but she's been hounding me nightly since you left the compound last weekend after finding Marcia's address."

Laughing, he knew Natalie, a Keeper as well as Leo's wife, was tenacious when ferreting out information.

Leo and Natalie had served together on the same Delta team for years, forming a lasting friendship while neither wanted to acknowledge their feelings went way beyond friends. Finally, last year, they'd both ended up in a place where they could come together after Leo headed to Guatemala to help Natalie with a case.

"Jeannie will want to invite her to a gathering before you know it," Adam added.

Carson's wife, Jeannie, managed to mother-hen the single men and include the Keepers' wives and girlfriends in the gathering, determined to foster the camaraderie that Carson worked hard to provide.

Rubbing his chin, he frowned. "I don't know about that. I'll need to talk to Jeannie when we get back. Marcia is shy... I don't want to force her into a social situation that would make her uncomfortable."

"Your protectiveness is already showing," Leo said.

Dolby noticed the look of approval on Leo's face. He accepted the comment as a compliment, knowing it was meant as such, considering Leo's protective instincts toward Natalie.

They checked the perimeter, satisfied at each stop that the system they'd designed, once put in place, would be more than what the client required.

"I'll be glad to get finished tomorrow and home on Friday," Leo said. He glanced toward Dolby and added, "Bet you can say the same."

Nodding, he didn't have time to reply before Adam piped up. "Hell, I don't have to have a woman to be glad to get home. I won't mind hitting the bar for a little recreation this weekend." As a fellow former Ranger, he and Adam had often trolled the bars in his younger years. He knew he'd probably accompany Adam if he hadn't met Marcia. Now, all that filled his mind was being back in California in two days. He'd even decided to drive to her place on Friday night instead of waiting until Saturday.

Pulling out his phone as they parked at the guesthouse, he fired off a text. **I'll call you tomorrow when we get in. Can't wait to see you the day after. Patience was never my virtue.**

He waited a moment to see if she'd reply, adolescent excitement coursing through him as the text bubbles appeared. She only answered with an emoji, but it was a smiley face with hearts for eyes, and he grinned. He knew that for her, the reply was a resounding agreement.

He pocketed his phone, a smile firmly on his face.

12

Marcia walked through the living space of Angela's house, flipping off lights and double-checking the doors. Angela was in LA to meet with her attorney, and Marcia let her mind drift to what her friend had told her. Marcia had never warmed to Roger, considering him to be a pompous ass, but had kept that tidbit to herself. When she and Angela first met, there was no reason for Roger to know she was an author. When her books began to hit charts, Angela had guarded Marcia's privacy, even from her husband. He'd often ignored her, obviously not impressed with Angela's introverted friend, which was fine with her.

Anglea must have had a productive day since she sent another text that only stated, **He's going down!** Marcia had grinned, assuming that Angela's attorney was ready to confidently handle her impending divorce.

Marcia's bare feet padded softly over the entry foyer's marble tile floors, the den's polished wooden floors, and the plush carpet of the upstairs hall leading into her guest bedroom. While her rental house was lovely, Angela's house was massive, elegant, and filled with high-end, expensive decor showcasing Roger's decorating influence of *ostentatious must be better*. Ornamental vases sat on antique tables. Framed works of art lined the walls. Heavy silver platters decorated the long dining room table with seating for twenty.

The owner's bedroom was over the top as well, but the guest bedroom that Angela had placed her in was warm and inviting, simple in its decor, and perfect. Angela had told her that Roger hated the room, but when Angela's mother came to live with them for a while, she'd wanted a bedroom that reflected her childhood and not Roger's aesthetic.

Angela had even confessed that she often slept in the room. With Marcia's silent, raised-brow questioning expression, Angela had shrugged, saying that she preferred it when Roger was out of town, or when he was getting in late and she didn't want him to wake her, or when she was pissed at him, which was more and more frequent.

Marcia loved it. A four-poster queen-sized bed with a white chenille bedspread. White lace curtains on the windows and a braided rug in hues of blue underneath her bare toes.

After her bath, she'd dressed for bed in warmer clothes than she normally would wear at her house. She'd discovered last night that Angela's house was colder than she was used to. Since Angela was coming back tomorrow, she didn't want to adjust the thermostat.

Long flannel pajama bottoms decorated in penguins, a camisole, and a soft, worn, long-sleeved T-shirt completed her sleep ensemble. Her toes were cold when she climbed into bed, so she hopped out and slid on a pair of thick, fuzzy yellow socks. Now more comfortable, she settled under the covers to read.

But as soon as she opened her e-reader to the romance she was reading, the only image that filled her mind was of Jonathan. She'd certainly written stories where the hero and heroine fell in love quickly—insta-love was the phrase the romance community used. Chuckling, she'd discovered some readers hated insta-love stories, calling them unrealistic. *Of course, I do write fiction!* But she'd had so many other readers email their real-life insta-love stories. Those were some of her favorite emails, filled with funny meetings, mishaps on first dates, and the knowledge that two people could meet, click, and fall for each other in a way that let love grow quickly.

Her e-reader landed on her lap as she leaned back against the pillows, remembering their meeting in the lighthouse. At first, the massive man covered from head to toe in mud with blood dripping down his forehead had terrified her.

And the first thing he did was to lift his hands and offer a calming assurance. *"Sorry, ma'am. I didn't mean to startle you."* He'd even started to leave to make her more comfortable. Sighing with pleasure, she was glad she'd gone against every instinct and insisted that he stay.

Her phone buzzed, and she grabbed it off the nightstand. Seeing a text from Jonathan, she grinned.

I know I said I'd call you tomorrow, but I hadn't said good night yet. So good night.

Laughing, she texted in return. **Good night. Can't wait to see you again.** No more bubbles came into sight, so she placed her phone back on the nightstand. It was soon followed by her e-reader, knowing that with her mind filled with Jonathan, no fictional character would hold her imagination tonight.

Turning off the lamp, she scooted down under the covers, a smile on her face knowing Angela was getting her life on track and Marcia could soon go back to her house. And most wonderful of all would be the day when she'd see Jonathan again.

Marcia jolted awake. Rolling over, she touched her phone to see the time—2:00 a.m.

Uncertain why she'd woken so suddenly, she barely breathed, listening. It was a habit borne from long ago. She waited, but nothing met her ears other than silence. Letting out her held breath, she lightly scoffed. This was one of the reasons she hated to sleep somewhere other than her house... getting used to the usual creaks and noises each house emitted. When she'd moved into the rental, getting used to the new environment had taken her a while. The daytime was less concerning when light flooded each room, and no dark corners existed where someone could lurk.

The urge to use the bathroom now took precedence over listening to continued silence, so she tossed the covers back. Hurrying into the en suite bathroom, she was glad for the night-light plugged into the wall next to the sink, providing a soft glow over the room.

She lifted her fingers to her lips, remembering the kiss she'd shared with Jonathan. Her lips curved upward at the thought that tomorrow would bring more kisses. At least, that was what she hoped it would bring. For the first time in a long time, the idea of spending time with someone new was exciting. And unnerving. *What does he see in me? Just the author? Is the chase more exciting than the real thing?* Professionally confident, she harbored personal fears that were sometimes crippling.

Gripping the edge of the counter, she leaned forward, holding her gaze on the reflection. *Stop, girl. You can do this. Let something amazing happen. And if it doesn't, then at least you took a step forward.* Sucking in a deep breath, she let it out slowly, her smile returning.

Finishing, she washed her hands and shivered in the cool air. She wrapped her arms tighter around her body and stepped back into the bedroom. Moving toward the bed, she hoped she could quickly get warm again once under the covers.

A slight movement on the right had her swing her head in that direction, but the hands that grabbed her came from behind. She opened her mouth to scream, but a large hand clamped over her face, cutting off any escape of noise while an arm around her waist kept her immobile.

"Got her."

The deep male voice came from next to her ear as she struggled in futility, unable to dislodge his iron-banded grip. Desperation flooded each nerve, and she kicked out, her fuzzy-sock-covered feet doing little damage other than to make his arm tighten even more.

"Settle down!"

Her body jolted as the man shook her like a rag doll in his arms. She wanted to scream that they could rob the house without hurting her, but she was still unable to speak.

"Come on," he growled.

"Hold her still," another man said from the side.

Spots formed in her vision, even in the darkness, as she tried unsuccessfully to breathe. Sure that she would suffocate in Angela's guest room, she dug her short nails into the man's arm nearest her face, and for once, she wished she had manicured talons that would have ripped his skin. His hand slipped down just enough to allow air into her nose while keeping her mouth clamped shut. Breathing deeply, she continued to struggle. *God, no! No! No!*

The man holding her twisted her head to the side, and for an instant, she thought he was going to snap her neck. Instead, the other man moved closer, and unable to move to stop them, a sharp prick jabbed her neck. Instantly, her muscles relaxed, and she slumped against the arms holding her. Her world went black.

Marcia's eyes slowly blinked open, but everything was fuzzy. She lay on a hard surface, wondering why Angela's bed wasn't soft. For a moment, she wondered if she'd fallen out of bed and slept on the floor.

She blinked several more times, trying to bring her muddled mind back into focus. Breathing deeply, she slowly cleared her vision and realized she wasn't in Angela's guest room. She tried to push to a seated position, but her arm seemed to be caught on something that clanked.

Hit in the gut with the realization, her breath rushed from her lungs as she looked down at the thin, plastic mattress underneath her, the small, dark, windowless room she was in, and the length of chain connected to a metal band around her wrist, tethering her to the pallet on the floor. Her stomach pitched, and she bent over, dry heaving as wracks of pain shot through her body.

Oh, God... not again.

Marcia looked down at the metal band around her wrist, and her chest heaved with the effort of breathing. The irony was not lost on her. The tight band was wrapped around her left wrist, opposite the one from the scars of her past. *I'll have a matched set.* She winced at the ridiculous thought, recognizing gallows humor as a coping mechanism. She'd learned a lot of coping skills over the years, some more effective than others, and some more socially acceptable than others.

A dim light bulb barely flickered above, but she'd take any light over complete darkness. The room was small, barely more than a closet. Looking down at her arm again, she observed the shaking and tried unsuccessfully to still the tremors. Her heart raced, and her breathing rattled in her lungs, making it impossible to calm down. *Why did they take me?*

She felt sure that no one knew of her birth identity. And even if they had, there would be nothing to gain from kidnapping her. Her father's company had been bought out after he died, taken over by other corporations, and what money she'd gained was mostly given away before she changed her identity. And certainly, Marcia Blackburn, the author, had no wealth worthy of a kidnapping.

She dragged another shaky breath into her lungs, hoping to tamp down the nerves rocketing through her body. No matter what, she was unable to dismiss another irony—getting kidnapped twice in her life.

But this time, it was different. She was alone. Tears pricked the back of her eyes, and she blinked at the sting. Scrunching her eyes shut in a tight grimace, she tried to hide from the memories threatening to overwhelm her. She should have known better—nothing made them lessen. The heartwrenching memories of surviving when her brother…

A sound outside the door had her eyes snapping open and the air stilling in her lungs. Then the footsteps moved farther away. She wasn't sure if she was disappointed or relieved. Swallowing deeply, she listened for any more sounds, wondering if she could ascertain where she was being held. Just the thought made her realize there was a huge difference between her childhood experience and now. Then, all she could do was cry. Now, she'd do whatever she could to survive. *Because it's all up to me.* No one else would know where she was. No one else could find her.

Closing her eyes again, she focused on breathing, and Jonathan's image came to mind. And for the third time, another irony hit her. *I just start seeing a man and get ripped away from him. And he'll never know what happened.*

Suddenly, the sound of footsteps was at the door again. Keys jangled in the lock, and the sound reverberated throughout the small space, including her stomach. The fire of anger flew through her. *I have to pay better attention to what's happening!* She shifted to her feet, refusing to be on the floor when someone entered. Even tethered with the cuffed wrist and the chain, standing gave her a modicum of control.

The doorknob turned, and her heartbeat, pounding in her throat, threatened to choke her. The door swung open, and a beefy man stepped inside, his expression neither smiling nor growling. He stared, saying nothing. She battled the urge to squirm but waited, not having a clue why he was there or what was expected.

"Toilet."

She blinked, still uncertain at his one-word comment. He lifted his hand and pointed down the hall. Dragging her tongue over her dry lips, she jiggled her left hand, and the chain rattled. "What about this?" She barely recognized the squeak of her voice.

With keys still in his hand, he grabbed her wrist to unlock the cuff. He stepped to the side and gave her shoulder a light push toward the door, so she hurried to step out into the hall. She glanced ahead, but other than tile floors and blank walls, the space gave no hint as to where she was being held.

Moving hesitantly in the direction he had pointed, she stopped when he grabbed her shoulder again, leaned past her, and threw open another door. It was a small bathroom with nothing more than a toilet and a sink, but she was grateful.

As she stepped inside, she wondered if he'd allow her to close the door. She was no risk to him, and without a window in the bathroom, she could hardly escape. She shut the door behind her, breathing a sigh of relief when he made no attempt to stop her. Not sure how long she'd have, she quickly used the toilet, then washed her hands. Not knowing if she'd get another chance anytime soon, she cupped her hands under the stream and sipped a small amount of water, relieving her parched mouth.

She glanced into the mirror, noting the bruising on her neck, and remembered being jabbed with a hypodermic needle when overcome at Angela's house. She had no idea how much time had passed since then or if Angela had even returned from LA yet and discovered she was gone.

A sharp rap on the door let her know her guard's patience was at an end, and she opened it quickly. Dipping her chin, she mumbled, "Thank you." It would do her no good to rant and rave. This man was following orders from whoever devised her kidnapping. Staying calm was her best offense right now.

He pointed back at her closet-sized room, and her

gaze continued to shoot around as they walked, looking for any clue as to where she was or what might assist her in escaping. But there was nothing. She could have been in any building anywhere in the world. And worse, her chance of escape at the moment was nil.

She hesitated at her doorway, but another slight push on her shoulder forced her inside. Her silent prayer that he'd forget about the restraint was not answered when he grabbed her wrist and fastened the cuff. He stepped outside and looked up the hall where footsteps approached. His low voice spoke a few words to someone, but she couldn't see who was there. He turned and came back into her room, holding a paper sack in his hand.

He lifted it toward her, and the scent of bread hit her. Taking the bag, she unfolded the top and peered inside to see a sandwich and a bottle of water. Once again, she forced her gaze to look into his dark, unsmiling face, dipped her chin, and thanked him.

His expression gave her nothing. No curving of the lips. No flash through his eyes. He simply turned and walked out of the room again. This time, he pulled the door shut behind him, and the sound of keys in the lock met her ears before his footsteps faded down the hall.

The urge to scream, cry, shake her wrist to rattle the chain, and even throw the bag across the room all slammed into her at one time. Dragging in a shaky breath, she let it out slowly. For now, survival included staying strong as well as staying alive.

Dropping to the pallet on the floor, she opened the

bag and pulled out her sandwich and water bottle, grateful for the trip to the bathroom and the food.

At least they don't plan on killing me right now. She pressed her lips together at that thought, and a tear slid down her face at the memories threatening to assault her.

13

Dolby walked into the LSIWC compound along with Leo and Adam. They'd left early, flown back to California, and were now ready for the report and debrief with Carson. Marcia hadn't answered her phone when he'd called last night, nor when they arrived back in California earlier. He knew she was busy but hated not having talked to her.

Stepping through the security panels, including retina scans, fingerprint scans, and keypads, they entered the main conference room and found the others there. It wasn't unusual to have all the Keepers together at once, but with so many missions going on at any given time, it also wasn't uncommon to have only a partial gathering.

Along with Leo, Natalie, Hop, Bennett, Rick, Jeb, and Adam, there were former SEALs Poole and Chris. Rick's fiancée, Abbie, had been a former CIA operative and was now a Keeper.

Half an hour later, the report was complete, and he

leaned back in his seat as Carson began going over upcoming assignments. He always looked forward to finding out what his next mission would be, but at the moment, all he wanted to do was talk to Marcia. Hopefully, she was back in her house, and he'd get there this evening.

Rachel stepped into the room, her gaze moving directly to Carson before darting over to Dolby and then back to Carson. His chin jerked down slightly at her ruffled demeanor, something rarely seen with Rachel. She was unflappable in most situations, and when she spoke, they all listened. Now, seeing the concern on her face, his attention was riveted on her.

"Rachel, what is it?" Carson asked, drawing everyone's focus to her.

"There's an Angela Mansfield on the phone. She says it's an emergency. She's a friend of—"

"Marcia," Dolby stated, his heart now pounding. "A friend of Marcia's. What's wrong?"

"She's asking to speak to you, Dolby," Rachel said. "When I questioned her, she admitted she needed our help. I've got her on video conference."

Jeb immediately turned, and with a click of his keyboard, the screen on the wall filled with the image of a beautiful, blond woman whose pale face and wide eyes gave evidence of her emotions. While they could see her, she would only have a blank screen in front of her.

"Ms. Mansfield, I'm Carson Dyer. I understand you need to speak to us."

Her face crumpled, agony deeply visible. "Please, you've got to find her."

"Who?" Dolby barked, rising to his feet, barely aware of Hop standing nearby, his hand landing on Dolby's shoulder.

"Marcia. Marcia Blackburn. She's missing. Kidnapped." A grimace twisted her mouth. "Oh God, this is all my fault."

"Ms. Mansfield," Carson said, attempting to calm her with his low and steady tone. "If she's missing, we need to gather all the information as quickly as possible, so I need you to take a deep breath and tell us everything you know."

She jerked her head up and down, swallowing deeply. "I... I didn't call the police yet. I knew she had talked of meeting Jonathan of Lighthouse Security. I'd heard of you... um... from security at a friend's place. Oh God, did I do the wrong thing?"

"Ms. Mansfield—"

"Angela. I hate... oh, just please call me Angela."

"Okay, Angela. Here's what we need. The location you last saw Marcia. And as succinctly as possible, tell me the facts. I've got a team that I'll send to you as soon as we know what we're dealing with. I have a contact with the FBI. As soon as you give us the information, I'll get ahold of him."

"I left Marcia in my house two days ago. Her street's water main broke, and I needed to go to Los Angeles to talk to my attorney. I haven't talked to her since the day before yesterday."

Carson looked at Dolby, who nodded in agreement. "Same here," he confirmed, trying to focus on Angela's discourse and not the pounding of his heart while praying she was wrong, and Marcia had just left early.

"When I got home, she wasn't here, but her purse and laptop were still in the den. I went to the guest room, and that's when I discovered her bed unmade, her toiletries still in the bathroom, her clothes still in an opened suitcase, and a small table overturned near the bathroom door." She squinted her eyes closed, her face contorting in a grimace again. Sucking in a deep breath, she opened her eyes and her features hardened. "I ran to our security system where the house is controlled and has video monitoring. I searched but found nothing." She grimaced again. "That doesn't surprise me. It seems my husband has a habit of messing with the system when it's convenient."

Dolby's eyes narrowed as he looked at the others in the room. Jeb was continually typing on his keyboard and on a separate screen. He had managed to get into the system located at her address.

"But I have a separate system in place," she continued, drawing everyone's attention back to her. "I'm beginning divorce proceedings and have to be very careful as I gather evidence on my husband. I installed my own system in each room in our house so that if he overrides our main security system to keep me from seeing what he might be doing, I can still observe. I looked at the video, and that's where I saw her. She was attacked in the room and taken!" A wail of anguish burst forth as tears rolled down her cheeks.

Dolby rushed forward, barely hearing the bootsteps

behind him. A hand clamped on his shoulder, and he whirled around to see Hop.

"Man, hang on. Let's get the intel so we don't waste time," Hop cautioned.

He heard the words and believed the concept, but with his heart racing and the breath halting in his lungs, he growled, "Let go of me."

"Dolby," Carson called out.

His training kicked in, and he looked over at his boss.

"Wait. Then you'll go in."

Understanding Carson's assurance that Dolby would be front line on the mission to find Marcia, he offered a curt nod, then looked back toward the screen.

"Angela, can you send us your security video?" Carson asked.

"Yes." She nodded. "It's on my computer." Her hands were shaking, but she managed to tap the keyboard, and after only a moment, she looked up. "I sent it."

"Got it," Jeb said. "Putting it up now."

Dolby and the other Keepers watched as two men entered through a door off the kitchen and made their way straight to the stairs. Dark clothes. Dark knit caps pulled low. Her system was room by room, but Jeb quickly keyed through the program so they could follow them in as they climbed the stairs and, without stopping, went directly to a door.

His heart now in his throat, he watched the video from the inside of the room where one man grabbed Marcia as soon as she stepped out of the bathroom. She began thrashing, but his hold was too strong.

The words "got her" only made Marcia struggle more, but it was easy to see the much larger man had a tight hold on her.

The kidnapper's order to settle down was followed by him shaking her, and Dolby's hands fisted at his side, knowing that man would pay dearly for his actions. Barely breathing as one man gave the order to hold her still, the other one jabbed her neck with a hypodermic, and she immediately slumped. "Goddammit!" he cursed, rage flooding his veins.

One of the men hefted her over his shoulder, and they retreated through the house the way they came, not taking anything other than Marcia. "Christ, who could've wanted her kidnapped?"

"What does she do?" Natalie asked, turning to look at Dolby.

"She's an author. She writes mysteries and romance under the names M.B. Burns and Marcia Black."

"Holy shit. I've read her work," Natalie said, brows lifted.

"Yeah, you and just about everyone else. She's also somewhat of a recluse, not going out very often. But this doesn't make sense!" Dolby argued. "I can't imagine her being held for ransom!"

"That's what I thought," Angela said, tears still streaming, "but keep listening."

In unison, the Keepers turned their heads back to the screen, where the two men carrying Marcia were just passing through the kitchen.

"Make sure you report that we got his wife. The angel package is on its way."

Dolby's chin jerked back again in shock and confusion. "Wife? Angel? What the fuck?"

"That's what I'm trying to tell you," Angela cried. "I think they were after me. I think my husband was having me kidnapped. The angel is a reference to my name."

The Keepers immediately jumped into action. Abbie, Rick's wife and their geospatial specialist, called out, "I'm pulling up the maps of Angela's house and surrounding area."

Natalie nodded. "I'll work with you. We can get our hands on info as to which direction they went."

"Why the fuck didn't the regular security system pick this up?" Rick asked.

Poole, like Rick, was a former SEAL and lifted a brow as he replied, "If her husband orchestrated this, he could have had someone fuck with their security system."

"He doesn't know about the extra cameras I put in the house," Angela interjected, her expression still holding terror.

"Well, thank God you did, or we would've had a fuck of a time figuring out what happened," Leo said.

"Let's not waste time getting to her house if nothing there will help us right now," Carson said, drawing Dolby's gaze. "I know you want to move, Dolby, but you know I'm right. We don't want to lose precious time that could be better spent using our resources to find out where they took her."

Another hand clamped on his shoulder, squeezing slightly. Bennett's calm voice spoke. "Hang on, man.

Carson's right. Let's do this methodically so we don't chase our tails and waste time."

"They're gonna pay," he growled, low and soft.

Another squeeze. "Yeah, they are."

Nodding, he looked around. Poole and Adam were already pulling up street cameras, and Jeb was tapping into the outside security cameras of the neighbors. Natalie and Abbie were busy with the logistics of where the kidnappers might have gone. Chris, also a former SEAL, and Leo were already searching for information on Angela's husband.

"We've got to get her out of there before her husband discovers she's at home and not kidnapped," Bennett said, drawing Dolby's attention to him.

"Shit, I didn't even think of that!" Dolby growled, his heart rate increasing.

"Angela," Carson called out. "Pack whatever you can that won't alert your husband to anything unusual. We'll jam the security system now. Since he'd already had it non-functioning to cover up the kidnapping, we won't let the system go back online. But you need to go somewhere to stay until we can complete the mission. Somewhere you won't be noticed or known or seen."

"I can find a vacation house to rent."

"We've got an available safe house about an hour south of where you are now. But you'll have to consider it a vacation and stay completely off the grid."

Angela nodded in haste. "I can do that easily. Anything for Marcia."

"We'll send the information securely. I'll have one of

my men meet you there to make sure you're safe and settled."

"It'll only take me about fifteen minutes to leave," she assured. "But there's more. Lots more."

At those words, all eyes shot back to the screen toward Angela. She dragged in a shaky breath. "I'll give you all the sordid details about Roger and his illegal maneuvers, plus what he has been trying to steal from my accounts. But it's Marcia... it's... it's just that she can't handle this. Not her."

"What are you talking about?" Dolby bit out.

"I was never going to tell anyone. She wanted to move beyond it. Not be tainted everywhere she went by it. But now... oh God... she won't be able to handle this."

"What the fuck are you talking about?" Dolby shouted at the screen, not caring that Angela jumped at his harsh demand.

"Dolby," Carson warned.

He jerked around. "We don't have time to bullshit. Every minute could mean—"

"Marcia Blackburn isn't her birth name," Angela blurted, once more gaining all eyes on her. "It's the name she legally changed it to when she was an adult."

"What are you trying to tell us, Angela?" Carson asked.

"Marcia Blackburn was Marcia Baxter. If that name doesn't ring a bell, then think back about sixteen years ago to the Baxter children's kidnapping. It hit all the national and international news at the time."

"Oh shit," Leo said, his chin dropping to his chest.

"Fucking hell," several others cursed, eyes wide.

It took a moment for Dolby to focus on Angela's words, but the importance of what she was saying finally took root. Breath caught in his lungs just as Jeb filled another screen on the wall with the news articles showing the picture of a bright, smiling pair of young teenagers with the headline screaming Baxter oil magnate's twins kidnapped. FBI manhunt ensues.

The next headline appeared on the screen. FBI raid saves Baxter's daughter. Twin brother's body found nearby.

Then all the oxygen rushed from Dolby as his stomach dropped at the idea that Marcia was living a nightmare all over again.

14

Marcia had no way of knowing how much time had passed. She ate and drank little, wanting to keep up her strength but also aware that another bathroom break might not come very soon.

She was almost thankful when the door opened, and the same man led her to the toilet once more. Finishing quickly, she washed her hands again and stepped out into the hall, expecting to go back to the small room.

Her body tensed as a heavy hand landed on her shoulder, halting her footsteps. Her wide-eyed gaze sought his, but his only motion was to grunt as he lifted his other hand and pointed down the hall in the opposite direction. With his grip tight on her shoulder, she had no recourse but to walk forward. At the end of the hall, he squeezed her fingers, and she stopped. Her imagination ran rampant with the image that he was getting ready to kill her, and it was harder to breathe as fear raced through her.

He slid his hand from her shoulder to her arm and

pulled it back while grabbing the other. She jerked instinctively, but her hands were zip-tied, rendering them immobile. Looking around, she barely caught sight of his movements before a cloth was whipped in front of her face and tightened around her mouth. Now unable to speak or move her arms, she stared wide-eyed at the large man.

He produced another strip of cloth and tied it over her eyes. She tried to scream, but the muffled sound couldn't carry farther than just a few feet. She heard another door open, and he held tightly to her upper arm, leading her forward. Unable to balance well or see where she was going, she stumbled. Her body was shifted, and more hands gripped her other arm. The efforts kept her from falling on her face, but she continued to stumble between them as they shuffled down the hall, went around corners, and then out through a loud-clanging door where the warm sun and fresh air hit her.

With the gag over her mouth, she breathed deeply through her nose. The sounds of machinery, the beeps of trucks backing up, and lots of talking and shouting in the background met her ears, but her escorts kept her continually walking forward. The blindfold had lifted slightly over one cheekbone, and she discerned asphalt was underneath her feet. Not wanting to alert anyone that she had a sliver of downward sight, she trudged along.

Heavily Slavic-accented voices nearby were heard, but she didn't understand what anyone was saying. After walking for what seemed like miles, she was lifted onto a metal platform, and then more hands took hold of her arms as a ramp was now underneath her feet. Going upward, she heard water slapping against the metal, and peering down, she realized she was being taken onto a huge ship. *Oh God, no!*

Having researched human trafficking for several books, she knew that her fate would be sealed once inside. *But why?* Women were often taken off the streets, campuses, or from bars where no one would notice right away. *I was taken from Angela's house in an elaborately arranged kidnapping.* Nothing made sense.

Her feet halted as her body stiffened, but the arms that now held her were not gentle as they half dragged her forward. In a few more minutes, she was taken through a large doorway, and the sounds of the dock fell to the background as she was met with other muffled sounds.

Down a hall. Into an elevator. Down another hall. And then she was brought to a stop before being led through another door where it was quiet. No sounds but the breathing of the men behind her and the congo drum pounding of her heartbeat.

Another door opened in front of her, but instead of being led through, her arms were jerked back just before her hands dropped free as her zip ties were cut. Her gag was removed next, and she gulped in the air as she was pushed forward a few steps. Her hands flew to her blindfold, expecting someone to stop her from jerking it off, but with no interference, she pulled it over her head and whirled around to see only one man still standing close to her. She simply stared, fear clawing up her throat.

Blue eyes and a square jaw met her eyes first. His dark hair was trimmed close to his head. He wore a suit, although ill-fitting with his thick chest and gut, and the unmistakable gun he had holstered underneath.

He inclined his head toward her, then rumbled with a Slavic accent, "You stay. You make a sound... you cry out... you try to get away... you will die." He lifted his hand and made a slashing motion across his throat. His lips curved maniacally as his gaze raked down her body. "But not before I have some fun." He stepped closer, adding a final warning. "A lot of men on this ship without a woman would love to have a piece of you. If you stay quiet, they will not know you are here."

He stepped back, turned, and closed the door. Her vision blurred again, and her chest heaved as her legs gave out from underneath her. Dropping to her hands and knees in the middle of the floor, she sucked in air. Finally, lifting her head, she stared around the small room dimly lit by a single ceiling light. A twin mattress was on the floor in the back corner.

Pushing to a stand, she braced her hand on the wall as she looked around. In the front corner was a tiled shower floor with a spigot on the wall. A portable chemical toilet was in the opposite corner.

A supply closet. She could imagine it would have had a shelving unit to hold cleaning supplies and a mop and bucket underneath the water fixture ready to be filled.

Jerking around again, she spied curtains high on the back wall and rushed forward to pull them to the side.

Whatever was on the outside stayed hidden since the window was boarded over from the outside. She tried to steady her breathing as she pressed her hand against her chest. *Think. Take stock of what's happened and think!*

She moved to the mattress and sat, her hands gripping the blanket on either side of her thighs. She felt certain that when Angela arrived home, she could check the security cameras and see that Marcia had been abducted. "Surely, the police will be looking," she whispered aloud, needing the sound of her voice to feel grounded.

Jonathan shot through her mind, and her eyes widened. "Maybe… maybe Angela will find him and get him to look for me, also. If only I had a phone."

The idea that she could steal someone's phone if she was let out of the closet had her blowing out another breath in frustration. She tried to remember everything that she'd noticed. "Docks. A warehouse. Now on a boat. Not a boat… a ship." Licking her lips, she squeezed her eyes shut and cast her mind back over the past half hour. "Slavic accents. Machines. Heavy lifters. Cargo ship?"

Nothing made sense, and she pounded the mattress with her fists before squeezing them together in her lap. Dropping her chin, she stared at the scars on her right wrist for a long moment before inhaling a rattling breath and letting it out in a shaky rush. "I'm not cuffed now. I'm not trapped in the dark. And I'm not being violated or dead. Whatever the hell is going on, at least I have that going for me."

Then struck with the memories of being held in the

dark with her brother, Marty, slowly dying on the floor nearby, a tear slid down her cheek.

Before she had time to meander down that horrid path, loud engines met her ears, and vibrations moved from her feet on the floor up through her body. Jerking her head upward, she waited, poised and tensed. Then she felt movement. *We're leaving port. Oh God... we're going out to sea.*

The overhead light went out, leaving her in total darkness. Clamping her hand over her mouth to still the scream that threatened to erupt, another tear rolled down her cheek.

Dolby and Rachel pulled up to the safe house, parking just outside the small house in the woods. Rachel had made little small talk for the hour-long trip. He was glad, not sure he had it in him for any conversation, considering his skin was tight and itchy with the heat of rage that had been with him for hours. He hadn't hidden his emotions from his fellow Keepers and was both shocked and a little pissed that Carson had ordered him to go.

Angela's car was not in sight when they arrived, but they climbed out, and he carried the provisions inside. It had been a while since he'd been there, noting the rustic decor and thinking it was probably unlike anything Angela had ever experienced. As Rachel busied herself with food, linens, and household items, he double-checked the security system. He knew it was in top-notch condition but felt the need to stay busy.

Finally, Rachel turned to him and planted her hands on her hips. "You know Carson was right."

He remained silent, unable to trust that he wouldn't snap, and Rachel sure as hell didn't deserve his ire. He'd wanted to stay at the compound and work with the others to discover where the kidnappers had taken Marcia, but Carson had ordered him to go with Rachel to meet Angela.

He had all the arguments in his head—he wanted to be at the command center; he wanted to be ready to leave immediately if they found where she was being held; he wanted to be in the center of the investigation. But Carson gave him a direct order, and when he looked at the faces of the other Keepers in the room, no one countered what Carson said. And it wasn't in him to disobey a direct order.

"I've just never felt so useless in my whole life."

"I know this goes against your grain, Dolby. It would go against the grain of any of the Keepers. But you can't do anything right now other than what the others are already working on back at the compound. And maybe, just maybe, meeting with Angela will give you something to not only do but help you feel a little bit closer to Marcia."

He jerked his head around, surprised at what Rachel had said. He hadn't thought of it that way, having only seen Carson feel the need to remove him from the planning as though he couldn't offer any assistance. Considering his mind was all over the place with fear, Carson was probably right. But it hadn't dawned on him that Carson understood that if Dolby could connect with Marcia's only friend, it would give him more insight into what they might be dealing with.

Turning to look at the iconic woman standing in front of him, he sighed heavily. "Thank you for that, Rachel." She reached over, and her hand squeezed his arm, her eyes full of understanding. "You're welcome."

Just then, the sound of a vehicle pulling in had his gaze shooting to the window. A BMW SUV parked next to him, and he observed a woman whose large sunglasses masked most of her face stepping out. He and Rachel met her as she ascended the porch steps, and the woman slid the sunglasses up on top of her head to push her hair back. He noted her red-rimmed eyes, and while her clothes were expensive, she appeared disheveled. As he was taking all this in, Rachel stepped forward with her hand extended. "Angela, it's nice to meet you. I'm Rachel from Lighthouse Security."

Angela nodded, her gaze darting back and forth between Rachel and Dolby before finally landing and staying on him. "Are you Jonathan?"

He nodded. "Yes, ma'am. I'm Jonathan Dolby." He observed Angela's tension seep from her body.

"I've heard of Lighthouse Security Investigations," Angela said, her hand gripping her purse strap as though needing to anchor herself with something tangible. "I know you keep a low profile, but I'm close friends with Senator Martinez's wife and heard glowing things about the security system in her house and the work you did when their daughter had a stalker. I couldn't ask for anyone better to help Marcia." She stepped closer, an assessing gaze roaming over his face, and he had the feeling Angela missed very little. She finally nodded again. "You're exactly the way she described you." Swallowing deeply, she blinked the moisture that had filled her eyes. "Please, please find her and bring her home."

"You can count on it." Dolby's voice must have given her the assurance she needed, and she stepped back and nodded. Glancing up at the quaint house, she smiled. "This is lovely."

"Rachel will take you inside, show you around, and give you what you need to order any supplies that aren't here. It will be paramount that you leave no digital trace of your location. No using your own phone, credit cards, or email. Basically, Angela, you have to think like the one kidnapped... you simply aren't here."

Angela's head jerked up and down. "I understand. I can do this. I wouldn't do anything to put Marcia in more danger than she's already in." She glanced up at the small but cozy cabin again. "Believe me, with all the events that have been going on, even before what happened to Marcia, I need to reevaluate who I am. How I managed to go from a woman who I thought was very strong to a woman who's been utterly used by the man who should've been taking care of me." She cocked her head to the side and peered up at Dolby again. "I know you and Marcia have only known each other a short time, so maybe I'm jumping ahead of myself. But I have a feeling about you. I have a feeling you'll be that kind of man she deserves."

He didn't respond. Honestly, he wasn't sure he had

the words. He watched as she followed Rachel into the house, knowing Rachel would have everything in hand. A few minutes later, he entered as well, bringing all of the luggage from Angela's vehicle inside. She carried most of it to the bedroom. After she came back into the living room, he made sure she was set up with a safe computer and untraceable phones and understood the security system. "Use these when we need to be in contact with you. These will leave no footprint."

Angela pointed at a small suitcase and laptop case still sitting by the front door. "I brought the things Marcia had at my house. I thought you could take them so she'd have them once you bring her home."

He stared at them for a few seconds, his fingers itching to open the case immediately to get a whiff of her soft vanilla scent. Clearing his throat, he said, "Thank you."

Rachel walked in from the kitchen to say goodbye as he bent to grab Marcia's belongings. Rachel assured Angela to call if she needed anything, but she waved her hand dismissively. "Don't worry about me. Just take care of my girl."

He dipped his chin, knowing how Angela had taken care of Marcia for years, holding her secret dear and counting her as a friend. "You can count on it."

As he and Rachel climbed into their SUV to head back to the compound, those words resounded as a vow in his head. *Hell yeah. I'll take care of my girl.*

15

Dolby tried to focus but discovered his mind was too fragmented to concentrate on what the other Keepers were doing. Scrubbing his hand over his face, he growled under his breath. "What the fuck is wrong with me?" He and Rachel had returned to find the other Keepers knee-deep in the investigation. So while they'd caught him up on what they'd discovered, they had nothing to send them out into the field with yet.

"Some of us have been right where you are," Rick said, standing nearby. "When Abbie was taken in Cairo, I wanted to kill whoever had put her in danger, yet couldn't seem to think past the next moment."

Dolby had been in Egypt with Rick at that time and now understood the feeling. Nodding, he sucked in a deep breath and let it out slowly.

"Let us handle the intel and logistics right now. You gather your wits, find out more about your woman, and then be prepared to go in strong as soon as we're ready."

He nodded again at Rick's advice and moved to the

computer at his station. Pulling up the news articles again, he hesitated. A part of him hated to read about Marcia's background, preferring her to tell him herself when she was ready to trust that he'd handle her with care. But, right now, he needed to know what he might be facing once they got to her. *And we will get to her.*

Taking another deep breath, he began reading. The articles ran from legitimate news sources reporting on the facts to gossip rags speculating on her captivity and subsequent family tragedies. And the more he read, the more his fingers curled into fists, and his heart pounded a rhythm that resounded in his head. And while he vowed they'd get to her, he wondered if this time she'd be destroyed.

Marcia and her twin brother were kidnapped from their family home when they were thirteen years old. As he looked at a photograph, they were so similar in looks, both on the cusp of adolescence. Even in the black and white picture, he could see the happiness in her eyes, something that had been missing when he'd spent time with her last weekend. The same light-hearted expression was mirrored on her brother's face.

It took two days before a ransom note was delivered and another day for her father to gather the money necessary to pay the kidnappers. *Three days for Marcia to be held in captivity.* Reading further, he discovered her brother had a medical condition that needed daily medication, as well as a strict diet, neither of which he received. When the FBI burst into the house they were held in, they found the two in a pitch-black basement, her brother deceased with Marcia nearby.

It was the bare bones of the story. Just the facts. But Dolby closed his eyes, imagining a young Marcia, in tears, terrified, hovering near as her brother grew weaker. He continued to read about how the three kidnappers were captured and sentenced to life. One had died in prison from pneumonia, but the other two were still enjoying the amenities of the state. Blood boiling, he forced his anger to the side as he scrolled down the article.

Their mother never recovered from the loss of her son and fell into alcohol, antidepressants, sleeping pills, and God knows what other drugs, dying just three years later when she passed out in her bed, never to awake. Marcia's father managed to live two more years, just seeing Marcia turn eighteen years old before dying of a heart attack. Many speculated he died of a broken heart. All of this tragedy left Marcia alone.

Uncertain he could stand reading more until he had a chance to hold her in his arms, he was glad for the interruption when the information finally started coming in.

"The vehicle seen leaving Angela's driveway is registered to a rental company," Chris called out. "Tracing them backward, the vehicle was dropped off at the lot after hours, but cameras show another SUV rental picked them up, then dropped them off at a remote location."

"Followed the security cameras and the street cameras," Jeb added. "The two men carried a still-unconscious Marcia into another SUV. This one was registered to Ivan Chanev. Bulgarian immigrant.

Followed it to Oakland Port, where it passed through the gates."

"I want to know everything about Ivan Chanev." Carson turned to look at the others. "Who does he work for?"

"Working on it," Chris called out, typing quickly.

"What Bulgarians are at the Oakland Port?" Natalie asked.

"Sposov International Transport is there. Warehouses and shipping," Poole replied from his station.

"Vladimir Sposov?" Carson asked. "He's the fuckin' Bulgarian Mafia."

"Bingo," Chris called out again. "Looks like Ivan works for the Sposov Transport company."

"What the hell do they want with Marcia, I mean, Angela?" Leo asked aloud, but no one had an answer.

"And what will they do when they realize they don't have Angela?" Dolby's stomach dropped at the thought. What might keep Marcia alive is if her kidnappers don't realize they have the wrong person.

"Get Angela back on the line," Carson ordered.

They'd had her assurance that she would be ready to talk at any time, and it was less than a minute when Jeb had her up on the screen again using their secure connections.

"Anything?" she blurted, her eyes wide.

"Tell us about your husband. The money. His dealings. You said you'd found things to bury him. We need that information," Carson ordered.

She nodded quickly, pressing her lips together for a few seconds before she started her rapid-fire diatribe.

"My husband is a financial planner. An investor. He worked for a major finance company for many years, then branched out on his own. While working for the company, he made good money, and we had what would be considered by many to be a very high standard of living. But once he went into business for himself, suddenly we were moving to an even larger house, new cars every year, and living an extravagant lifestyle. At first, I believed him when he said he was just very fortunate with his clients. But he began to change, and I didn't like the changes."

Her face scrunched. "I'm sorry. I think I'm rambling. None of this probably matters, does it?"

"Time is of the essence for us to find Marcia, but in order to do so, we need to understand exactly what your husband was into. Whatever it was, my assumption is that whoever took Marcia, thinking it was you, did so because of your husband. We need to discern what that was."

She nodded, let out a deep breath, and continued. "I had suspicions about his fidelity first. I wasn't even thinking about the money, but the more I was sure he was having affairs, I began to notice other things. Because of his background, I tended to leave our financial accounts in his hands, but it didn't take long to realize he was shifting money from our joint accounts into investment accounts that only had his name on them. I started checking his emails and phone messages, and call logs. I realized I had only scraped the tip of the iceberg."

Tears formed in her eyes, but she blinked several

times, appearing to fight them back. Blowing out a deep breath, she continued. "We had a top-of-the-line security system, but I noticed it was not working once when I returned from a weekend trip. I wondered if he had disengaged it on purpose. I installed basic hidden cameras with audio in each room, and on my next trip out of town, I discovered he and one of his mistresses in our home. I engaged a private investigator to do a more thorough job of gaining evidence of his affairs that would stand up in court. And I hired a top forensic accountant to delve into Roger's finances. That's when we discovered he had shady dealings with laundering money."

The Keepers shared a look. "Money laundering," Dolby growled in a low voice.

"Do you have the evidence gathered by the accountant?" Carson asked.

She tapped on the laptop they'd provided. "Yes. I can send it. Just give me a minute. I've got it in the cloud and can use your computer."

After a few minutes, Jeb nodded. "Got it."

"One more question, Angela," Carson said. "Have you ever heard of Sposov International Transport?"

She nodded, eyes wide. "Oh yeah. That was one of Roger's biggest clients."

Carson placed a call to his FBI liaison, Landon Sommers, updating him on the new information and assuring him that Angela was at their safehouse, secreted away so that no one would know she hadn't been the one taken. The local office near Angela had already been inside her house, taking prints, reviewing the security, and gathering their own intel while the security system was still inoperable. But Landon knew that Carson and his Keepers weren't bound with the same constraints the FBI placed on their investigators.

While they talked, several Keepers pulled from as many Oakland Port security cameras as they could, and several others dug into the information that Angela's forensic accountant had amassed on Roger's dealings.

Crawling out of his skin, Dolby stalked out of the room, needing space. He prowled past Rachel's desk and headed to the patio outside the lighthouse overlooking the waves crashing below.

He wasn't sure how long he might be able to escape before someone would come check on him, but he was grateful as the minutes passed. He had the privacy to suck in fresh air to hopefully activate his focus. He snorted, shaking his head. Focus. Something he'd always managed to do before. Until this mission.

The door behind him opened, but he heard a lighter step instead of heavy booted footsteps. Keeping his eyes facing the water, he was aware of Natalie stopping beside him, staring out at the same magnificent view. She was much shorter than him, and he glanced over, surprised at the serious expression replacing her usual quick wit and snark.

"You the one who drew the short straw to come rein in my ass?"

She snorted and grinned. "Nope. I volunteered." He

sighed heavily, and they continued to look out over the water for another moment without speaking.

"It doesn't make any sense, Nat." She turned to look up at him but remained quiet, so he continued. "What I feel. It doesn't make any sense. I've only known her for a week. How can I have these feelings for someone? How can I be so terrified for her after knowing her for such a short time?"

"You told Leo that the two of you talked for hours while stuck in the lighthouse."

He nodded, waiting to see where she was going with this line of thought.

"There are people who meet, barely share anything about themselves, fall into bed after only a couple of hours, and start having feelings while knowing less about each other than you and Marcia do. I guess what I'm saying is that I don't think it's that unusual at all. You actually spent a week taking the time to learn a lot about her, talk to her, and discover who she is behind the persona she projects."

He chuckled, the tension in his shoulders lessening slightly. "You know, that's kind of strange coming from you. It took you and Leo years to get together."

She stepped forward and turned, leaning her head back as she held his gaze, her hands on her hips. "Do you want to know how long it took me to fall for him?" He didn't have a chance to answer before she kept going. "I noticed Leo instantly. I was instantly attracted and started falling for him within the first week of knowing him. But it took ten years of our working together on a Delta team, where we couldn't act or even admit our feelings. Nothing could happen until we finally came to a place where we weren't either teammates or on opposite sides of the world. But I guaran-damn-tee you that if I hadn't had those external restrictions, he and I would've been together after only a week."

Duly chastised, he offered a rueful smile. "You're right. Anyway, it wouldn't matter if we were together or not. Knowing what she's been through, I want to kill whoever hurt her. In the past and now."

She held his gaze and then finally nodded. "I know you're itching to get going, boots on the ground, ready to find her. But you have to know that it makes more sense to make sure we know where to send you guys. Having you run around, chasing false trails, and wasting time could cause her harm. If the kidnappers get wind that someone's after them, and for whatever reason, they thought they were taking Angela but have Marcia, her life might not be worth the trouble."

The idea that Marcia could not only be injured but killed sent shock waves through his body, and he dragged his hand over his face before sliding it around to squeeze the back of his neck.

"But we've got this," Natalie continued, placing her hand on his arm. "We're going to get her back because we've got her, and we've got you."

He nodded, letting out a heavy sigh, then jerked his head behind them. "Where are we at?"

"Carson has Landon on board. The FBI has officially asked us to assist." Shrugging, she grinned. "Of course, Landon knows that's just a formality. We're going to do things our way. But between the others, it's taking a while to dig through the maze of security cameras on the port, but it looks like she was taken to the warehouse at Sposov's."

"Goddamn fucking Roger. I don't even know the man, but once I take care of the Bulgarians who took Marcia, I'm going after him."

With a nod, Natalie grabbed his arm and tugged. "Let's go see what they've got. We're getting close to being able to figure out where she is. And then, as far as Carson is concerned, we go in heavy."

He dipped his chin and threw his arm around her shoulders, guiding her back inside. "Thanks, Nat. You're the best. I hope Leo knows what a lucky fuck he is."

She laughed. "Any time I think he forgets, I'm sure to remind him."

As they stepped into the main building, Rachel met them. "I was just coming to get you. Jeb has managed to get a visual of Marcia."

With that information, he and Natalie rushed through the security panels, hurrying back into the main conference room. "What have we got?" he barked, then turned to look up at the widescreen on the wall.

"At five thirty-three yesterday morning, the SUV went into one of the warehouses of Sposov Transport. Chris is trying to get into their warehouse security cameras, but I was able to move forward in time to see if I could find anything else on the outside. At two forty-nine, watch," Jeb said.

Every eye was pinned to the screen as two men emerged from a back door, walking with a woman held between them. She was wearing pants with a pattern and a mismatched long-sleeved T-shirt. And on her feet… "Fucking hell, she's in socks!" he growled at the sight of the yellow socks on her feet. A beige blindfold was over her eyes, and another one wrapped around her mouth. The beige color made it difficult to tell that she was blindfolded and gagged. She was walking of her own accord even though her wrists were secured behind her, and the two men had ahold of her upper arms.

All around her, the activity of the dock continued, and no one seemed to pay any attention to the three walking toward one of the massive cargo ships. Barely breathing, he never wavered from the screen as he watched while they maneuvered her to a ramp at the side. They held her between them as they walked up the ramp before disappearing into a doorway leading into a cargo ship that had to be close to three-hundred meters long. When she was no longer in sight, he whirled around to look at the others, his thoughts a tangled mass of anger, fear, and despair.

"We know the ship! Can we get the Coast Guard to hold it until we can get there?" he barked.

"Shit, Dolby. That's not all."

He swung his gaze back to the screen where Jeb fast-forwarded. "At eleven fifty-one last night, they left the port."

He watched as the massive cargo ship maneuvered expertly out of the Oakland Dock, heading out into the Pacific Ocean.

"But they can't be far. They've been underway for

less than twenty-four hours. Surely, the Coast Guard can make them stop and board them."

"They're outside the CG jurisdiction," Carson answered, his jaw tight.

Rick clamped his hands on Dolby's shoulders, pulling him in close so that they were eye to eye, blocking out almost everything else in the room. "Man, hang in there. Stay with us. We're a fuck of a lot closer than we were. We now know that she's alive. We know that whether or not they realize they don't have Angela, she's alive. We know she's on the *Skrita Kralista*. We also know now where the ship is heading. A stop in Hawaii just for fueling."

"Can't the Coast Guard hold them in Hawaii?"

"We can't take that chance," Carson said.

Dolby stared at his boss, frustration threatening his sanity. Slowly nodding, he sighed. "If they see they're getting boarded, they might harm her."

Rick continued, "Look, their next stop is the Marshall Islands on their way to Hong Kong. But guess who has a house on Majuro in the Marshall Islands?"

His jaw squared as the muscles tightened. "Fucking Roger Mansfield."

"Hidden Queen." Abbie spoke softly, gaining the attention of all the other Keepers. She looked up, searching for and holding Dolby's gaze. "The *Skrita Kralista*. The boat she's on translates to Hidden Queen."

He closed his eyes slowly, swallowing deeply. Hidden queen. *Yeah, I'm coming for you, baby.*

The Keepers continued to work for hours, long beyond the normal day, but no one was ready to leave.

As soon as they knew when the *Skrita Kralista* would dock in the Marshall Islands, they began the planning and logistics.

While Dolby wanted to jump into action, he knew they could do little at the moment. And he sure as fuck knew their chances of complete success would be improved with their mission planned.

"They will stop at Honolulu Harbor Oahu in five days," Natalie reported. "They'll dock but won't unload or accept more cargo other than provisions, then travel on to Majuro Port in the Marshall Islands. They will arrive there two days later."

"I've got the ship's online deck log," Abbie said, her gaze pinned on her screen. "There are thirty-two crew members listed. Thirteen are main officers, nineteen crew members." She looked over her shoulder. "With a cargo ship, most of the space is taken up with containers. That'll make it easier to check out the shorter accommodations decks."

The group was silent for a moment, and Dolby knew what was on each of their minds. *What if Marcia is being held in a container and not a room?*

"They can't take a chance on her being in a container," Poole said, holding Dolby's gaze. "We watched them walk her on board to the crew decks."

With his fists on his hips, he offered a curt nod. "We can fly to Oahu and get me on board. I'll locate where they have her, so I'll be ready when we land at Majuro."

"I'll get it coordinated," Carson stated. "Landon will smooth the way with the Marshall Islands US embassy, their police, and Interpol."

"I've got the Honolulu Harbor plans," Abbie said. "I'll work up the best way to navigate onto the ship based on which dock they pull into."

"We'll need to get a team to Majuro," Rick added. He looked over at Abbie. "We'll also need the plans for Roger's place there."

"What about Vladimir Sposov?" Poole asked.

"He's still in Oakland. My guess is that he is as physically far removed from the actual dirty dealings as he can be. As of today, his private jet logged his second in command, Aleksi Milanov, as heading to Hawaii," Chris said, leaning back in his chair.

"So did Sposov take Marcia… well, *Angela*, to get back at Roger, or did Roger orchestrate this because he discovered his wife wanted to divorce him?" Leo asked, rubbing the back of his neck.

"He and Roger working together on this?" Poole lifted his brow and looked over at the others.

Jeb sighed. "I've just started going through the financial reports, but I'll do more work on them tomorrow. If Roger's been working with the Bulgarian Mafia, he's in deep. I'd say he got Sposov to take care of his wife for him."

"Why not just have her killed?" Adam asked, then shot a wince toward Dolby.

"Roger must need something from her. Maybe to sign more of her wealth to him or something," Bennett surmised.

Dolby nodded. "That works for Landon and us. We can get them all."

Carson stood. "Okay, I want everyone to go home.

Get some sleep. We'll meet back here tomorrow morning to finish the planning."

Dolby accepted back slaps, chin lifts, and clasped hands as everyone filed out of the room. When it was just him and Carson, he walked over to the man who was as much a friend as he was a boss. "Carson, I know I don't have to say it, but I will. This mission means everything."

Carson placed one hand on Dolby's shoulder. "You're right. You don't have to say it, but I know. Felt the same when it was Jeannie. There's a lot at stake, and we'll need our heads in the mission. But you've got all of us behind you."

They walked out together, and for another moment, Dolby stood and looked out over the horizon. All he could think of was that Marcia was somewhere out there on the ocean. *I'm coming. I promise, babe. I'm coming.*

16

Marcia had once again lost sense of time. Without being able to see out of the window, she discovered that since the wood didn't fit tightly against the glass, the barest hint of light filtered around the edge. She couldn't see anything outside, but it was enough that her eyes could adjust to the dark room, making it less pitch black. She didn't know what time it was, but exhaustion pulled at her body, making her yawn widely while trying to stay alert.

She'd been in the room for what felt like hours when a light knock on the door had her leap to her feet, heart pounding. The door opened, and she squinted at the light shining in from the outer room. A short, stout man entered, and the overhead light flickered on. Continuing to squint, she finally could see that his expression was blank, although he dipped his head in a small greeting. His dark hair was trimmed, and wearing a blue shirt and khaki pants, he appeared to be a worker on the boat and not a crazed kidnapper ready to end her life at a second's notice.

Staring blankly at him, she waited for him to speak. Instead, he stepped to the side to expose a petite woman standing behind him. Her dark hair was pulled into a ponytail, and she was wearing a shirt like the man's, but her bottom half was covered with a loose skirt that hung to her shins. Her eyes darted around the room before settling onto Marcia, uncertainty filling them as her gaze moved from the top of Marcia's head down to her yellow-socked feet.

Marcia had the strange sensation that the woman was as afraid of Marcia as she was of her visitors. The woman moved forward hesitantly with a small metal tray in her hands. Glancing up at the man, she waited until he pointed at the bed. She hurried to place the tray where indicated and then stepped back in haste, nearly tripping over her feet. No one spoke, but the two backed out of the room, the door closing behind them, and the outside lock clicked.

Marcia stared at the closed door before shifting her gaze over to the bed, grateful that the light was still on. She walked forward, the scent of food wafting past, and her stomach growled. Reaching out, she lifted the top of the plate cover, blinking in surprise at the sandwich of thick, buttered bread and a slice of roasted chicken inside. A water bottle on the tray completed the meal.

She sat on the bed, and her mind raced to try to make sense of what she was experiencing. While the meal could not be considered a luxury, it was vastly more than she had expected. In truth, she wouldn't have been surprised if they'd barely fed her at all. Suspicious, she stared at the food for a moment, wondering if it was a trick.

Finally shaking her head, she reached for the sandwich and took a nibble. She used her fingers to tear the chicken into smaller pieces, finding the meat tender and delicious. The bread was a bonus, but the butter smeared on top had her ravenously tearing into it. By the time she finished the meal and half of the water, she leaned her back against the wall, her mind still reeling, but her stomach sated.

Closing her eyes for a moment, she snorted. *Maybe this is my last meal before being executed.* Once again, gallows humor emerged. But then, considering she had no idea what was happening or why, she couldn't discount the real possibility that she wouldn't make it out of this situation alive.

With her fingers sticky, she walked to the shower and turned on the spigot, washing her hands and face. With no towel provided, she grabbed the bottom of the blanket on her bed and dried off. She wished she had a mirror, but figured if she caught a glimpse of her reflection, she'd be shocked at the way she looked. *It's better not to know.*

Glancing at the chemical toilet, she pressed her lips together, hating the idea that she might have another visitor while taking a potty break. But nature called, and she decided it was better to have the toilet than to be expected to relieve herself on the floor. She shivered with another memory, wincing until she shook her head and let out a shaky breath.

Once finished, she managed to wash her hands again before the light switched off, and she was once more plunged into darkness. Crawling over to the bed, she sat down and tried to calm her tumultuous thoughts. Tears pricked her eyes as she pulled back the covers. She'd already discovered that the sheets appeared clean, and still wearing the pajamas she'd had on since being taken from Angela's house, she covered herself with the thin blanket.

It was frightening to allow herself to be so vulnerable as to fall into bed and sleep, but her body was at the end of alert consciousness. She wouldn't be able to stop anyone who came inside the room to harm her, even if she stayed awake. A flash of memory from when she was thirteen bolted through her mind, and her hand lifted to her chest, pressing against the ache. She'd seen what depravity someone would stoop to and lived to have the horror embedded in her soul. *Never underestimate someone who will kidnap and imprison another human.* Forcing her thoughts away from the past, she breathed deeply.

"Tell me about him, sis."

She startled at the sound of Marty's voice. He sometimes came to her, talking as if he were still beside her. Staying perfectly still, she waited.

"Come on. Tell me about him."

A tiny smile creased her face as she pulled up the image of Jonathan. Her heart jolted slightly as she remembered seeing him sleeping after the night they'd spent together in the lighthouse. "He was masculine and utterly gorgeous, yet his face appeared boyishly cute in slumber."

Feeling Marty's presence next to her, she continued. "When I walked away the next morning, my heart ached with each footstep that carried me farther away from him. I constantly looked over my shoulder to see if he was racing after me." She snorted and shook her head. "But when I made it to my house, I couldn't decide if I was glad that he hadn't followed or sorry I was still alone."

"What happened then?"

"His arrival the next day sent my heart fluttering and my hopes soaring. It was as though I could finally admit that seeing him was what I secretly longed for. Does that sound silly, Marty?"

He didn't answer, but she didn't really need him to. He'd managed to get her thoughts solely on Jonathan. She lay on the mattress, and her mind wandered to him as a child. She imagined him with his brothers… Frazier and Dalton. The image of three little boys climbing trees, playing carefree and happy. Another image of them as teenagers, flexing their muscles, flirting with girls, and sticking up for each other moved through her mind, and a lighthearted smile crept over her face. *I was once carefree.*

Rolling over, she curled into a tight ball, her arms hugging her aching chest. *Oh, Jonathan, do you know I'm missing? I feel certain that if you do, you're trying to find me.*

She swallowed deeply as fatigue filled her being, and tears threatened to fall under the weight of her exhaustion. If Jonathan was looking for her, she feared that now she had gone far beyond his reach.

Rest. If I'm going to be able to work to stay alive and possibly escape, I've got to rest. With that in mind, she closed her eyes.

The following two days passed much in the same way as the first. The same man and woman came twice each day with a meal tray, turned on the light, and each time the meals were more than Marcia expected. She assumed the food was probably served in the ship's cafeteria for the workers, and she was grateful for the gesture by whoever was in charge of her imprisonment. Each time they came in after knocking, they served the food and took away the empty tray from the previous meal.

But when the first meal came today, the woman cast her eyes up and down Marcia and then turned and whispered to the man. He also raked his gaze over Marcia, but it didn't feel sexual. She pressed her lips together, knowing what she looked like. She'd used the water spigot to clean herself, but without any soap, she'd simply had to rely on the water, grateful it would get warm. She'd washed out her panties each evening and had washed out her camisole just last night, letting them dry while she slept.

But she still had her long-sleeved T-shirt that was unwashed because it gave her a layer of warmth. It also felt like protection since she didn't want to only be wearing a camisole. She had become accustomed to the meal delivery but wasn't about to let down her guard.

Without speaking, the man and woman left the room, and Marcia ate the hard-boiled eggs and buttered bread. Today, there was coffee along with the water bottle, and she wrapped her hands around the cup, inhaling deeply.

The warm, bitter drink wasn't sweetened like she normally prepared it, but she wanted the shot of caffeine. While grateful for a toilet, running water, light during part of the day, and the way the wooden window covering allowed her to have a bit of vision during the rest of the time, and the food, she knew change could come. Her minutes were filled with the ever-present fear that, at any moment, she could find her nightmare situation worsening.

She'd just finished breakfast when a light knock sounded on the door, and instantly alert, she jumped to her feet. The door opened, but the man didn't step inside this time. The woman entered alone, and Marcia's gaze dropped to her hands which held folded cloth. Her brow crinkled as she sought the woman's face again.

"For you."

Marcia blinked but stayed still. The woman stepped hesitantly forward, her hands extended. Marcia realized she was holding several items of folded clothing. She reached out before the woman could decide to take back the offering. Looking down, she saw at least two shirts and possibly a pair of pants. Her breath rushed out as she clutched them to her chest, holding them tightly. "Thank you."

The woman nodded, her expression softening. She glanced over her shoulder toward the man whose expression had not changed. Looking back at Marcia, she pressed her lips together before sliding her hand into her skirt pocket. She pulled out a small plastic bag and held it out as well.

Marcia's lungs depressed when the air rushed out at the sight of a small bottle of shampoo, conditioner, body wash, toothpaste, and a toothbrush. "Oh," she breathed shakily. Her fingers clasped the bag and pulled it against her chest along with the clothes. "Thank you, thank you."

The woman's shy smile widened.

"Tudora. Come," the man said, his words curt.

While it was an order, Marcia noted it wasn't harsh. The woman nodded, then patted her chest. "Tudora."

"Thank you, Tudora," she whispered. She watched as Tudora gathered the tray, and they left, the door closing behind them and the lock clicking into place.

Marcia stood still for a moment, then with more excitement than she thought she possessed under the circumstances, she hurried over to the water spigot. While waiting for the water to warm, she sorted the small pile of clothes Tudora had brought. The pair of dark blue pants with elastic at the waist was functional, which was all she cared about. There were two T-shirts and a small plastic package with two pairs of panties inside. She was stunned, but a cotton bra was included. It wasn't new, but it was clean. And on the bottom was a thin towel.

Stripping quickly, she stepped underneath the stream of water, thrilled with the body wash, then shampooed her hair, luxuriating with the conditioner. Stepping out, she toweled off and slipped on the underwear, pants, bra, and T-shirt. Using the old bar of soap, she washed her pajamas and socks, wrung them out, and draped them across the floor. Carefully placing the small bottles on the tile underneath the spigot, she stared, tears pricking her eyes.

She sucked in a deep breath, then let it out slowly. Her mind was a mixed bag of gratitude for the toiletries and clothes while knowing she was a prisoner trapped on a ship that must be far out into the ocean going who knows where.

She'd spent the past couple of days being scared out of her mind, unable to think past the next meal or the next knock on the door. Rubbing her head, she grimaced. *Time to think more clearly.*

Moving back to her bed, she sat on the mattress and once again tried to think of why she had been kidnapped. She wished she had paper and pen to write down her thoughts the way she plotted her mysteries but talked through the facts she knew out loud.

Channeling Inspector Marley, she closed her eyes, blocking out her cell so she could see him standing before her, just the way he did when she created a new book about her fictional character. Brown hair was now sprinkled liberally with gray, particularly at the temples. A slightly messy mustache. Dark brown eyes that were a little small for his face gave him a beady appearance, but he never seemed to miss anything in a room. A quiet man, he observed everything around him, not speaking unless he had something to say. But he absorbed evidence like a sponge.

His brown suit was slightly rumpled, but he shunned buying a new one, preferring what he was accustomed to. Familiar things gave him a sense of calm. *And a calm mind allows us to think more clearly, Marcia.*

He talked to her at times… usually when she needed to work through a difficult plot point or scene. But now, he seemed to want to guide her again. *Ask yourself why, Marcia? Why did they take you?*

"Someone knew I was at Angela's house. Who knew? Angela. Well, she certainly didn't have me kidnapped. And… Jonathan. Nope, not him either." Racking her brain, she couldn't come up with anyone else who knew. "How did someone find out that's where I was? In fact, the only people who knew Angela wasn't also at home were her attorney and me. She didn't want Roger to know what she was doing and had mentioned that she didn't trust any of their friends."

Sighing, she leaned back against the wall and stared at the wooden board over the window, wishing she could see the sky. "Why didn't they seem concerned about Angela being somewhere in the house? They should have been prepared for her to be there when they came for me."

An inkling of an idea began to form, but just like when plotting and writing, an exhausted, anxious brain was not the best for analyzing. Snorting, she stood and began pacing the floor. Another knock on the door halted her, stunned at today's extra visits. Once more, the same man stood there, but Tudora stepped in, her gaze sweeping over Marcia's new clothes. Tudora smiled, then said, "Outside. We go outside."

Her brow lowered as she tilted her head to the side in confusion. "Outside?" Her heart pounded again at the fear of why she was now being summoned out of her room.

"We go outside."

About to refuse the offer, preferring to stay in the room since it seemed safer, the man ordered, "Come. Now."

Shooting her gaze back to Tudora, the other woman was smiling, but Marcia wondered if that was because Tudora had no idea what might be happening. Looking down at her bare feet, she said, "I have no shoes." As soon as the words left her mouth, she realized that kidnappers and possible murderers couldn't care less about her bare feet.

"Here."

Lifting her chin, she saw the flip-flops in Tudora's hands and the smile still on her face.

"Come. Now," the man repeated, his voice less soft this time.

Not knowing what she was facing, she steeled her

spine, clenched her fingers tightly, and reached for the footwear. Slipping her feet into the flip-flops, she glanced around, wondering if she'd ever see the room again. Like a prisoner heading to a firing squad, she forced her feet to move and followed Tudora and the man out of the room.

17

Dolby headed home after another day of the mission, planning to pack before meeting with the others who were flying out with him. He'd hated the time it took to make all the arrangements but knew that, in the end, he trusted his Keeper team explicitly. Before leaving the compound, they'd met with Teddy to make sure they had the equipment and weapons necessary. With handshakes, he'd left the ones working the mission from their home base.

Now, in his bedroom, he grabbed his duffel, which he kept pre-packed for missions. Walking back into his living room, he caught sight of Marcia's luggage that Angela had taken from her house and given to him.

He unzipped the larger piece and was immediately hit with the vanilla scent he remembered so well from the night they were in the lighthouse to the way her sweet smell surrounded him when she was in his lap as they kissed. He picked up each piece of clothing, seeing that she'd packed light for her few nights at her friend's place.

His fingers met and curled around a small, hard object as he lay her clothes back into the suitcase. Withdrawing it, he stared at the dove figurine. He remembered her words when he spied her collection at her house.

"They remind me of hope and encouragement from... well, they just make me feel less alone."

Slipping the figurine into his duffel, he grabbed his phone. He typed "dove" into the search engine, and the air seemed to thicken, making it hard to breathe. Clicking through every site, they all said basically the same thing– according to lore, seeing a mourning dove, a person senses a message of encouragement and hope from the deceased loved one.

Her family. Gut punched again with the reality that her entire family had passed. He wondered what message she received when she thought of her twin brother. *Christ, she's so much stronger than she realizes.*

Sucking in a deep breath, he jerked out of his musings, knowing they had their time and place. And right now, he needed to get his head on the mission. Hearing the approaching vehicle, he grabbed his equipment and duffel and secured his house.

As one of their pilots, Adam would be on the active mission. Poole, with explosives expertise, and Bennett, as a former Ranger sniper, would round out their on-the-ground team with Dolby. They had a plan, but not knowing what they were going up against, they wanted strength in numbers.

Natalie, Abbie, Jeb, Chris, Hop, and Rick would be back in the compound in shifts, sending in the intel as well as the ever-changing mission logistics, working with Carson and Leo, who would be directing the mission. As far as Carson was concerned, this was a full team effort until Marcia returned.

Storing his bags in the back of Adam's SUV, he climbed into the back seat, greeting Poole and Bennett. Landon was meeting them at the airport.

The first leg of their trip would be a chartered mid-jet to Hawaii. The flight would only take about six hours, and Landon would accompany them. The others chatted on the way to the private airport in Los Angeles, but Dolby just leaned his head against the window and stared out. He tried to imagine what Marcia was doing, how she was holding up, and whether she was being taken care of or abused. Squeezing his eyes shut, he attempted to hide the shiver that raced over his body. He was used to controlling all his movements, but it seemed his feelings for her had crept deep inside, making it impossible for him to keep his emotions in check.

Finally arriving at the airport, they drove straight to the private jet Landon had arranged for them. After meeting him, they all went through the introductions and then boarded. The jet accommodations were more than adequate, with leather seats that could recline flat, a bar and food service, and two large bathrooms.

Settling in, he was anxious to get started and felt a sense of relief when they were wheels up in the air on their way to Honolulu.

Marcia followed the man out of the closet and looked around in surprise. A clinic. She was in the ship's clinic. It was pristine and very empty. Surprised that she'd been placed in a supply closet in an area that could have easily had crew members around, she remembered the threat given. Not that it had been very far from her mind.

Before she had time to wonder more about her place of captivity and threats of violation, the man led her out and down a short hall with Tudora at her side. Her heart pounded as they came to a heavy metal door. She stopped suddenly, and the man pushed open the door, stepping through it. Filled with trepidation, she flexed her fingers again. She followed him, her steps hesitant, and then her feet stumbled to a halt. They were outside on a small deck, the brilliant blue sky above, the sun beaming down, and the strong breeze blowing across her face causing her to gasp. If this was serving as a last meal, then she wanted to soak up the warmth and light.

"Oh," she exclaimed, lifting her face upward, feeling the fresh air and sunshine.

Tudora's soft voice came from behind. "You like?"

She nodded. "Yes." The deck was very small, and there was no one else around who could see them. The sound of engines as the ship sliced through the water met her ears, and she knew that even if she screamed as loudly as she could, no one would hear her. *And who would come to my rescue?* For all she imagined, the other crew members were all part of the kidnapping.

"I'm glad," Tudora said.

Jerking around, she stared at the woman who nodded shyly, having no idea what to say in response. She knew that Tudora was referring to the trip outside, but it was so evident that Marcia was a prisoner. *How can she be glad for me?* Her earlier fear was now replaced with anger that threatened to choke her. *You want me to be happy that you've snatched me from my life? That I'm a prisoner being held in a closet?*

No words came forth, so she simply turned and lifted her face to the sun again, trying to still her racing heartbeat. The light was blinding, and she dropped her chin to look over the railing where the massive containers were methodically stacked. She would have found the ship fascinating if she hadn't been in such a strange situation. As it was, she could only stare out to the side at the wide expanse of ocean as far as she could see. She had made it outside her cell, but an easy escape was not possible. But there was a certain strength in knowing she would not give up.

She sucked in a deep breath, her body relaxing as she allowed her mind to filter through possibilities. *Who brought me here? And why?* Once more, human trafficking moved through her mind, but she dismissed that. *Women are herded like cattle and held in horrendous conditions, certainly not in private cells with a toilet and running water.*

"Pitar says we go in now," Tudora said, breaking through Marcia's turbulent thoughts.

Swinging her head around, she realized Tudora was

talking about the man who'd always accompanied them. "Pitar?"

"Pitar. My brother."

Marcia wanted to ask how she and her brother could work for kidnappers, but instead asked, "You work on the ship?"

"Pitar does now. I am, uh... new."

"So... um... what do you do on the ship besides bring me food?"

Tudora blushed, her gaze darting to the side. "I here for you."

Here for me? More confused than ever, Marcia wasn't able to ask any more questions before Pitar repeated his order. "Come."

They retraced their steps, and she spied no one else in the hall. Once back in the closet she was being held in, she turned, determined to risk finding out more. "Why are you here for me?"

Tudora's brow was crinkled. "Pitar said woman needed."

Marcia's chin jerked back, licking her dry lips.

Tudora nodded. "Pitar's boss said woman was needed for angel."

Before Marcia had a chance for more questions, Pitar motioned for Tudora. She turned to hurry after her brother, slipping out the door, leaving Marcia to stand in the center of the room with more questions than she'd had before.

Sleep came fitfully that night as the ship rocked with waves, and she could hear the wind whipping past her window. Nausea hit with the rolling, and twice she rushed to kneel over the drain under the spigot as she threw up during the night. Lying awake, she wondered how the containers managed to stay on the ship. When she finally did sleep, her dreams were filled with the horror of memories, and she woke with a sweat. Crawling from the bed, she padded to the faucet and splashed cold water on her face before lying back down.

A sliver of light came from the upper corner of the window, which she'd never seen before. Unable to discern what she was looking at, she stood on her tiptoes and pulled the curtain back farther, gasping at the light shining through. The wooden board that covered her window must have slipped during the night's storm, and now she had a corner triangle of a view available. Placing her face against the glass, she could observe the light coming from the main deck of the ship with the dark sky in the background.

A thrill ran through her. *I can see out!* It was a small concession, but she'd take whatever snippet of hope she could get at this point. Not willing to miss anything, she stood on her toes for as long as she could, watching the sky grow lighter with the dawn. Shifting around slightly, she could see the tops of a few brightly colored containers on the main deck and realized that there was a small deck just outside her window. She prayed that no one would walk by and notice the skewed board. Shifting again, she watched the water in the distance as it changed color with the sunrise.

She sucked in a deep breath and let it slowly leave

her lungs. As much as she'd appreciated walking outside yesterday, the gut-wrenching anxiety of wondering what was happening overshadowed the enjoyment. But this? This tiny peek outside that she hoped no one would notice and take from her gave her hope.

It was still early, but she didn't want to be caught at the window when Tudora and Pitar came with her breakfast. She pulled the curtain over the edge just enough to cover the small gap in the wood and turned back to the center of the tiny room.

Dressing quickly, she stood in the middle of the room, waiting for them to appear. Since yesterday's outing and chat, it seemed that Tudora was more comfortable and greeted her warmly as she handed the tray to Marcia. With Pitar waiting just outside the doorway, she decided to extract what information she could. "Where are we going?"

Tudora looked up sharply, a crinkle between her brows. "Hawaii."

"Hawaii? That's where I'm going?"

"Oh, no. We stop for fuel but no get off. We keep going."

"Tudora! Come!" Pitar ordered, his head swinging back and forth, keeping an eye on the clinic and the hall.

Tudora blushed and ducked her head before darting out of the room with a quick nod, whispering, "Goodbye, Angel."

Now alone, Marcia simply stared at the closed door in stunned silence before she dropped down onto her mattress, her breakfast ignored. Not even the scent of the food could tempt her out of her mind's racing, turning over the snippets she had been exposed to. Fatigue and stress had wreaked havoc with her ability to think clearly, but now the lines between the dots started to take shape.

In her mind, Inspector Marley stood near the window and turned slowly, his small eyes not leaving her face. *"What were you thinking yesterday, Marcia? You cannot ignore the signs in front of you."*

She remembered what she was pondering before Tudora had come to let her outside. *The kidnappers weren't concerned about Angela being in the house when they grabbed me. They should have been prepared for two women if they thought we were both there and they were after me.*

"Why weren't they prepared?" Inspector Marley asked.

She startled. *They weren't expecting two women! The kidnappers couldn't have known I was at Angela's house.*

"And who were they expecting?" he prodded.

Tudora called me Angel. She gasped. "Angela... Angel. They weren't after me! They thought they were kidnapping Angela!"

Inspector Marley bestowed a mustachioed nod toward her. *"And now?"*

For a few seconds, relief exploded as the air fled from her chest. *Angela is safe, and they don't want me. Once they know they have the wrong woman, they'll... they'll...*

Another gasp escaped from her lungs. "Oh God," she moaned, her stomach clenching. "They'll have no use for me!" Her gaze shot around the closet, but Inspector

Marley had disappeared from her mind. While her prison this time was more comfortable than what she'd endured years ago, she had little hope that anyone would be able to find her in the middle of the ocean... even if they realized she was gone. *Not even Jonathan has a reach this far.*

18

The wheels of the plane touched down on the runway of the private airport outside of Honolulu. Disembarking, they walked toward the two extra large SUVs provided. Separating, they stowed their bags and equipment before climbing inside. Landon had already briefed that they would be staying in a hotel that overlooked the harbor where the ship would dock. They had already planned the mission, but as Dolby turned every scenario over in his mind, he knew the others were, too.

Once ensconced in the hotel, he ignored the accommodations and stalked to the window, throwing back the curtain and allowing his gaze to roam over the vast harbor.

He would've found the view interesting if he had just been interested in the workings of a major international harbor. Instead, all he could think of was how close Marcia would be to him tomorrow and how their plan needed to proceed for the best chance of success. Because he knew, without a doubt, of all the missions he'd ever been on, he would accept nothing less than complete success in her rescue. And whatever demons she would face from her experience, he'd make sure to be there with her each step of the way.

"You'll get her," Adam said, coming up behind him.

He turned, seeing the others already setting up secure laptops and in contact with the Keepers back at the compound. He nodded, uncertain of his voice, before they walked over to join the others.

"Jeb's got an update," Bennett called out.

They watched the screen on Bennett's computer. "Just discovered that Roger Mansfield isn't in Hawaii at the supposed conference that he told Angela. He was there with his assistant, sharing a hotel room with her, so Angela was right on that account. But he's already flown to his place on Majuro."

"That's good news," Natalie interjected. "You won't have to worry about him realizing they have the wrong woman while in Hawaii. Unless someone there figures it out."

"Has there been any unusual activity with him at his place in the Marshall Islands?" Poole asked.

"No, and in fact, Chris has managed to intercept emails between Roger and his attorney. The dumb fuck is putting this in writing. His plans are for Angela to be brought to the house, probably drugged, then they'll take a few pictures of how happy they are together, make sure others see them, then he says he'll get her to sign a new will listing him as sole beneficiary."

"He knows she's changed things on her end," Adam

surmised. "Wonder if he knows she's seeking a divorce or that she has evidence of his criminal activities?"

"That would explain the kidnapping," Dolby added, a renewed flicker of hope burning in his chest. "And would make it likely that Marcia is alive and well, still on her way to the Marshall Islands. Since we'll get to her before she's taken to his place, we can keep him from discovering that he's taken the wrong woman until it's too late."

Landon got off his call and turned his attention to Dolby. "You and I will head to the harbor tomorrow morning. My contact at the FDA, who checks the food containers brought onboard, will get you in one, and once you're on the ship, you'll have the uniform for Sposov Transport so you can move about the ship. But you won't want to be seen by too many people."

Dolby nodded. "Don't worry. I'll get the cameras on each deck. While you fly to Majuro, you can monitor what's happening."

Teddy had provided Dolby with the smallest cameras available for him to attach at the end of each hall as he made his way along the ship's corridors. Unlike a large cruise ship, most of the space was taken up with the flat main deck stacked containers. The crew lived and worked on only a couple of floors.

"Christ, I just hope she's been protected," he groaned.

"Roger's in tight with Vladimir Sposov, and the last thing the Sposov mob family wants is something to be discovered on their watch, and that includes their ship.

They won't do anything other than plan to turn her over to him," Bennett surmised.

Sucking in a deep breath, he held the oxygen until his lungs burned, then let it out slowly. Turning, he walked over to the bed and lay on the covers, throwing his arm over his eyes. Sleep would be welcome but unexpected as he turned the mission over and over in his mind until he'd memorized each step, refusing to consider failure or error to be a possibility.

By the next afternoon, Dolby and Landon had already arrived at the dock where the *Skrita Kralista* was moored. The fuel tanker barge had loaded the fuel onto the ship while it was outside the port. The massive cranes were lifting some of the containers from the top, but Dolby was safely ensconced inside a wooden crate filled with vegetables all around him. Landon's contact was bustling around, checking the other food crates bound for the ship. Finally, when ready, Landon secured the top onto the crate, giving Dolby plenty of coverage while providing him a way to escape easily.

Landon tapped on the top of the crate twice, and Dolby heard, "Good luck. See you in Majuro."

The container wasn't huge, and with Dolby's size, it was a tight fit. He shifted slightly, crouching, ready to defend himself if his hiding place was discovered, but all he felt was the rocking and bouncing of the crate as it was rolled up the ramp, and when it leveled off, the sounds of the busy dock fell away.

When the movement stopped, he grimaced as the crate rocked back and then seemed to be dropped as the sound of two men with Slavic accents moved farther away. Several minutes later, he was bumped again as it appeared more food crates were being delivered. Finally, the noise stopped and didn't return. He continued to wait until the sound of the engine rumbling increased, and the vibrations were felt throughout his body as well as the room. It wasn't long before he could feel the ship's movement as it pulled away from the dock.

It was now midafternoon, and he wanted to be away from his hiding place and somewhere secure before the crew member in charge of cooking would possibly open the crate.

Unsecuring it from the inside, he lifted the top and looked around, seeing he was in a refrigerated room. Stepping out of the crate, he turned and shifted the vegetables around before placing the top back on and refastening it with the FDA's seal, clearly stamped on top.

Moving to the refrigeration room door, he cracked it open and observed the empty kitchen. Thankfully, with most cargo ships, the food preparation would be shared by a couple of crew members who also had other duties. He quickly moved around the stainless counters to one door that led to a dining area that held three long tables with ten chairs around each. Reaching to the doorframe above, he attached one of the miniature cameras provided by Teddy. He tapped on the screen of his watch, noting the camera number and location.

Hastening to the next door, he moved into the hall and placed another camera at the end, noting its placement as well. The hall was empty, and using the stairs, he moved up and down the four decks, placing cameras on each so that LSIWC would have video from the inside of the ship. Coming to the clinic, he opened the door and saw that it was empty. He stepped inside and glanced around. Cargo ships didn't sail with a doctor, but several crew members would be trained in first aid. It appeared the clinic wasn't in use for anyone, so he slipped back out.

He finally entered a supply closet filled with cabinets and shelves. Attaching a lock to the inside, he slid to the floor and settled in to wait and watch.

For the next two hours, he watched as a few crewmembers moved about the halls, but for the most part, the accommodations decks were empty as everyone attended to their duties. It was amazing a ship this large could be run with only about thirty people. A few would work in shifts, but many other duties would be during the day.

Just as he suspected, two crewmembers entered the kitchen, tied on aprons, and began the meal preparation. He continually switched between camera views, constantly looking for a clue as to Marcia's whereabouts. He also knew that other Keepers would be monitoring the cameras as well so nothing would be missed.

The image of Marcia's shy smile that she finally graced upon him in the lighthouse ran through his mind. How can a strong connection be felt in such a short amount of time? It was like being hit by a truck or jumping from a plane without checking if your chute would open. It was like running a race, not worried about where the finish line was. It was the gut punch from the hit not expected. It was the shot through the heart from a weapon you never knew was being fired. He knew he'd fallen for Marcia the instant he discovered she battled through her fear of him and took care of his wound.

Staring at the screen on his watch, he jolted at the sight of a woman entering the kitchen. Women crew members were rare, only making up about two percent of the maritime industry. But the fact she wasn't dressed in uniform like the other workers was what captured his attention.

She didn't speak as she waited while one of the crew members plated food onto a plate set on a metal tray. She walked to the refrigerator and retrieved a water bottle, then set it on the tray as well. She carried the tray out of the kitchen, walked down the hall to the elevator, and entered. Once she stepped out on the floor above, she was met by a man who escorted her down the hall, stopping at the clinic. They entered, and then a few minutes later, the man came back into the hall, followed a moment later by the woman, her hands now empty. When he'd peeked inside the clinic, he hadn't seen anyone. *So who received the food? And why was a woman delivering it?*

Radioing to Jeb, he asked, "Are there any women crew members listed on the deck logs for the *Skirta Kralista?*"

After a moment, the succinct reply was given. "No."

So the woman wasn't an official crew member. Calculating how he could get to her without the escort, he watched the man leave the area while the woman continued to help in the kitchen. Most of the crew entered the dining room, ate, then left while she remained. She cleaned the kitchen and dining room alone. He followed her movements as she also mopped the halls and two of the bathrooms. She moved between two floors only for several more hours, just cleaning, not interacting with any of the crew members she came in contact with.

The two kitchen crew members returned and began the supper meal, and he watched as the woman repeated her earlier procedures with the covered food plate on the metal tray with a bottle of water. Leaving the supply closet, Dolby moved with stealth, and when she stepped into the elevator, he shot out his arm and stopped the door from closing. Stepping inside, he towered over the woman who was staring, eyes wide with terror as she backed into the corner. The door closed, and knowing he only had a few seconds, she looked down at the tray, which was rattling in her shaking hand.

Pointing at the tray, he asked, "For the woman? Woman in clinic?"

She didn't say anything as fear oozed off her. He repeated, his voice a little sharper. "Is food for the woman in the clinic?"

She jerked her head up and down. Pulling the small

dove figurine from his pocket, he lifted the cover over the food, and set it on the plate, then recovered the dish.

She still said nothing but lowered her brow in question.

"Gift to woman." The elevator stopped, and just before the doors opened, he repeated, "Say nothing to anyone but give to the woman."

Her gaze jerked back to his face, but with less fear in her eyes. She jerked her head up and down again, then stepped out of the elevator, and the doors closed behind her. As Dolby slipped back to the supply closet, he watched her on his screen as she met the man outside the clinic door. When they stepped inside, he held his breath, waiting to see if the woman had told the man what he'd done.

But after a moment, they came out again, and the man gave no indication he'd seen anything untoward. He walked down the hall while she made her way back to the kitchen.

Now, he waited. But not for long.

19

Marcia was restless, pacing back and forth. Her nerves were heightened more than at any time since she'd woken into this living nightmare. Her body ached from the poor mattress, and she shivered from the chill. She'd spent time staring out the corner of her window, but the cloudy day gave little hope. She'd paced for as long as she could, determined to work her muscles in the cramped space. She knew they'd docked, and according to Tudora, they were supposed to be in Hawaii, and she wondered if she could rush out when her meal was served, finding a way to jump ship... *without killing myself in the process!*

But a surprise at lunch had greeted her. When Tudora came with the tray, Pitar wasn't with her. Instead, another large man with a hard expression and a scar down the side of his face had been at the door when it opened. And his countenance had not been welcoming in the least. Shocked at not seeing Pitar, her heart skipped a beat at the glare this man had sent her way, causing all ideas of rushing out to shrivel.

But as soon as Tudora scooted into her closet cell with the tray, it was evident the young woman was unnerved. Marcia wanted to ask where Tudora's brother was, but the vibe pouring from the new guard gave evidence that she shouldn't speak. Or even if she had asked, she doubted Tudora would have replied.

Tudora had managed to send a wide-eyed, scared look toward Marcia, but she didn't know how to interpret what was happening. Simply mumbling her thanks, she watched as Tudora was sent out of the room. The man stayed and stared at her for a long moment, and Marcia could feel the sweat forming underneath her clothes. She couldn't tell if he was divining that she was not Angela or if he was simply trying to offer a threatening tone. Standing perfectly still with her hands clasped in front of her hoping to imply her acquiescence, he finally turned and closed her door, locking her in.

She released a long breath as her body shook, not having realized she could barely breathe while in his presence. Pitar and Tudora had been a shock to get used to, but she had become familiar with them. Now she felt as though her situation had changed again, and definitely not for the better. The tremors rocked throughout her, and fear slithered along her heightened nerves.

Her legs gave out, and she plopped onto the mattress, then looked down at the meal. Trying to settle her stomach, she'd eaten quickly but remained ill at ease for the rest of the afternoon. *So close, but no way to escape.*

Now, as she waited for the evening meal to be delivered, her stomach clenched as she wondered what would be presented to her. The knock came, followed by the door opening. Once again, the harsh man stood back, allowing Tudora to enter. This time, Tudora was visibly shaken, and Marcia could only imagine what was happening to the young woman—her brother was missing, and this new escort appeared volatile. It struck Marcia that while she was undoubtedly a prisoner, perhaps Tudora was also not on board of her own accord. At least the man moved back toward the hall to speak to someone.

While she pressed her lips together, the two women stared at each other, neither speaking. Then Tudora's gaze dropped to the tray in her hand, barely lifting the cover. Surprised, Marcia glanced down to see something nestled next to the vegetables on the plate. "Wh—"

Tudora whimpered, giving an almost imperceptible shake of her head.

Marcia took the tray in her hands and peered closer. A gasp left her lips at the sight of a dove figurine. One of her doves. The one she'd had at Angela's house. *Oh God!* As quick as a flash, she knew where it came from... *Jonathan!*

Unable to keep her lips from curving, she moved to where only Tudora could see her smile. Tudora's expression morphed from confusion to wide-eyed surprise. Then her lips curved slightly as well.

"Pitar?" Marcia whispered.

Tudora's face fell. "Hawaii. Was made to leave ship. We weren't supposed to let you walk outside."

She winced, hating that Tudora was separated from her brother having assumed he'd given his sister some protection.

"What are you waiting on?" the man barked, causing Tudora to jump.

"Thank you," Marcia whispered, watching as Tudora nodded, then turned to hurry out of the room. This time, when the door shut and locked, Marcia was giddy with anticipation. She dropped to the floor, not even bothering to make it over to the bed. Plopping the tray on her lap, she lifted the plate cover again, and the figurine was there, assuring that she hadn't imagined it.

Carefully lifting the carving, she cradled it in her hands. The dove. *One of my doves.* A sign of encouragement and hope from a loved one who has passed. *Oh, Marty... Jonathan has to be here... somewhere on this ship!* For the first time since she'd been attacked in Angela's house, she felt a sense of hope that she'd be saved. She couldn't imagine how Jonathan had gotten on board or where he was, but she didn't care. Just knowing he was close was enough to make her almost giddy as renewed energy flowed through her veins.

Suddenly, a fat tear rolled down her cheek. Giving in to the emotions that rocked her as she hugged the figurine to her chest, she allowed the tears to fall, then swiped them away. Eating quickly, she wanted to be prepared for anything. She had no idea what he planned for her rescue but was determined to be an asset, not a liability. *Oh, Marty. I promise I'll do whatever I can to get out of this.*

She paced back and forth, occasionally peering out the corner of her window to see the darkness of the night creep onward. She had no idea what the crew normally did but felt sure that Jonathan would want to approach her at a time when the risk was low. As the minutes ticked by, her imagination began to take over. *Is it him? Is there someone else? Will anything happen on the ship? Maybe, I have to wait until—*

The doorknob jiggled, the sound reverberating in the small space sounding much louder than she remembered. Her heart skipped a beat before it began a staccato pattern threatening to leap from her chest. The door swung open, and she winced at the light behind the large silhouetted figure filling the space. And then it spoke. "Marcia."

She'd dreamed of the moment she might see him again, but the reality was far more intense than her imaginings. His dark shirt stretched tightly over his torso, his bulky arms barely contained in the sleeves. Dark pants gave evidence to his powerful thighs. And his eyes not wavering from hers.

"You're here," she whispered, afraid he was an apparition that might disappear.

"I'm here, babe."

Her eyes squeezed shut as her face scrunched, tears leaking down her cheeks. Her legs gave out from under her, and she began to crumple to the floor, unable to speak, much less stand.

But before she could drop to her knees, strong arms

banded around her body, pulling her tightly against a broad chest. She felt lips against her forehead and then was shuffled along with him as the door closed, shrouding them in darkness. But this time, she wasn't afraid.

"I've got you, Marcia. It's going to be okay. I've got you now."

She continued to cry as he held her, giving in to the emotions while he offered soothing words.

"I'm going to take care of you. We're going to get out of here."

"H... how? Wh... when?"

"Shh," he whispered, rubbing her back. "As soon as we get to the next stop tomorrow. But I'll be close and can keep an eye on you. I won't let anything happen, I promise."

She felt her body shifting again and, this time, found herself sitting on his lap as they both reclined on the mattress. His arms had not loosened his embrace, and she kept her face nestled under his chin, pressed to his chest. As the tears finally subsided, she leaned back and wished for the room to be bathed in light so that she could see his face more clearly.

It took several minutes for her eyes to adjust, and as they did, his features came into focus. The same thick muscles she remembered. The same square jaw she'd cupped with her hands. The same lips she'd kissed. But unlike before, she could now feel the tension in his muscles and anger radiating from him, but she had no idea what to do to alleviate his stress. So she did exactly what she'd dreamed of.

She clutched his face with her hands, feeling the coarse stubble underneath her palms. "I'm okay," she assured. "I promise I'm okay. I wasn't harmed." Moving closer, she angled her head and sealed her mouth over his, wanting to take what strength she could from him while offering what understanding she could give. If he was surprised at her bold move, he didn't show it. Instead, his arms tightened, pressing their chests together, until she felt sure that their hearts must be beating as one.

He groaned, and she swallowed the vibration, welcoming his tongue sliding into her mouth as she did the same. If this was a dream, she never wanted to wake. She wanted to memorize his taste and feel of him. Everything he had to give, she wanted to take deep within her soul. His body. His affection. Even his pain, having recognized his fears for her.

"Christ, babe," he mumbled against her mouth. "Since Angela told us that you'd been taken, I've been lost. Fuckin' crazy, pissed, and lost."

She leaned back slightly to hold his gaze in the darkened room. "And now?"

"Now, I'm fuckin' found."

Ignoring everything else around them, she dove in for another kiss. She wanted to crawl inside him, be surrounded by the safe harbor he offered. Yet as her tongue tangled with his, she poured everything she had into the kiss, wanting him to feel down to his very bones that she was safe and alive.

Leaning back slightly, she gripped the bottom of her shirt. Lifting it, she whipped it over her head before he had a chance to speak. Not caring that the only thing underneath was a plain, white cotton bra, she reached behind the clasp.

He jolted, then grabbed her hands behind her back. "No, Marcia. Not now. Not this way. You deserve—"

Shaking her head, she argued, "Yes, Jonathan. I want this. I need you."

"Babe, you've got me. When we get together, I want it to be what you deserve. Not here in this place of bad memories."

She spied his anguished hesitation. Bringing her hands forward, she cupped his jaws again. "I'm bruised but not broken. I've cried, but I've survived. I have no idea what tomorrow brings, but right now, I want to feel alive with *you*. I want *all* of you. If you want to rid my prison of the memories, then let me have you now."

She waited, his gaze boring into her eyes, and even in the dim light, she was sure he could see into her soul. Barely breathing until his lips slowly curved, she finally let the air rush out. Unclasping her bra, she let it fall from her arms, then clutched her arms around her. Brow furrowing, she confessed, "I've been able to wash off, but with no razor, I haven't shaved in a week."

Snorting, he growled, "Babe, do you think I give a fuck about not shaving?"

She grinned and thought it was the perfect answer as she lifted her arms around his neck. His gaze finally dropped to her chest, and now that her eyes were more adjusted to the dim light, she could see the flare of desire move through his eyes. She shifted around to straddle him, his erection pressing against her core.

"I should be pissed at myself," he said. "I have control of my body, yet when I'm around you, even in the middle of this fucked-up situation, my dick has a mind of its own."

A soft giggle slipped out. "I'm glad. Both for your typical restraint and the fact that he"—she wiggled on his lap—"can't wait."

Dolby, with his arms still wrapped around her, fell back onto the mattress, pulling her on top of him. In that position, she felt free. Freer than she'd been in a long time. She knew he was giving control over to her, knowing how much control had been stripped away.

Their mouths melded together again, then she finally mumbled against his lips. "I want you. We have too many clothes between us. I want nothing."

He rolled to the side, his grip loosening around her as he sat up and whipped his shirt over his head. He stared down for just a moment before bending and sucking and kissing along her jaw, down to the bottom of her neck, where her pulse fluttered underneath her pale skin. He continued kissing a trail to her breasts, and she gasped when he pulled a hard-budded nipple into his mouth.

As his lips worked magic, she started to close her eyes and then realized she didn't want to miss one second of their first time together. He moved between both breasts before trailing kisses down to her pants. Still wearing the elastic-waisted pants, she felt them shimmy over her hips and down her legs. Soon, she was naked and exposed to his heated gaze.

They lay facing each other, chest to chest, gaze to gaze.

Kissing again, she welcomed his wandering hands as they skimmed over her breasts, palming their fullness, slightly tweaking her nipples. He swallowed her moans and little gasps, and his fingers danced tantalizingly close to her mound. She pleaded, "Please, Jonathan."

His forefinger circled her clit, and she knew he'd discovered how wet she was for him when his hand continued lower and he slid his fingers through her slick folds. Opening her legs wider, she welcomed his exploration.

And he didn't disappoint. Gliding his finger through her wetness, he inserted it deep inside. She immediately felt the coil tighten in her womb. He leaned forward to kiss her again, his tongue now in rhythm with the movements of his finger. She felt more fullness as he added another finger, scissoring the two digits, touching her in a way that her vibrator couldn't even begin to pleasure.

Groaning again, fingers clutched his shoulders, her ragged nails digging into the skin as her orgasm came closer. Playing her like a fine instrument, he hit just the right spot, and her inner muscles quivered as her release slammed into her. Whatever sounds she would've made were muffled as he sealed his mouth over hers for another kiss.

She lay for a moment, basking in the euphoria of her body's humming from his hand, and wondered what heights of pleasure she'd feel when she had all of him.

Her hands moved to his belt buckle, but he shook his head. "Babe, we can't."

"Jonathan..." she begged, not caring that she was whining.

"It's not that I don't want to, but baby, I don't have protection."

"Protection?" Her brow lowered as her sluggish brain tried to discern his meaning.

"A condom. I don't have a fucking condom," he growled.

Suddenly, she bolted out of his arms and jumped to her feet. Bending, she snatched his shirt from the floor and pulled it on, grinning at how it covered her to her knees. She headed to the door, but he jumped up behind her and stopped her with his hand on her shoulder.

She twisted around and looked up. "No one is going to come into the clinic at this time. I've hardly heard anyone on this entire trip. But believe me, you're going to want me to do this."

His gaze narrowed as he gently moved her to the side and opened the door before peering out. She darted around him into the empty clinic and headed to one of the supply closets on the side of the room. Opening it quickly, she scanned the inside before moving to the next one. On the third shelf of the second cabinet, she reached out and grabbed several condom packets. Turning, she lifted them in her hand like a trophy before darting around him and back into her little cell.

He closed the door behind her, but before he had a chance to ask, she grinned. "I figured the ship's captain wouldn't want his crew to come back from the shore leave with STDs. I just knew the clinic would have to have some!"

It only took a second for his smile to widen as he stalked toward her. She was still smiling when he gathered her into his arms, lifting her before crawling back onto the mattress. With his muscular body now covering hers, she felt his full protection. And her heart soared.

20

Dolby's always-on-the-mission brain was about to short-circuit. He'd gone from stealth to risky in less than an hour. And right now, with his body lying over Marcia's with her legs spread, welcoming his hips, he didn't give a fuck about anything other than she was safe and in his arms. Their mouths sealed again, and he thrust his tongue in time with his hips pressing his cock against her pelvis.

She began to squirm, and when he lifted, she complained, "I want your pants off."

Chuckling, he stood and shucked his boots, pants, and boxers. Snagging one of the condoms, he ripped the package and rolled it on before dropping back onto the mattress. Gathering her in his embrace, he flipped once again, pulling her on top. He wanted her in control. She'd had so much taken from her, and he wanted her to only do what she wanted.

But with all things about Marcia that surprised him, she immediately straddled his hips, lifted on her knees, and then slowly lowered her body onto his cock, not stopping until he was fully sheathed. She rode him with abandon, throwing her head back, and as his gaze roamed from her beautiful smile down her full breasts to the curve of her waist, she rocked his world as much as his body. Dropping her chin, she held him with her heated gaze and leaned forward, her hair creating a curtain.

He knew she needed to feel safe... alive. And was thrilled she wanted him to be the one to offer that to her. "Take what you need, babe," he groaned as his cock swelled and thickened.

"I am," she assured. Leaning closer to where her nipples brushed against his chest, she added, "I'm taking what you're giving... all of it. And giving you all of me in return."

Christ, this woman was undoing him. Gripping her hips tighter, he lifted her as she became tired and thrust his hips upward, loving each hitch of her breath and each moan that slipped from her lips. Knowing he was close, he slid one hand forward, pressing his thumb on her swollen nub, and watched her cry out softly, her hand covering her mouth. Knowing she was trying to stay as quiet as possible, he couldn't wait to make her come in a place where she could scream as loudly as she wanted.

She was beautiful in the faint light from the corner of her window. Her silky pale skin glowed. She'd been through so much yet was giving him the greatest gift possible... to feel completely alive with the one person who made his heart pound.

As her core convulsed around him, he continued to

thrust for another minute until his release hit, and he could have sworn stars filled the room.

She fell on top of him, and they lay, fully connected from their tangled legs, his cock still inside her channel, chests pressed together, and her head tucked close to his neck. Her breath puffed against his skin as their heartbeats gradually slowed, still beating together, the rhythm as old as time.

Finally, she shifted off him, and as much as he hated to lose her warmth, he stood and pulled off the condom. While tying it off, she pulled her shirt over her head again, slipped on her panties, and stepped into her pants. Without speaking, she rushed back into the clinic and grabbed a paper towel. Handing it to him, she grinned. "Here you go."

Pulling on his boxers and pants, he pocketed the wrapped condom. He bent to kiss her, then said, "You're resourceful."

"I can't imagine how. I feel like my brain has been mush for days."

His grin fled, thinking of what all she'd gone through. Sighing heavily, he said, "Babe, I'm so sorry."

Her hand landed on his arm, and she squeezed. "You're here, Jonathan. I know I'll be okay now."

He finished dressing, stunned but not sorry at how they'd spent their reunion. "I can't believe we did this now. I've wanted you since we were together at the lighthouse, but I wanted it to be special."

"This was special," she said, her gaze boring into his. "I've been so scared. So alone. I… I…"

His gaze dropped to where she rubbed her right

wrist. "We need to talk. I need to let you know what the plan is. But first, I want to know everything that happened."

Her head snapped up to look at him, anguish marring the happiness she'd exhibited before. Neither spoke for a moment, and then she slowly nodded.

"Everything... now... and before," he added.

Her breath caught, then she continued to nod. She dropped to the mattress, and he joined her, sitting close so he could keep his eye on her face while making sure they were touching.

"Did Angela call you?" she asked.

"Yes. She called my boss. She came home, didn't find you, and looked at her cameras. The ones she put in that Roger didn't know about."

Her brow lowered, and he continued. "Roger had control of the main house security cameras, but she'd put in ones without him knowing to see what he was doing when she wasn't there. Thank God she did. They recorded the images of you being..."

"Abducted," she supplied, breathing heavily. "I came out of the bathroom and was grabbed. They didn't say anything but jabbed me in the neck with a hypodermic. When I came to, I was in a room bound."

He gently rubbed her hands.

"When I woke, I was blindfolded, gagged, and brought on board. I didn't realize where I was at first, but they must have held me in a warehouse at the docks."

He nodded. "We followed the car that took you and discovered you were at the docks. But by the time that happened and we had the dock security pulled up, the ship had left the port and was out to sea."

She pressed her lips together tightly, and he wanted to ease her distress, but they had much to cover. Continuing gently, he said, "We've... the whole Lighthouse Security team has been on this. Since the moment Angela called us, and she did that as soon as she got home."

After another moment of silence, she whispered, "Why?"

"LSI would have taken the case even if I didn't know you, Marcia. But we were starting out... you and me. When Angela called, it was like I'd been punched in the heart. I know I'd told you that we were an *us*, but I didn't realize until that moment that I already considered you mine. Mine to hold. Mine to have. Mine to protect."

She dropped her gaze, and he gave her that moment of privacy, then, with his knuckle under her chin, he lifted so he could see her eyes again.

She swallowed, then nodded. "I was brought into this room and left. But before they closed the door, they threatened me. Told me that I could stay here and be alone, but if I called out or tried to get someone to help me, then I'd be used to service the crew—"

"Fuck!" he growled, his hands tightening around her.

"I didn't know I was in the clinic until the door opened the first day, and Tudora brought me food. But I wasn't about to try anything. Not with the threat he made." Her breath hitched, and she shuddered. "I was so scared. I know you think I must be crazy, jumping you like I did, demanding sex. But..." Her face crumpled. "I was just so glad... so relieved. I've thought of you. Oh, Jonathan... thinking of you is what kept me sane. And when you walked in, it was as though my skewed world had righted again."

He pulled her close. "Oh, babe, I've done the same. You've been on my mind continuously. I just wanted our first time to be somewhere worthy of you. Not here. Not when you've been traumatized."

Blowing out a breath, she glanced around the room. "I had no idea why I'd been taken. I tried to think it through, like one of my plots. I know it might sound crazy, but Inspector Marley helped me muddle through a few things. I came up with that they'd meant to take Angela. And that would make it Roger who set it up."

Nodding, he agreed. "You're right. Exactly right, babe."

"But I had no idea where we were going."

"Roger has a place in the Marshall Islands where he hides money for some of his less savory clients. Angela was to be brought there, where, probably drugged, he would have made it looked like they were very happily vacationing, and then she would have had an accident."

"Oh my God," she gasped, her fingers digging into his shoulders.

"I got on the ship in Hawaii and have been watching the halls until I saw the woman bring a tray of food to the clinic."

Lifting her head, she bit her quivering lip. "And you slipped the dove onto the plate."

"It was to let you know I was here. I couldn't get to

you right away, but I wanted you to know you weren't alone."

She pressed her lips to his, and this time, he took the kiss slow and gentle, soft and sweet. It wasn't a kiss of desperation or a precursor to sex. It was just the simple human connection of his heart to hers.

As they separated, he resettled her over his lap, shifting her so that his arms could band tightly around her.

"Can you stay all night?" she asked. "No one comes in until Tudora brings breakfast."

"I don't want to be anywhere else."

She nodded and melted closer to him. He hated to bring up more trauma but didn't want there to be secrets. "I want full disclosure between us, babe. Angela told us who you were as far as your childhood. I read what I could about you so I'd know how this experience might affect you."

"Oh." She sighed heavily, looking down.

"But I only know what the articles said."

Lifting her gaze, she stared at him, her eyes searching. "Do you want more?"

"I want to know everything about you, baby. What makes you happy, and what keeps you up at night. What gives you joy, and what gives you nightmares. I want us to be together, and that means wanting to take care of you in all ways. To answer your question… if you're willing to give me more, then yes, I want it all."

After a moment of silence, she whispered, "Okay."

Heart pounding, he waited.

21

Marcia's body was still sated from their lovemaking, but now her mind began to churn with the past. It was a place she tried not to visit often, but being a part of her, it was never very far away. *What was the saying? You can't escape your past.* She understood that sentiment because our past is always part of us. The experiences, good and bad, are what make us individual and unique. Pretending something didn't happen doesn't make it go away. Refusing to look under the bed doesn't mean there aren't monsters.

Years of counseling had taught her that it was only by facing the past that she could learn to live with it and move forward. Maybe the same words applied to the relationship she was starting with Jonathan.

"I've never done this before… not everything… not even with Angela." She dragged in a rough breath. "I don't know where to start."

He lifted his hand, his knuckles gently gliding over

her cheek, and she leaned her head into his hand. Holding his gaze, she waited.

"Start at the place that makes you happy," he said.

Nodding, she said, "That's a perfect place." With another cleansing breath, she began. "Daddy was such a funny man. Larger than life, with a booming laugh and a sparkle in his eyes. He came from old money in Texas. He married the woman he fell in love with after seeing her riding over the fields. Momma didn't come from money. Her parents worked with horses on other ranches, but once he'd seen her on the back of a horse, he declared that was the woman for him."

She smiled softly, her memories coming to the forefront of her mind. "Growing up, I didn't realize how wealthy we were. I just knew I was happy. While our house was large, it wasn't pretentious. It was just a big ranch house. Our spread had a lot of acreage, but I had friends whose parents had oil fields much larger than ours. My father didn't walk around with a pompous air that said, "I'm rich." Most days, I saw him in jeans and a work shirt as he would handle business on the ranch, and then he'd wear a suit only when needed. My mother was as down to earth as the day he met her. She helped anyone who needed it, gave her time and energy to charities, and, like my father, was often found in jeans while taking care of the horses we raised. I know to many people it sounds like a charmed life, but my parents worked hard."

She shifted around a little more to get comfortable. "My twin brother, Marty, was my best friend. We were raised to appreciate what we had. Daddy used to always say, "no matter how lofty your goals are, always make sure to keep one foot on the ground." A little smile slipped across her face as she thought of her father's words.

"Sounds like you came from good people."

She nodded, swallowing past the lump in her throat. "I was lucky. They were the best."

"Marty had a rare illness that never really let him live life to the fullest the way he wanted. He tried doing all the things a normal boy would want to do but was unable to maintain his physical stamina for very long and needed special medication. He and Momma formed a bond over their love of horses. I loved to hang out with the ranch hands and listen to their stories, sometimes writing them down so they'd be recorded and last forever. I think Daddy loved that I would do that. I still have some of those notebooks."

Looking down at her hands in her lap, she knew the story was about to take a turn for the worse. "One night, when Marty and I were thirteen years old, my parents were gone for the evening to an event. My brother's room was across the hall, and we were both asleep. Our housekeeper was downstairs. I don't remember much about that night, but according to the FBI report, she heard someone in the kitchen, and when she went to see if one of us were hungry in the middle of the night, she was hit on the head. Three men had entered the house, two went into Marty's room, and one came into mine. I remember waking up when someone leaned over the bed, but I thought it was daddy. Then nothing. Just nothing."

"You were drugged?" he asked, his voice soft and hard at the same time.

She nodded. "That's what I was told. They did the same thing to Marty. When I woke up, I was in the dark." A shiver moved through her whole body, and his arms tightened. Letting his warmth soothe her fears, she leaned into him. "Things were very fuzzy at first. The memories come to me in little snippets. I remember the pitch black. I remember being scared. I remember crying. I remember hearing Marty trying to breathe, and I'd reach out to see if I could get to him, but there was something on my wrist that kept me from moving too far."

She gently rubbed her right wrist, a slash of pain seeming to hit where she'd been tethered. His fingers wrapped around hers, creating a new kind of band around her wrist. One made up of their joined hands providing protection and comfort.

"It was so dark that my eyes couldn't adjust. There was a blanket on the floor, and as I felt around, I heard moaning and realized Marty was in a bad way." She winced, her head beginning to ache. "A door finally opened, but the light seemed blinding. A man walked in, and I was finally able to discern that we were in a room about the size of a large closet. The man brought us a water bottle and two pieces of bread. I had no idea how long we'd been there, but I knew Marty needed his medicine. I cried to the man to help us, telling him that Marty was sick and begging him to get the medication.

The man just told me to shut up, and then as soon as Daddy would pay, we'd be out of there."

Jonathan's face grew tight, and she felt his entire body coil, ready to spring into action. But she knew there was no action to be taken. The events were years before. They couldn't be erased. They couldn't be denied.

"The hours ticked by, and Marty grew weaker. I don't know how much time passed, but I tried so hard to break free from the chain and band around my wrist. I even remember clawing at my skin, trying to get free. I thought if I could somehow escape, I could save Marty. But time slipped by, and Marty finally slipped away. His last words to me were, 'It's okay, sis. I love you.' It was sometime later that day, as I held Marty in my arms, that the door was broken open with a loud crash, and men rushed in, their weapons drawn. They shouted that they were the FBI, assuring me that I was safe. Looking back, I should've been afraid, but with Marty no longer breathing, my will had ceased to matter. I knew that even though I'd been rescued, I was far from safe."

"Christ, babe, I can't imagine." His hands gripped her even tighter, making it almost hard to breathe, but she didn't want him to let go.

She hadn't even realized that she began to cry until the tears on her cheeks dropped onto her hands in her lap. It wasn't that she never cried over the past anymore, but with time, she tried to remember her family through the good times and happy moments, working hard to push the tragedies behind.

"Of course, I learned more later. At the time, I just

knew that they had to pry Marty out of my grip, and we were separated. While in the hospital, I was checked out, and other than my wrist, dehydration, and hunger, there were no other physical injuries. My parents rushed in, their grief written on their faces even while they held me. I later learned that while we were land rich, my father was working desperately to get the cash that the ransom note required. Friends and relatives were helping, but the kidnappers had delayed getting the ransom note out, and by the time they got the money ready, and the FBI knew where to go, it was too late for Marty." She was silent for a moment, then added, "My parents never recovered."

"You know none of that is your fault, right?"

Her head moved up and down, but while she knew the facts, it was sometimes hard for the heart to believe. "I'm assuming you've read about my parents." He didn't have to answer because she could see the response on his face. Sucking in a deep breath, she let it out slowly, hitching halfway through as she fought to keep the emotions in check.

"My mother, who'd never been a heavy drinker, started self-medicating with sleeping pills and vodka. I sometimes hated that was how she coped. She's been such a strong woman, full of life, ready to take on everything. But the addiction to sleeping pills, and then the alcohol, was a combination that managed to bring a strong woman down. One night, she went to sleep and didn't wake up. When I was sixteen years old and really needed my mom, I was burying her."

She loved the closeness of having Jonathan hold her,

but suddenly needed to move. She pulled out of his arms and stood, grateful he didn't try to hold her back. She walked over to the window where the sliver of dawn was shining through. Without looking back at Jonathan, she continued. "And just a few years after that, my father had a heart attack, but honestly, he died of a broken heart. I know he loved me, and he loved my mom, but he was never able to get over the guilt. Parents are told that it's their job to protect their children no matter what. But I think there's evil in the world that sometimes touches us no matter what we do. But daddy could never seem to forgive himself that he and mom had gone out that night. And that he wasn't able to get the money as quickly as needed." She sighed. "By the time I was entering adulthood, I buried the last of my family."

She turned slowly as Jonathan pushed up from the mattress and came to stand near her. She could see his face clearly in the dim light. His blue eyes seemed to see deep inside her. His muscular body, she now knew, was exquisite, especially when making love to her. And his smile filled her heart with joy whenever he bestowed it on her, which was often. He lifted his hand and cupped her cheek.

"And now this," he said, his voice cracking.

She nodded slowly, then said, "I'm not downplaying what this has been like. Not the fear, the unknown, the anguish. But I've been to the darkest place I could've ever been and somehow survived. At least here, I haven't been bound. While the room was often dark, there was enough light that I could adjust. And they supplied a woman who gave me some clothes, toiletries, and food. Although if you hadn't walked through the door, I'd still be terrified. But with you here, I know I'll be okay. I feel like I can do anything knowing someone is in my corner." She smiled and added, "Especially if you're that person with me."

"You're the strongest woman I know, Marcia. I'm humbled. So fuckin' humbled."

"Oh, you're looking at the result of some expensive counseling," she said with a little smile. "It was my therapist who suggested that I start writing as a way to cope. I found that I wrote about what I wished the detectives and investigators had been able to do a little faster. Gotten to me quicker." She shrugged, "That was how Inspector Marley was born. Somehow the idea of a plodding older man who could read people and always figure out the crime before anyone else just made me feel better."

"It's a brilliant coping mechanism." His voice was soothing, and the warmth surrounded her.

"I've learned that, in truth, no matter how we cope, our traumas and tragedies define us as much as our successes and happiness. I've learned we are all affected by the human emotions and events that make up our lives."

He wrapped his arms around her, and she rested in his embrace with her hands clutching his shirt, her cheek now pressed against his chest, hearing the rhythm of his strong heartbeat.

Finally, she leaned back and said, "What's the plan?"

He chuckled, and the sound vibrated against her chest. "We get out of here."

Her eyes brightened, a spark of renewed energy and confidence moving through her. "And how do we do that?"

Smiling down at her, he said, "Together."

22

Dolby hated to leave Marcia in her cell, but with another day until they docked at the Marshall Islands, he needed to keep her safe. So after the memorable night they'd spent together where she'd given him her painful past, and they'd made love, sealing their vow for a future, he was back in his hiding place. She'd assured him that her days passed the same– complete solitude broken up by meals brought by Tudora. She said that Tudora's brother had taken out her chemical toilet once and brought it back, assumedly after emptying it. Other than that, she had been left alone.

He prayed this day was no different but had his eye on the camera outside the clinic just in case. He'd been in contact with the Keepers, then felt guilty that he had something to concentrate on when Marcia had endured days with nothing to do to fill her time but worry, pace, and remember.

By nighttime, his skin was practically crawling with the need to get back to her. Thankfully, Tudora was just now leaving after delivering the evening meal. The man who'd escorted Tudora stood and stared at Marcia, and Dolby's fists clenched as his body was primed to go after him if he didn't get the fuck away from her.

Using his radio, he questioned LSI. "ETA?"

Natalie replied, "Queen at two forty a.m. Majuro. The birds have flown in."

Nodding to himself, he was thankful for the other Keepers who'd landed at the Majuro airport and were in place. Now, he just needed to get Marcia off the ship safely and knew the timing would be of utmost importance. For himself, he wasn't concerned. But for her? She'd been through more than enough. More than what anyone should ever have to experience, and if it took the rest of his life, he wanted to give her nothing but good memories from now on.

Signing off, he waited until most of the crew had gone to their rooms unless they were working the night shift. Then, slipping out of his hiding place, he re-entered the clinic with stealth, easily unlocking the door to the closet that had held her captive for a week. This time, he was expected and greeted exuberantly the instant she saw him. He barely had time to spread his arms out before she flung herself at him, leaping into his arms. She wrapped her legs around his waist, and he carried her easily into the room as he closed the door behind him.

"God, I missed you," she said. "Each day has been interminably long, but today, just knowing you were close had me pacing frantically."

"I know what you mean, babe. My closet didn't give

me room to pace, but I was coming out of my skin and couldn't take my eyes off the camera I'd placed outside the room to make sure you were okay."

"I felt safer just knowing you were on the ship."

"Tell me more about the man who came with Tudora today."

Still in his arms, with her hands clutching his shoulders, she shook her head. "I don't know what to tell you. For the first part of the trip, I had her brother, Pitar. He never talked much except just to say a few words to her. But he was with us the day we stepped out onto the deck to get a breath of fresh air. After we left Hawaii, he wasn't there, and this other man came. His voice is much harsher, and he looks at me with a lot of suspicion. I hated the way he talked to Tudora. I managed to ask her about Pitar, and she just said that he'd been left behind in Hawaii. Something about he was being punished for letting me walk out."

"I couldn't see the man's face, but he stared at you for a long time from my camera angle."

"I've been terrified that they'd discover I wasn't Angela. I mean, I knew it was going to happen sometime, but I guess I'd hoped that I might be able to escape before I was found out. Not a realistic hope, I know, but I knew if they discovered it too soon, my life would be easily expendable."

He hated that he'd put the worry lines on her face. Bending, he kissed her lightly, then slid his tongue between her lips, loving the way she leaned into him, plastering her front to his, giving her trust to him.

Nibbling the edge of her mouth, he leaned back and said, "Tonight, it ends."

"We're docking?"

"We dock in about three hours."

"I remember the plan you told me last night," she said. " I guess I spent today thinking of all the things that could go wrong. I just don't want to screw up, Jonathan, and put your life in danger."

"Babe, no chance that's going to happen. My job is to take care of you, not the other way around. And believe me, I'm used to missions going fubar, so we can make this work no matter what."

"When this is over, I think I need to write a new series. New heroes who are larger than life and swoop in to do all the active work."

"No way. You've got to keep Inspector Marley going!"

A giggle slipped out, and she nodded. "Oh, I'll keep him going. But maybe I'll write romantic suspense as well."

"I've got some clothes for you to change into. It's a basic uniform that the other crew members are wearing. We'll have your hair pulled up in a cap, and while it wouldn't fool anyone up close, if someone happens to catch a glimpse of us from a distance, they won't think anything about it."

With her feet on the ground, he shrugged off his small pack and pulled out the pants, shirt, and black high-top sneakers that, from a distance, would look like boots, as well as be serviceable. When he turned to hand them to her, he grinned at the sight. She whipped her shirt over her head, and with her thumbs hooked into the waistband of her pants, shucked them to the floor. Now standing in a plain white bra and panties with a trusting smile on her face, she was more beautiful than any woman he'd ever seen.

Lifting a brow, she asked, "Do I have to get dressed now, or do we have time for anything else."

Not knowing what the next day would bring, he hesitated. He never ventured away from the absolute mission until the previous night, and having had a taste of her, he wanted another.

She stepped closer, placing her hands on his shoulders. "I don't want to put us in danger, but if we've got time to kill, I want to spend it with you. Really *with you*. I'm tired of playing it safe, Jonathan. Tired of being afraid of my own shadow. Just for once, I want to do something unplanned and unpredictable on my own terms."

"Babe, you know I want you. And if you need this, too, I'm all in."

She finished stripping, and he lifted her in his arms after freeing his cock and rolling on another condom. With her back pressed against the door, she wrapped her legs around his waist, and he dragged his finger through her slick folds, finding her ready.

"Don't wait," she begged.

With a thrust upward, he impaled her on his cock, and her head flung back as she gripped his shoulders, a smile on her face. Dropping her chin, she held his gaze as his strong legs held both of them, and his massive arms easily kept her in place.

"What would you say if I told you that this had been a fantasy of mine since I first met you?" she asked.

"What would you say if I told you that I want to make all your fantasies about me and you together come true?" he countered.

Grinning, she sealed her mouth over his, then mumbled, "Then I'd say we're both getting our wishes."

Their conversation fell away as their lips melded and their bodies joined. With her back pressed against the door, he slid one hand between, lightly pinching her clit as he bent to take a nipple in his mouth. Her body tightened, and her legs squeezed tighter around his waist. She grunted before burying her face in the crook of his neck, muffling the sound of her pleasure. As her core was still convulsing around his cock, his own release hit at the same time, and he continued to thrust till every drop was emptied.

Both panting, gasping for breath, he held her weight easily. Slowly, he pulled out and let her legs slide to the floor, holding her steady. She peered up at him and grinned.

"That was better than a fantasy, Jonathan."

Chuckling, he nodded, dealing with the condom before refastening his pants. Wrapping his arms around her, he kissed her wishing they were a thousand miles away, just the two of them. "I couldn't have said it better myself, babe. Let's get dressed. It should be just about time to start the next phase of rescuing Dolby's woman."

Brows lifted, she stared. "That's what this mission is called?"

"No, not officially. But unofficially... yeah." Suddenly

unsure, he hesitated. She seemed preoccupied, her eyes averted. Lifting her chin with his knuckle until her gaze hit his, and he tilted his head to the side. "What are you thinking about?"

She hesitated, chewing on her bottom lip, but he pushed. "Really, Marcia, I want to know."

"What's a typical Dolby dame?"

"Wha... what?" Suddenly, he remembered his phone conversation with Hop the night he was with Marcia in the lighthouse. The conversation that he had no idea she'd heard. Sighing heavily, he kept her close while he admitted, "It's a stupid phrase that I ended up with years ago. I wasn't very discriminating with my hookups as long as they were pretty, willing, and understood that it was only for a night." He winced, hearing himself, knowing he looked like an ass. "And often, the women who'd pursue me were the same. So typical Dolby dame became a moniker for a woman who was only going to be a one-night thing."

She nodded slowly, but her expression was unreadable. Panic crawled up his throat, threatening to choke him. Cupping her face, he pleaded, "Please, Marcia, that was all before I met you. And, honest to God, in the past year, those women have been few and far between. I was looking for something lasting but never found it until I scared a beautiful woman in an abandoned lighthouse during the middle of a rainstorm."

"I'm sorry, Jonathan. I shouldn't have been listening to your conversation."

"No, babe, I should have been more discreet. But, believe me, you are nothing like that. You are everything that I want to be with. Yeah, I'd love for you to be Dolby's woman. My only woman. At least, I hope that's who you want to be." His breath held in his lungs as his gaze held hers, desperation filling his entire body as he waited in anticipation.

She pressed her lips tightly, rubbing them together, before finally offering a tiny smile. "I'm a lot of things with a lot of different names. By birth, Marcia Baxter. By choice to protect my privacy, Marcia Blackburn. M.B. Burns as Inspector Marley's creator. Marcia Black is a romance writer. But now, I'd love to add Dolby's woman to the others. That might just be my favorite name of all."

His heart leaped as he kissed her again, with his heart as engaged as his mouth. Tongues tangled and danced as he memorized the taste and feel of her. Only the knowledge that he needed to get her out of here forced him to separate. Their hot breaths panted as their gazes locked.

She stepped back, her kiss-swollen lips holding his attention as she slipped on the slightly large uniform he'd managed to procure from Landon. The khaki pants were long, so forcing his thoughts away from her mouth and to the task at hand, he bent to roll them up from the bottom. The blue shirt was also large on her, but at least it was much smaller than her wearing his shirt.

He handed her a hard hat, and she reached up to twist her hair into a knot and then plopped the hat on top. "Are you ready, babe?"

She sucked in a deep breath and looked around the

room before turning back to him. Nodding, she replied, "More than ready."

Tapping onto the radio on his watch, he reported, "I've got the dove."

With his hand on the door, he halted when she reached out and touched his arm. Looking down, he waited.

"The dove? Is that me?"

"When I was asked if I wanted a codename for you, I told them dove."

Her smile widened. "I think that's perfect."

Squeezing her hand, he opened the door to the clinic, and they slipped into the main room. He locked the door behind them and then moved to the outer door. Checking his cameras, he found the way was clear, so they moved out into the hall. Continuing to monitor their progress with his hidden cameras, they made it to the dining room and then into the kitchen unseen.

"This is where we're going to hide until we dock. I don't know when someone will go in to get you, but I can't imagine it will be when everyone else is running around. Of course, that's a chance we'll have to take. But we should have the opportunity to slip out the door over there," he said, pointing at the wide doorway at the side. "That's where supplies will be coming on board, and we should be able to leave and get to the dock."

"That seems so risky to think someone won't see us."

"Let's just say the Keepers have a few tricks up their sleeve. No matter what, make sure you follow my directions. Whatever I tell you to do, wherever I tell you to go, I need you to do that for me. Okay?"

"Absolutely," she promised.

With that, they slipped into one of the kitchen supply closets closest to the door. He was even more vigilant this time than when he'd come on board. It didn't take long for them to begin to feel the change in speed through the vibrations and noise of the ship. Keeping an eye on his wrist screen, he could see no one had come to the clinic.

More and more crew members had left their rooms and were moving about the ship in preparation for the docking. Since it was the middle of the night, they wouldn't have to contend with anyone in the kitchen immediately. And what the Keepers had planned should keep them away. He'd kept Marcia in the dark about the next step, not wanting her to worry while they were still in deep water.

The engines cut, and he knew it would take time for the tugs to push them to the dock. Looking down at Marcia, he could see her growing increasingly anxious. Wrapping one arm around her, he pulled her against his side. Kissing the top of her head, he said, "It's all good."

"This seems to be taking forever. I didn't pay any attention to what it was like when we were docking in Hawaii. But now that I'm terrified someone will find me missing, and they'll come looking for us, it seems like each moment drags on."

"Just remember that everyone on the crew is busy getting the boat docked. Even the crew member who was with Tudora earlier has a job to do. Right now, no one is looking for you."

She nodded, letting out a long breath. "I'll be fine, Jonathan. Don't worry about me."

"Babe, you're the most important thing for me to worry about."

She gifted him with a wide smile, and he couldn't resist. Bending, he took her lips in a quick kiss, vowing to make it last longer as soon as they were safe.

"I can't help but wish I could get Tudora off this ship. I know that she was not involved with the kidnappers. She was just brought on board as Pitar's sister."

"My guess is that while Roger plans for Angela's demise, he needs her... which is you, for now. He probably didn't want her to be molested but didn't exactly care about how she was transported out of the country."

"He's such a shit!"

Chuckling, Dolby agreed. "Well, he's gotten in bed with the Bulgarian mob, but he's getting ready to find out they make for poor bedfellows."

Eyes wide, she asked, "What's going to happen?"

"I'm afraid I can't tell you right now," he said. "But when it's over, I'll let you know."

As the ship rocked side to side gently with no forward motion, he said, "We're docked."

She nodded but remained silent, pressing her lips together. He cursed as two crew members walked through the kitchen, standing near the door that would lead outside. Staring at his wrist screen, he grimaced as they remained near the door, just talking. "Looks like we're going to have a little excitement." Shifting his gaze to her, he curved his lips. "Ready to get out of here with me, babe?"

Her breath hitched as she nodded again, her eyes wide but lips quirking upward.

He tapped his earpiece and said, "Need the fourth." With his hand on the door of the supply closet they were in, he turned to her. "As soon as I move, you stay with me."

A muffled boom was heard from the other side of the ship, and he watched as the two crew members looked at each other before jumping into action and running out of the kitchen.

"Let's go," Dolby said, throwing open the door. Racing to the main door at the dock, he pulled on the automatic handle that allowed the door to lift. With Marcia right on his heels, he looked down to see the dock ramp had not made it to the door. They were about thirty feet above the dock. Pulling a thin rope from his pack, he tied the end to the door handle before sliding on gloves. He looked over his shoulder. "Hold on, babe, and don't let go."

She nodded and, without hesitation, did exactly what he asked. With her wrapped around him piggyback style, her ankles crossed at his waist, he swung out of the doorway. Hand under hand, he used his thick arm muscles to scale down the rope until he could drop safely to the concrete deck of the small port.

Several people at the dock were running toward the ship but focused on the front where the explosion had sounded. Grateful it was still dark, Dolby patted her leg. "Okay, you can let go."

She slid down his back, and once her feet were on the ground, he grabbed her hand, and they began running.

Seeing a flashing light ahead, he veered to the left, and they darted behind containers, still running toward the light. Keeping to her pace, he tried not to rush her faster than she could go. She was already slowing, but they made it to the end of a warehouse building nearby when a shot was fired, and Marcia screamed and dropped to the ground.

23

Marcia sucked in air as she ran, holding tight to Jonathan's hand while he led them past massive container crates and dodged the dockworkers running toward the ship. Thoughts raced through her mind, but it wasn't time to ask anything. He was much more athletic than she, but adrenaline kicked in, and she forced her body to keep going, determined not to hold them back. A growing excitement replaced her fear, the desire to escape giving wings to her empowerment.

"Almost there," he said, glancing down at her.

She wasn't sure if he meant those words or was just trying to encourage her. She nodded, unable to speak. Suddenly, shouts came from behind them, and two shots rang out. Terror ripped through her, and she dropped to the ground, covering her head.

Dolby dropped to the ground next to her, his massive body bending over her back and his lips close to her ear. "Babe, are you okay?"

She nodded, her body shaking.

"Are you hurt?"

She jerked her head back and forth and twisted around to look at him. "No, but I heard gunfire!"

"It's okay. We've got to get out of here. I'll carry you."

While her heart still pounded in a furious beat, she shook her head again. "No, I can do this!" With more force than she knew she had in her, she pushed upward, standing on the legs that threatened to give out underneath her again. She was terrified that she'd cost them precious time. Before she had a chance to apologize, her hand was once again wrapped in his, and she had no choice but to follow as he began running again.

They rounded a corner of a building and came upon several large men with weapons right in front of them. She stumbled to a halt, then opened her mouth to scream when Jonathan clapped his hand over her mouth, pulling her close to him. "It's okay, babe. They're with me."

Shivers ran down her body. She knew he felt them when he jerked his hand away. "Christ, I'm sorry, Marcia. But it's okay," he repeated. "I've got you."

The other men stepped back as he pulled her closer to him, tucking her into his side. "This is Marcia Blackburn. Marcia, I'll make introductions later, but these men are with me. They're going to get us to safety."

One of the men stepped forward and clasped forearms with Jonathan. "Dolby, good to see you."

Stepping into the dim light, Marcia could now clearly see the three men standing before them. Terror was still in her heart as it pounded, despair mixed with hope still rushing through her veins, and fatigue combined with adrenaline still battling for primacy. But throughout all that, it did not miss her attention that the three men were tall, broad, built, and devastatingly good-looking. Once more, the thought flew through her mind that she needed to memorize and commit this to pen and paper.

A squeeze on her shoulder brought her back to the current moment. Looking up at Jonathan, she managed a weak smile. While the others were drool-worthy, only one man had captured her complete attention and already held her heart. "Yeah, I'm good."

Good sounded like a ridiculous descriptor, considering everything she'd gone through. But at the moment, it was the only word she could come up with. She squeezed his hand and nodded. "Really, I'm good. But I don't mind saying I'd like to get out of here."

His arm tightened, and she loved the feel of being surrounded by him. Turning toward the others, she smiled a little stronger. She wanted to ask how they would get off the island but thought it best to let the ones in charge just do what they needed to do. As though reading her hesitation, he looked toward the others and said, "We're ready."

The men nodded and turned to continue hustling around the end of the warehouse, away from the dock.

"The *Skirta Krislista* is the only ship docked at the Uliga Pier right now, and it looks like they're *busy*," one of the men said, and the others chuckled.

"Needed a diversion," Jonathan said, chuckling. "Thanks for the fireworks, Poole. Just when I thought we wouldn't need them, I had two guys in the kitchen who wouldn't leave."

She jerked slightly and twisted her head to look up at him. "That was you?"

His gaze softened as he looked down. "Poole took care of a small explosion on the dock away from where we needed to escape. It worked."

"And the gunfire?"

"Two men from the ship climbed down after you. When they started chasing, I winged them," one of the other men said. "Sorry to scare you."

Her eyes widened, and her mouth dropped open. "Oh... it's okay. Um... thank you."

It was still dark, and the dock lights had disappeared behind the warehouse. With Jonathan's hand holding hers again, they followed the guys to an SUV parked at the side. "I can't believe you came so prepared."

He grinned, his gaze sending warmth through her cold body. The door of the SUV opened, and Jonathan ushered her in. Nerves still tight, relief moved through her as the others piled in. It was crowded with the large men, but tucked next to Jonathan, she let out a shaky breath. They had a long way to go to get home safely, but a sense of calm now moved through her as the SUV started down the road, taking her farther away from the pier.

"It's nice to have you with us, Marcia," the driver said, having twisted around to smile at her. "I'm Bennett."

The man next to him shifted around as well. "And I'm Adam."

She nodded, then looked at the man sitting next to her.

With a chin lift, he added, "Poole. Good to meet you."

She leaned forward slightly to look outside the window next to Jonathan, but she discerned very little with only a few streetlights illuminating the area. Seeing Jonathan look down at her, she shrugged. "I don't really even know where we are."

Poole shifted slightly to give her more room. She wanted to tell him not to bother. Usually, feeling confined by people she didn't know made her uncomfortable. But right now, with Jonathan on one side, and these men risking their lives to rescue her, she felt nothing but safe.

"The Marshall Islands," Poole said. "When you look at a map of the Pacific Ocean, unless you move in close, you'd never even notice all the tiny tops of volcanoes and mountains that have pushed just above the water creating islands. This one is a chain making a donut shape. Except for a few areas that are wider, it's really encompassed with only one road and buildings on either side before you get back to the water. But it has a small port and an airport."

"And Roger has a place here?" Unable to keep the incredulity out of her voice, she couldn't imagine why Roger had purchased a house in such a remote area.

"We know from the accountant that Angela hired he has offshore accounts in various islands for himself and some of his clients," Jonathan said.

"A man like him can live like a king here. His house

isn't huge compared to what he has in California, but it's big. He has a staff but no guards. As far as he's concerned, he has nothing to fear here. It's a place for him to come, bring his mistress or friends, and be a big fish in a little pond," Poole added.

She nodded, understanding what Poole was saying. "I was never around him much in California, but when I was, I always got the feeling he wanted more, even though they had a big house. Angela never cared about any of that. I can imagine for a man like him, he'd prefer having a woman who thought he was a big deal." She shook her head and sighed. "I never understood why they were together."

"Did she love him?" Jonathan asked.

Twisting to look at him, she chewed her bottom lip. "I think at one time, yes, she did. They had actually met years ago in college. I think he was impressed with some of her author clients and wanted her to be impressed with his wealth."

"Did he know who you are as an author?"

She shook her head. "No. He just knew me as Marcia, Angela's shy little friend." As soon as those words left her mouth, she realized they made her sound pathetic. She quickly amended, "Not that I minded. I preferred my own company over the crowded company of people I didn't know. And Angela protected my identity and pen names, so she never let him know who I was."

It only took about ten minutes before they pulled into a driveway leading to the back of an airport. She followed Jonathan's lead and scooted over after he climbed down. He turned and grabbed her hand, gently assisting her down. They all seemed to know what they were doing and where they were going, so she simply moved along with them. It didn't escape her attention that they formed a human shield around her as they walked into the small hangar.

She couldn't imagine why but remained quiet until they were inside, and the men led them into another room with a small table, a counter, a mini-refrigerator, and a sink. When the others had stepped to the side, she leaned up and whispered, "Why the security on me? After all, they kidnapped me and got the wrong person. I'm no one to them."

He turned and then glanced at Bennett and Poole, who walked back to them, their hands full of water bottles. He waited until they passed the bottles around, then ushered her over to the table. They sat down, and the others stood leaning against the counter. She licked her dry lips, then opened the water bottle and took a deep gulp.

Another man walked into the small room. She gasped as her body jerked, and Jonathan's hand landed on hers. "Marcia, this is Landon. He's part of our team on this mission and is with the FBI."

Her brows lifted, but she remained quiet, only nodding toward Landon. She'd often researched law enforcement for her books, especially writing Inspector Marley, but knew little about international law enforcement. She was surprised that someone from the FBI was in another country on a mission to rescue her.

Lifting her hand, she wiped the drops of water from her lips and waited.

"It's nice to meet you, Ms. Blackburn," Landon said, walking farther into the room to sit down as well.

"You might not be the one the kidnappers wanted to take," Jonathan began, "but Roger is desperate to get his wife to sign everything over to him. And desperate men make desperate mistakes. As soon as he realizes the error, he could try to use you as a hostage to get Angela to do his bidding."

Landon nodded. "And the Bulgarian mob will not want you around as a live witness. After all, Angela was going to have a fatal accident here. Now, with you no longer in their captivity, their screwup by taking the wrong person would come back to bite them in the ass."

Like trains hurtling toward each other on the track, her thoughts collided too quickly in her mind to sort each out. Roger wanting Angela dead. Roger hiring people to kidnap her. Those people being an actual organized criminal group. Her ordeal on the ship. She was terrified of being taken again and was not sure she could survive a third kidnapping. Spots begin to form at the edge of her vision.

"Breathe, babe," Jonathan said in her ear, his large hand rubbing her back between her shoulder blades.

The air rushed out, and she struggled to steady her breathing, embarrassed at her weakness. When the spots abated, she looked down to see her hands gripping the water bottle. "I'm sorry," she mumbled.

"Don't apologize," Bennett said. "You've been

through an ordeal, and you came out on the other side. That makes you fuckin' amazing, Marcia."

Her head jerked up, surprised to hear his words and even more surprised when the others in the room nodded. Jonathan squeezed her hands. With all the competing voices in her, she was calm. *I'm not alone.* It was freeing to know just how having someone else on her side could make her feel.

"What have we got on him?" Jonathan asked Poole.

A laptop appeared on the table, and it was turned so she and Jonathan could see it with the others gathered around. "Roger has been pacing most of the night. Guess he figured Angela was about to be delivered to him, and the next part in the plot would begin."

She stared at the screen, seeing the front of a large home compared to the ones she'd seen around the airport. The early dawn light gave evidence of lush grass in the front yard, and trees, palms, and flowering bushes filled the area. Open-air porches surrounded the two floors with shuttered doors that opened onto the decks. With a tap on the keyboard, another view came into sight—that of Roger walking around while talking on his phone in what appeared to be a home office.

The knowledge he was waiting for Angela to be brought to him to coerce her to sign over her inheritance and then kill her caused Marcia to inhale sharply.

"You okay?" Jonathan asked, his hand squeezing hers.

Nodding, she looked at the others and then turned to him. "Yeah, sorry. It just really hit me about what he's expecting. What he'd planned. It's hard to wrap my head around it."

"Well, he'll soon get a surprise," Poole said, grinning.

Glancing to the side, Jonathan mirrored the grin as he looked down at her. "He's been laundering money for the Bulgarian mob out of LA for several years, taking his extra cuts and putting it in offshore accounts so he didn't pay taxes and buying properties such as the one you see on the screen. That's how he got them to agree to kidnap Angela and bring her here on a cargo ship. Of course, them getting you instead was their mistake. But he also skims a bit from the top."

Eyes wide, she blurted, "So the thief steals from the thieves?"

"Perfect way to put it, Marcia." Bennett laughed.

Landon chuckled. "And this is why I love working with you all." Turning to Marcia, he said, "I'm here at the US government and the American Embassy's discretion to make sure you're officially brought back to the States. And with the backing of the Marshall Island government and Interpol, I'll deal with Roger." Standing, he said, "I'm heading out. Time to make sure I'm covered."

She cocked her head to the side, glancing out the window, seeing the dawn now casting its glow over the airfield. "What now? Do we leave?" Her question could be answered by anyone, but she was looking at Jonathan.

"For you, it's over," he replied. "For us, we've got a score to settle."

She didn't speak but continued to hold his gaze. He

leaned forward until his forehead touched hers. Still holding gazes, he amended, "I've got my own score to settle."

Before she could ask more, he stood and pulled her to her feet, ushering her to the mini fridge. He pulled out a container and set it on the counter. "Here, you need to eat to keep up your strength."

She peeked in to see several hard-boiled eggs. He also placed energy bars, as well as soft, local rolls on the counter with another water bottle.

Nibbling on an egg, she said, "You haven't been here, so how did you know there was food?"

He grinned, then bent to place a light kiss on her lips before inclining his head to the other Keepers. "Because part of their job was to make sure we had what we needed to take care of you. I knew they'd take care of everything."

She couldn't help but smile. "These people you work with... a well-oiled machine, right?"

Poole walked over and leaned around to snag an egg from the container. "Damn straight." He smiled down at her, adding, "Glad that food was all that's needed right now."

Her brow furrowed as she shot a questioning gaze toward Jonathan. He grimaced, then offered, "We weren't sure what medical care you might need, so we were prepared."

She could see he hated the explanation, but she reached out and placed her hand on his. "I'm good. Really. I mean, thank God that you all were ready for anything, but I'm good."

As Poole moved back into the hangar with the others, leaving just Jonathan and her, she walked to his side and placed her hands on his waist. "Okay, now that it's just the two of us, tell me what you can. How are we getting off the island? We're obviously in an airport. Are we flying? And what did you mean when you said this isn't just a case of you rescuing me, and now the FBI wants more evidence on Roger?"

"One thing at a time, babe. Yes, when it's time, we'll fly off the island. Adam flew the others on a private jet from Hawaii, so they'll use it to take us all back as well. Landon is working with the local police. They would like nothing more than to get rid of Roger, someone with such a dubious background. How he'll make that work, I'll leave that up to him."

Her fingers dug in slightly, and she lifted on her toes. "Okay, but you left out the part about the score to settle."

"Roger and the Bulgarian mob took something that belongs to me."

Blinking, she jerked her chin back slightly. "I have to tell you, Jonathan, that sounds suspiciously like something I might have written in one of my romance novels. You know... alpha male speak."

"And why is that?" he countered. "Why would something like that end up in one of your romance novels?"

Her mouth opened and closed several times as she realized his question was harder to answer than she had initially imagined. Finally, she replied, "Because, in romance novels, our heroes are usually larger than life. Of course, I try to make them believable while filling many readers' fantasies. And yes, an alpha male makes a great character in a romance novel, but he also has to be sweet, or else the reader gets pissed and wants to throw their book across the room, leave a bad review, or decide that they won't read you anymore."

Squinting her eyes closed, she shook her head. "Christ, this is harder to explain than I thought." Sighing, she continued. "But one thing in a romance novel is that the man... the hero would do anything to save the woman he loves."

"Roger and the Bulgarian mob took something that belongs to me," he repeated, holding her gaze.

Brows furrowed, she shook her head. "I still don't understand."

"Look, I know we're not ready to declare love for each other right now," he admitted. "But I know what I feel for you already is more than I've ever felt for another woman outside my mom. You and I had already decided that we were at the start of something amazing, and someone came in and ripped you away from me. Even if it makes me sound like an alpha asshole to declare that you belong to me, I still say they took something of mine. They took the woman who I was falling for. They took the woman who I wanted to protect. They took the woman who I was getting to know, someone who was going to trust me with her secrets in her own time, not have them forced upon her to relive. Someone who could choose when and who they wanted to know about their past, and that includes my coworkers and friends. All that got fucked up when they took you. And I spent days in agony wondering what was happening to you, what they might be doing, or whether you were even alive, and terrified for you. I had no idea what I might have to deal with to help you through all of this but was sure as fuck going to make the commitment to take care of you." With his hands on her waist, pulling her closer, he leaned down. "They took something of mine, and they're going to pay."

Stunned at the words that came out of his mouth, she knew she couldn't have written a speech as heartfelt as what he'd just said. And she couldn't say anything to refute those words. They were wrapped around her heart as much as his arms were wrapped around her body. Nodding slowly, she said, "Well, alrighty, then. I guess they're going to pay. But I have to throw this in there— I'm pretty excited about making them pay myself, although I'm not sure what I can do other than put them in my next book and kill them off."

She watched his face morph from severe into a wide grin, making him even more gorgeous. Lifting on her toes, she initiated the kiss that he quickly took over, and ignoring the men just outside the room, they stood in the middle of the kitchen and became lost in each other.

She didn't know how many minutes had passed until one of them called out, "Roger is on the move. Looks like he's heading to the airport."

24

Dolby grabbed Marcia's hand as the others hurried back into the room. He wanted to protect her from whatever was going on, but he also wanted her to be a part of what was happening.

"What's up?"

"He got a call to come to the airport. We've identified the plane in the other private hangar besides this one… Aleksi Milanov. Vladimir's second in command. He flew in here just before the ship arrived at the dock."

"My guess is that Vladimir has discovered something and called Roger in," Poole said.

It took almost fifteen minutes of watching the tracer Landon had placed earlier on Roger's vehicle to see it stop close by. Then they watched the screen as he climbed out of the vehicle and walked into the hangar that appeared identical to the one they were in. The short, stocky man stood for a moment, settling his suit coat over his bulk, covering the holstered weapon Dolby knew he'd have with him.

"Yep, that's Aleksi," Dolby said as a man stepped out to greet Roger.

Dolby hated seeing the fright in Marcia's eyes. Taking both hands in his, he bent closer. "We know Roger has been skimming off from the money that he launders for the Bulgarians. As much as they paid him, that was a pretty stupid thing to do because these men were not the ones to steal from. And if he's here, that means his trying to kidnap Angela will be the least of his worries."

"What are you going to do?" she asked, her fingers gripping his arm tightly. "Shouldn't Landon or the authorities handle this?"

"We want to see what they know and what they're going to do about Roger. And see what evidence Landon can obtain. Don't worry. He's working with the embassy and Interpol's National Central Bureau in Majuro."

The gathering grew quiet as the voices could be heard.

Roger walked into the room and looked at Aleksi with shock on his face. "I was surprised to get the call from you. Is she here? Did you bring her?"

"My boss thought this was too important of a job not to follow through with. I've been in close contact with the *Skrita Kralista* since Hawaii." Ignoring the question about Angela, Aleksi walked over to the counter and pulled out a flask.

Roger snorted. "It's a little early to be drinking, isn't it? Of course, if you've been around my wife, you probably need a drink." He swung his head around, repeating his question. "Is she here?"

Aleksi downed his drink in a large sip, then turned around, his unsmiling face in a hard expression. "We have a problem. Actually, we have more than one problem. An error on your part. An oversight on ours. And then a choice you made that you will regret. My boss is not happy."

Roger's hands landed on his hips, and he scowled. "What the hell are you talking about?"

"I'll begin with the error on your part. It seems you were uninformed that your wife was not going to be home that evening, and instead, another woman was there."

"Wh… what?" Roger stammered, his eyes bugging.

Aleksi's hand shot up, quieting Roger. "Unfortunately, our men did not realize the error and took the wrong woman."

Roger's mouth dropped open. "Are you fucking shitting me?" He stalked forward, then turned and paced in the other direction. "Who the hell would have been in our house– oh my God. Her stupid little friend, Marcia. Christ, that's who you took?" He barked out a laugh. "You won't need to worry about her. She's a mouse. Easily disposable. Are they still in California? Why wasn't I told?"

"Now is not your time to ask questions. It's your time to shut up and listen," Alesksi growled before turning the flask up and slamming back another drink.

"The error was not discovered in time. This woman

was taken and boarded on the ship according to the plan, and the only people who saw her once there were the man and his sister, that was hired just to see to your wife's needs. She was a prisoner, kept in a room at the back of the ship's clinic as agreed, but she still had food delivered to her several times a day. They were paid well to see that your wife was fed and her basic needs met. As it turns out, they gave her the opportunity to step outside one day. One of my boss's men noticed the woman had dark hair… not blond. That was when I was contacted and had a man fly to Hawaii to board the ship there. He's been keeping an eye on her until we receive further instruction."

Roger shook his head, his expression still in awe. "So where the fuck is Angela?"

Aleksi took several steps forward, sending Roger backward. "We don't know. She hasn't been seen anywhere. So my guess is she must have made it back to your house, realized whoever was in the house was taken, and managed to contact someone besides the police. Just an hour ago, a small explosion occurred on the dock near the ship, and the woman was seen running from the ship. Two men pursued them only to be shot at. There's no way your wife could've arranged that on her own, so we know she must've had assistance."

Roger dropped onto the chair behind him, and with his elbows on his knees and his head resting in his hands, he groaned. "This is a fucking nightmare! I can't believe Vladimir hired these morons to do what should've been a simple job. If Angela knows and is in hiding, that means somebody's got to be looking for me!" He lifted his head and sent Aleksi a glare. "You can tell your boss that I hold him responsible. I won't be continuing our association anymore!"

Aleksi walked over and sat in a chair facing Roger, his expression calm. "I think you forgot, Roger, that I said that you also made a choice you would regret. We transported the wrong woman, and she now poses a threat. But you, someone my boss trusted, made a very poor choice."

Roger licked his lips and stared without speaking. "I don't know what you're talking about."

"Oh, I think you do. It didn't take my boss long to realize that not only were you handling his money, you were also taking a little extra for yourself." The man leaned closer. "You should count yourself very lucky. For that offense, the boss would normally have you tortured before killing you. But he's willing to let bygones be bygones as long as you return the money you took. You get to keep your life and can consider your association with our business to be over from this moment forward once payment with interest has been returned." He glanced around and smiled. "This is a lovely little island in the Pacific. You should be very happy here."

Roger jumped to his feet. "What are you talking about? This was just a cheap place to invest in. A place to be off the grid for me to come to. I'm not living here!"

"I have a feeling that whoever your wife hired to rescue the woman who was kidnapped in her place will also let the authorities know. I doubt you'll even have a home to go back to in California. Or a business."

"You can't do this to me. I had everything planned out." Roger's pitch rose with each word until he was squeaking.

Aleksi chuckled. "We're not going back empty-handed. But remember, we know where you are, and your life will be worth nothing if you don't pay back the money you stole."

With a shared look among the others, Dolby nodded and then turned to Marcia. "Stay here." Giving her a quick kiss, he and the others slipped out the back door, darting toward the other hangar nearby. The early dawn-lit sky now gave illumination but also took away their cover of darkness.

They entered the hangar and spread out to guard the exits. Roger gasped, and his eyes widened as Aleksi's eyes narrowed. Roger turned and raced toward the nearest door, and it was Dolby's pleasure to stop the fleeing man with his fist to his face.

Roger cried out, dropping to the ground. Dolby leaned over, grabbed Roger by his shirt, and hauled him up. Getting in his face, he growled, "That was for Marcia, asshole," just before he hit him once more. Letting him drop, he stepped back as Landon walked into the hangar. His brow lifted.

"He was trying to escape. Must have run into me," Dolby said without a hint of sarcasm but had no doubt Landon could see the amusement in his eyes.

Hauling Roger off the floor, he looked in disgust at the man who'd orchestrated the situation that resulted in Marcia's traumatic experience. Leaning close, he growled, "You took my woman, asshole. Consider yourself lucky. Two punches are all you get from me."

"I... I didn't know anything about it. She wasn't the one—"

"If you had taken your wife, it still would have been fucked up and would have still hurt the woman I care about." He shoved Roger back toward the middle of the space, and Landon, as another suited man walked in.

"Who are you?" Roger asked, his gaze moving around the room. Landon stepped forward, drawing Roger's attention.

Landon pulled out his identification. "FBI."

"I—"

"You are a bit out of your jurisdiction, aren't you, Agent Sommers?" Aleksi asked, his body taut but not giving off the air of someone trapped the way Roger was.

Landon looked over. His expression was almost bored. He inclined his head toward the other man who followed. "Not for him."

The tall man, dressed in a suit, pulled out his identification as well. "Thomas Baldwin. Interpol."

At that, Aleksi tensed but lifted his chin in defiance. "You have nothing on me."

"I'll take you in for questioning about Vladimir Sposov's expanding empire throughout the Pacific, and now that includes kidnapping."

"I was not involved in any kidnapping," Aleksi argued.

Thomas continued, "We have a lot to uncover and evidence we're still gaining, including from the *Skrita*

Kralista. But for now, Roger Mansfield, you're under arrest. You will be taken with Agent Sommers to the police office in Majuro. And you, Mr. Milanov, are to be taken in for questioning."

Dolby and the others watched as Thomas moved forward, signaling behind him where several armed law enforcers hustled in and took the two men away in handcuffs. Dolby sighed, ready to get back to Marcia. With a grin, the Keepers followed the others out of the front of the hangar.

25

Marcia had watched the events play out on the screen left for her. While she'd jumped when witnessing Jonathan hit Roger, a giggle slipped out at seeing Angela's soon-to-be ex-husband drop to the floor. She'd wanted to do that herself since figuring it out that Roger had orchestrated the kidnapping.

As it seemed the action was finally drawing to a close with Roger and the Bulgarian being led off by Landon and the police, she leaned back against the counter and glanced out the window at the blue sky painted with the brilliant colors of the sunrise. She could now see the public area of the airport, including the tower, in the distance. Lush trees were beside the high fence that encircled the runways. It was a small airport, but from what she'd been told, it was a tiny island. *I'm in the middle of the Pacific Ocean on an island.* Suddenly, the events of the past week had her inhaling a shaky breath. *If Angela hadn't discovered I was missing. If she hadn't added extra security cameras to her house. If she hadn't gone straight to Lighthouse Security. If I hadn't met Dolby the previous week and had a connection to him...*

The *what-ifs* threatened to overtake her as thoughts of being discovered and killed caused spots to reappear at the edge of her vision once more. Gripping the counter, she forced her gaze to the window, determined not to fall apart again.

Let it go, sis. You can't live your life with what-ifs. Sucking in a breath, she let Marty's words dig in deep. *It's time for you to have a future, and I like him, sis.* A little gasp slipped out as her vision cleared, and she smiled.

Breathing easier, she leaned closer to the window as movement captured her attention, and she shifted to the side to see who was there.

A man was coming from behind the hangar, dragging a gagged woman by the arm. The woman wasn't bound and was trying to dig her heels in to keep from going.

Marcia gasped as she leaned closer, and her palm landed on the glass as her gaze took in the scene in front of her so reminiscent of her own experience. Then the woman was jerked around, and she could see it was Tudora, and the man was the one from the ship who'd taken Pitar's place. The one Aleksi said he'd sent.

He was trying to drag her behind the building toward the trees. Not having any idea where the others were, she whirled and raced out the door, hoping to find Jonathan or one of the others. Once outside, she saw no one other than the man still dragging a struggling Tudora.

Racing forward, she screamed as loud as she could,

causing the man to jerk around just as she launched herself at him. It was like landing against a brick wall. He shoved Tudora to the side and, facing Marcia, grabbed hold of her arms as she fought and kicked, managing to scratch his face.

Suddenly, more arms and legs joined the melee, and she realized Tudora was attacking him from behind. While the man was much larger than both of them, they had the element of surprise on their side, as well as the strength of women fighting for their lives.

They managed to take him to the ground, and as he struggled to stand with both women on top of him, he fell over again.

A roar sounded from the side, and she barely had time to look up before Jonathan raced around the corner of the hanger toward them. The others were right behind, weapons drawn.

Poole lifted Tudora onto her feet as Bennett pulled Marcia back, giving Jonathan room to jerk the man to his feet before knocking him back on his ass with a single punch to his jaw.

"I looked out the window when he was taking her!" she wheezed, rushing forward to wrap her hands around Jonathan. He pulled her in tight, both cursing and mumbling assurances in her ear.

Looking to the side, she watched as Poole gently removed the gag from Tudora. Hating to leave the comfort of Jonathan's arms, she rushed forward as Tudora did the same. The two women threw their arms around each other, holding tight, sobbing as they reassured themselves that they were safe.

Turning to look at Jonathan, she said, "This is Tudora, the woman hired to look after Angela on the ship. She was trying to make things so much easier for me. She brought me clothes and toiletries and made sure I had food. She wasn't part of the kidnapping... she was just hired. We can't leave her—"

"It's okay," Jonathan assured, pulling her gently into his arms. "Let's get to the police station where the statements can be made, and then we'll get out of here."

She nodded, and they made their way to the SUVs lining the airstrip. It took another ten-minute drive to get to the station, where they were led down a hall.

"You! You're the one they took?"

She jerked at Roger's roar and looked into one of the rooms to see him being pushed back into a chair by a policeman.

Jonathan stepped between her and the doorway, using his body to protect her, though she could still hear Roger's blustering. They were ushered into a large room. Looking behind her, she winced as Tudora was taken through another door.

As Jonathan, his coworkers, Landon, Thomas, and a woman from the US Embassy listened, she went through her ordeal from the moment she was kidnapped from Angela's house until Jonathan showed up, and they escaped the ship here in Majuro.

Landon was on the phone with others, and when all was finished, he turned to say, "We want Roger Mansfield to return to the United States with me to face every charge we can throw at him." The embassy liaison nodded, and Thomas agreed.

"Now, for Tudora," Landon said, looking at Marcia.

Pressing her lips together, she was uncertain what crimes they wanted to charge her with, but she couldn't leave the young woman without an advocate.

"I don't know what she was told before coming on board. I don't even know what position her brother, Pitar, normally had. But as far as me, it seemed as though he was there to make sure his sister was escorted when she was taking care of me. From the first time Tudora saw me, there was sympathy in her eyes. I was dressed in socks and pajamas and had nothing with me. She spoke to her brother, and then brought clothes and toiletries. She always brought my food, always added something extra to the tray, and was even able to get Pitar to let me walk outside on one of the upper decks, for no one could see me one day."

She looked around the room but could not discern the expressions on anyone's face other than Jonathan's. And with him, she could see gratitude, knowing he felt that toward the young woman who'd helped her.

The need to plead for Tudora was overpowering, her voice now shaking with emotion. "I have no idea what her role is, if she even has one, with the Bulgarian mob that you were after. But I can tell you that from what I've seen, she was given a job to bring food to another woman on the ship and, without knowing anything about me, tried to make my stay more pleasant. For that, she has my heartfelt thanks."

Thomas nodded, seeming unsure what to say for a moment, then finally leaned forward with his forearms on the table and his hands clasped as he held her gaze.

"From what we've deduced, her brother, Pitar, has not been in the United States for very long but immigrated and was able to get a job on the docks. He was recently offered the opportunity to learn how to become a ship's crewman if he could handle a special assignment. If he and his sister could watch over a woman who would be on the ship, not ask any questions, and follow the directions precisely, then he would be afforded the opportunity to become employed with Sposov Transportation, and his sister would be compensated. The job offer gave her much more stability and benefits than just being a house cleaner."

Nodding, Marcia said, "I could tell they were surprised to see me dressed the way I was. But they gave extra care and comfort. I just don't understand why Pitar was taken off the ship in Hawaii."

"At the same time Dimitar got onto the ship, Pitar was taken off. The FBI in Hawaii, as well as Interpol, was watching. He was not kept under guard by anyone, and we were able to get to him. He said that he was being fired from the job because he didn't follow the rules when he let you walk on the deck. It was a decision he and Tudora made, both hating to see you stuck in a dark room. He said the treatment of you was not right and not what he had agreed to when he accepted the job."

She turned and gripped Jonathan's arms. "I knew it. I knew they were good people!"

"I've interviewed Tudora, and what she says backs up what Pitar told the agents in Hawaii."

"So what will happen with them?"

"We're looking at offering them a chance to go into a protection program if they're willing to testify against the Sposovs."

"But what—"

Jonathan leaned forward and wrapped his arm around her, halting her words. "Babe, you've got to let this play out the best for them. They did good by you, and now the agency will do good by them."

She knew what he was saying, but her heart still ached. "Will I be able to see her one last time?"

Landon nodded. "You can do that right now."

She jumped to her feet and followed him out of the room with Jonathan right behind her. They were just leading Tudora out, and the two women once again hugged, crying as they clung together.

"I never wanted them to hurt you," Tudora cried, tears streaking down her face. "Pitar and I knew something bad was happening, and we didn't like it."

"You helped me," Marcia said. "Just giving me comfort helped me."

"I don't understand everything happening," Tudora said, "but they say if I tell the truth like Pitar did, he and I will be taken care of and safe."

"That's right," she assured. "I won't be able to see you, but you'll be able to start over somewhere safe."

They hugged longer and finally said goodbye as a female agent escorted Tudora out. Landon walked over and shook hands with Poole, Bennett, and Adam. "I'll be flying back separately with Roger. Tudora will fly back to Hawaii, where she and her brother will be reunited and then taken care of."

He stepped over and clasped hands with Dolby. "Good working with you, man. Hope to do more in the future."

Turning, he smiled at Marcia, taking her hands in his. "You did good, Ms. Blackburn. I'm glad you're returning home safe and sound." Bending, he whispered, "Perhaps there's a part for me in the next Inspector Marley novel."

She didn't have a chance to respond before he straightened, winked, and then left the room. Her mind whirling, she grinned as Jonathan's arms wrapped around her again, pulling her in tight against his chest.

Two days later, she peered out the window of the private jet as they left the Marshall Islands. The sight was breathtaking, with the purest blue water below dotted with the tips of underwater mountains that created the tiny islands. She decided at that moment that she needed to have Majura as a setting for one of her romance novels... the new series that she'd been plotting ever since she'd discovered what it was like to have men like the Keepers swoop in to rescue her.

She and Jonathan had rested, eaten, and played on the beach until he was convinced that she wouldn't collapse right in front of him from her ordeal. And with a private hotel room, they'd made love long into the night.

Now, flying home, she heard the men talk about a layover in Hawaii for her to rest. "Please," she interrupted, drawing their gazes to her. "I know we need to stop and refuel. But I really just want to get back to the States. Please don't prolong the trip for me."

Jonathan searched her face and must have been satisfied with what he saw because he smiled, squeezed her hand, and then turned to the others and nodded.

It was another day before they landed in California, but she was met with a reception when Jonathan drove into the driveway of her rental house. Angela burst from the front door, screaming with her hands waving in the air, enveloping Marcia in her tight embrace. They were followed by another couple, greeted enthusiastically by Jonathan.

Fellow Keeper Chris and his artist wife, Stella, had brought Angela from the safe house. They walked out smiling and, after hugs from Jonathan, were introduced to Marcia. Angela had taken it upon herself to order dinner to be delivered from a restaurant nearby that declared they had the world's best chicken parmesan.

Soon settled, they ate, talked, and related the stories over again. After the meal, Chris and Stella said goodbye, Chris man-hugging Jonathan while Stella gushed, "I can't wait for you to come meet the others. All the women are dying to get to know you!"

Jonathan peered at Marcia over Chris's shoulder, but she just offered a heartfelt smile, accepting Stella's exuberant hug. Angela left after a tearful hug, filled with guilt that Marcia had been kidnapped due to Roger. Assuring Angela he wouldn't be a factor anymore, they parted with promises to talk soon.

Walking back into the house, Marcia could tell that

Jonathan was on edge, and she realized he was waiting for her to break down. But she wasn't. No tears. No spotted vision. No gasping for breath. This ordeal was over.

Taking his hand, she led him into the living room overlooking the beach. She stood for a moment, just staring out at the ocean.

"What are you thinking?" he asked, encircling his arms around her, one across her stomach and the other over her chest.

"I look out over the ocean, and it seems so very different to me right now. It's always appeared vast, but now having seen it from a ship in the middle of the Pacific, this beautiful view can't begin to capture how small we really are in the world."

He didn't respond but rested his chin on the top of her head, pulling her deeper into his embrace.

"I've spent so many years trying to keep from letting anything happen that could bring fear back into my life. And now, I know that bad things can happen at any time. But I don't want to live a life where I constantly look over my shoulder for something to happen. I just want to live my life."

She turned within the circle of his arms, which now wrapped around her back. She placed her palms on his chest and looked up into the face of the most handsome man she'd ever seen. "I know my parents and Marty would never have wanted me to have become so isolated." Snorting slightly, she rested her forehead on his chest. "I hardly see myself becoming the life of the party type, but I don't want to hide from everyone anymore."

"What are you saying, babe?"

Tilting her head back, she stared into the blue eyes that held her captive. She reached up with one hand, cupping his jaw and gliding her thumb over his cheek. "I'm saying that I'm ready to take a chance on us. Wherever that takes me, wherever we go, I want to have a chance to really live a life with you in it."

She felt a slight pressure of his arms tightening as he lifted her off the floor and twirled in the middle of her living room. Throwing her head back, she laughed, clasping her hands behind his neck as she held on.

As his feet slowed, he continued to hold her feet off the ground as he angled his head and kissed her deeply. The kiss spoke of yesterdays and tomorrows, burying the past and looking into the future, reaching out to grasp everything life had to offer. It was a kiss that celebrated the couple they'd become.

Turning the page of my life to write a new chapter with this man. And, oh yes... a new series is on the horizon. She grinned against his lips, giving herself to him as all other thoughts left her mind.

26

Dolby was the first Keeper out of the SUV when it stopped, wanting to hustle inside to check on Marcia. A hand landed on his shoulder, and he looked back at Rick.

"She's fine," Rick said, smiling his understanding.

"I know. I just worry. This group... she's not used to—"

"Trust that our women understand," Hop said, walking over. "It takes someone special to be with a Keeper, so trust that they've got Marcia's back."

He'd made a trip the week before, only telling Marcia that he had a mission, but in actuality, he'd gone to the prison holding the two remaining kidnappers from when she was a teenager. His size was enough of a warning, but he made sure they knew that their lives inside prison would no longer be secure, and if they got out, they'd see him again. He had no doubt that Carson knew what he'd done, but his boss said nothing.

And today, he had taken a special trip with Rick and

Hop volunteering—or rather insisting they tag along. Dolby had tracked the two Bulgarian men who'd broken into Angela's house and kidnapped Marcia. They were in a bar they frequented near the harbor in Oakland. By the time he finished with them, their broken noses and the few broken fingers told them he was serious when he informed them that there wouldn't be a next time or no one would find their bodies. He didn't worry about his boss, knowing he had the backing of all the Keepers.

Hustling around to Carson and Jeannie's backyard, he stopped to take in the view in front of him. The patio overlooking the water was filled with comfortable chairs and settees, all filled with bright cushions. If a stranger had walked up, they would've also seen the area filled with beautiful women. But for the men bearing gifts of food and more wine, it was a sight of beautiful, intelligent, accomplished women who had all forged a bond.

Dolby's eyes immediately sought Marcia, his heart lighter as he spied her head thrown back in laughter as she sat between Stella and Natalie. Her hair was pulled back with a scarf, but tendrils had escaped in the breeze. Her long-sleeved pink T-shirt and jeans gave a casual air to her natural elegance.

He had to chuckle at the difference between the two women on either side of Marsha. Blond Stella was an artist who had her head in the clouds as she spied color and beauty all around her and wore a wild-colored printed shirt. Natalie was a no-nonsense former Army operator with Leo's Delta team, had worked as a Los

Angeles bodyguard, and now worked for LSIWC. She was dressed in jeans, boots, and a Go Army sweatshirt. Yet with Marcia in the middle, the women's differences didn't matter as they were obviously enjoying their time together.

Jeannie and Rachel were setting another platter of food among the others. Lori sat with her feet up, her hands resting on her pregnant belly. Abbie was next to her, smiling as she turned to listen to Natalie's story. It was true… it took a special woman to be with a Keeper or work with them, and Marcia fit right in.

As soon as the Keepers' presence was made known, the women looked over, their smiles greeting them. It didn't take long for the gathering to grow rowdier as the huge group laughed and talked, ate and drank. All through it, he kept an eye on Marcia. She was quiet, but he could tell she enjoyed herself, preferring conversations with a few at a time as she made her way around the others.

By evening, the party broke up as the Keepers headed home or out to bars. Goodbyes were said, and hugs ensued. As Marcia was involved with her goodbyes, Dolby looked to the side, observing Bennett and Carson talking. He made his way over and clapped Bennett on the back, knowing he was preparing to go on a mission.

"It must be hard being assigned a mission to Las Vegas," he joked.

Bennett shook his head slightly. "Honest to fuck, I can't think of any place I'd rather be less. Lights, noise, crowds… I get a headache just thinking about it."

"Well, you'll be stuck at a boring-ass conference for most of the time," Carson said.

Bennett nodded. "Fine by me. I can stand all day and just keep my eye on the target." With goodbyes, Dolby watched him walk away. Bennett had been a sniper for the Army, and while one of the best men Dolby knew, he always felt the serious Keeper carried his scars deep inside.

He and Carson turned to look at Jeannie and Marcia chatting. "I get it now. What you wanted to build. Not just a business. Us, not just employees. And not even just a team like we'd had in the military. But something more. Deeper. I don't know." He shoved his hands into his pockets. "Something just *more*."

Carson clapped him on the shoulder. "I can't take credit for the idea," he said. "Mace Hanover with the original LSI in Maine had the vision."

"Might not have been your original concept, but you were the one here in California who brought LSIWC to fruition. Us. The team." Inclining his head toward the others, he grinned. "All of us."

"I haven't had the time to tell you, but I really like Marcia," Carson said. "She's brave, strong, smart. The women have really given her a chance to have something she hasn't had before. A family of friends."

Saying good night, he walked over and slung his arm around Marcia's shoulders, and together they said their last goodbyes before heading home.

Two months later

Marcia leaned back against the pillows piled against the headboard, slipping off her reading glasses and setting her pen and notebook to the side as Jonathan walked into the bedroom, fresh from the shower. With Angela no longer living in the house she'd shared with Roger, Marcia had no desire to stay in the neighborhood either. So with Dolby's plead for her to move in with him, she decided to throw her former caution out the window and agreed. And she hadn't regretted one moment of it.

She still saw Angela frequently at her new condo in San Francisco. She'd integrated into the Keepers more easily than ever imagined, now finding a group of women friends filling a space inside her that she hadn't realized had been empty. In fact, today she'd had lunch with Stella, Jeannie, and Lori, planning Lori's twins' baby shower.

Jonathan had been keen to introduce her to his parents, and they'd visited them in their home in Northern California. His mother had swept her into a hug at their first meeting, and instead of feeling ill at ease, she'd battled the tears that threatened at the warmth that moved through her. She'd rediscovered that the memory of her own mother's arms around her were not gone forever but just buried. And it was lovely to have them resurface once again.

And after meeting his parents, she couldn't wait to

be surrounded by the entire Dolby clan whenever Frazier and Dalton could make it home.

And moving to Jonathan's house, she found that the new location with the mountains in the distance and the ocean not far, new stories seemed to flow from a well of excitement and fresh ideas.

Now, she grinned as Jonathan walked closer. She admired his body as she had since the first time she'd laid eyes on him. Being with him every day unless he was on a mission, she still hadn't gotten over her initial appreciation of the sight of his body, which she considered to be a work of art. Priceless art that was all hers.

Wearing just boxers, he walked to the side of the bed and grinned before striking a pose and flexing his muscles. She laughed and threw a pillow at him, her aim having not improved. He managed to keep it from hitting him right in the face before laughing as well.

"What's got you all man-posing?" she asked, still grinning, her gaze raking over his muscles before landing on his gorgeous face.

"I talked to Frazier and Dalton today," he admitted, crawling under the covers, his large body surrounding hers as he moved over her. "They'll try to take leave this summer at the same time and can't wait to meet you at Mom and Dad's place. Then Dalton said you could see that you'd chosen the wrong Dolby brother."

A giggle slipped out, and she pressed closer. "Well, I will have to make a comparison– No! Don't tickle me!"

"You'd better not check out my brothers," he warned, his fingers dancing close to the sensitive skin of her stomach.

She leaned up and cupped his jaw. "You're the only man for me."

He grinned and held her close to him. "Did you have a good time with the girls today?"

"I did. It's been a long time since I've had real friends besides Angela. It's nice to feel like I have a group I belong to. And considering I admire and care for every one of those women, it's a great group to be with."

He wrapped his arms around her, and she thought back to the first time she'd seen his biceps and wanted nothing more than to feel them pull her close. She murdered her appreciation as she nuzzled against his throat. "I finally got around to ordering a new desk," she said.

He leaned back and held her gaze, a wide smile on his face. "Thank fuck!"

She giggled and shook her head. "I just felt bad about you giving me the office space to use as my writing office. But then, once I got used to it, my old furniture just didn't look right there."

"You can get anything you want and make this place as much yours as it is mine." He kissed her, then muttered against her lips, "Because this place is now ours."

With that, he rolled on top of her, breast to chest, his cock nestled between her thighs, and their lips sealed together. It was her favorite way to start the night, knowing their lovemaking would keep them busy for a while. And as far as she was concerned, this love story would never have an end.

Because just like in fiction, with true life, love stories can live forever.

>For the next exciting LSIWC...
>Bennett

>Join my FB reader group!

ALSO BY MARYANN JORDAN

Don't miss other Maryann Jordan books!

Baytown Boys (small town, military romantic suspense)

Coming Home

Just One More Chance

Clues of the Heart

Finding Peace

Picking Up the Pieces

Sunset Flames

Waiting for Sunrise

Hear My Heart

Guarding Your Heart

Sweet Rose

Our Time

Count On Me

Shielding You

To Love Someone

Sea Glass Hearts

Protecting Her Heart

Sunset Kiss

Baytown Heroes - A Baytown Boys subseries

A Hero's Chance

Finding a Hero

A Hero for Her

Needing A Hero

For all of Miss Ethel's boys:

Heroes at Heart (Military Romance)

Zander

Rafe

Cael

Jaxon

Jayden

Asher

Zeke

Cas

Lighthouse Security Investigations

Mace

Rank

Walker

Drew

Blake

Tate

Levi

Clay

Cobb

Bray

Josh

Knox

Lighthouse Security Investigations West Coast

Carson

Leo

Rick

Hop

Dolby

Bennett

Hope City (romantic suspense series co-developed with Kris Michaels

Brock book 1

Sean book 2

Carter book 3

Brody book 4

Kyle book 5

Ryker book 6

Rory book 7

Killian book 8

Torin book 9

Blayze book 10

Griffin book 11

Saints Protection & Investigations

(an elite group, assigned to the cases no one else wants…or can solve)

Serial Love

Healing Love

Revealing Love

Seeing Love

Honor Love

Sacrifice Love

Protecting Love

Remember Love

Discover Love

Surviving Love

Celebrating Love

Searching Love

Follow the exciting spin-off series:

Alvarez Security (military romantic suspense)

Gabe

Tony

Vinny

Jobe

SEALs

Thin Ice (Sleeper SEAL)

SEAL Together (Silver SEAL)

Undercover Groom (Hot SEAL)

Also for a Hope City Crossover Novel / Hot SEAL…

A Forever Dad

Long Road Home

Military Romantic Suspense

Home to Stay (a Lighthouse Security Investigation crossover novel)

Home Port (an LSI West Coast crossover novel)

Letters From Home (military romance)

Class of Love

Freedom of Love

Bond of Love

The Love's Series (detectives)

Love's Taming

Love's Tempting

Love's Trusting

The Fairfield Series (small town detectives)

Emma's Home

Laurie's Time

Carol's Image

Fireworks Over Fairfield

Please take the time to leave a review of this book. Feel free to contact me, especially if you enjoyed my book. I love to hear from readers!

Facebook

Email

Website

ABOUT THE AUTHOR

I am an avid reader of romance novels, often joking that I cut my teeth on the historical romances. I have been reading and reviewing for years. In 2013, I finally gave into the characters in my head, screaming for their story to be told. From these musings, my first novel, Emma's Home, The Fairfield Series was born.

I was a high school counselor having worked in education for thirty years. I live in Virginia, having also lived in four states and two foreign countries. I have been married to a wonderfully patient man for forty-one years. When writing, my dog or one of my four cats can generally be found in the same room if not on my lap.

Please take the time to leave a review of this book. Feel free to contact me, especially if you enjoyed my book. I love to hear from readers!

Facebook
Email
Website

Made in the USA
Las Vegas, NV
31 March 2023